'*Gravel Heart* is one of the beautiful novels that lingers in the mind long after reading. Gurnah writes about the clash of worlds with such pathos and elegance' Amanda Foreman

'The measured elegance of Gurnah's prose renders his protagonist in a manner almost uncannily real ... Gurnah's portrayal of student life in Britain is pleasingly deliberate and precise, and also riveting ... Even the minor characters in this novel have richly imagined histories that inflect their smallest interactions – one of the loveliest pleasures of this book, and a choice that makes its world exceptionally full' *New York Times*

'A colourful tale of life in a Zanzibar village, where passions and politics reshape a family ... Expect echoes of *Measure for Measure*, which provides the book's title, in two hundred pages of powerful narrative' *Mail on Sunday*

'Abdulrazak Gurnah's latest novel on identity, immigration, and the long fraught legacy of colonial rule, is poetic and gentle as ever, yet unshrinking in its cool appraisal of how London works now' *Financial Times*

'A work of post-colonial literature that entertainingly intertwines migration and a tale of family drama ... Gurnah has rightly been praised for his masterful storytelling ... An emotive tale about betrayal, families and the East African diaspora' *Sunday Herald*

'Powerful, moving' *Times Literary Supplement*

ALSO BY ABDULRAZAK GURNAH

ABDULRAZAK GURNAH is the author of nine novels: *Memory of Departure*, *Pilgrims Way*, *Dottie*, *Paradise* (shortlisted for the Booker Prize and the Whitbread Award), *Admiring Silence*, *By the Sea* (longlisted for the Booker Prize and shortlisted for the *Los Angeles Times* Book Award), *Desertion* (shortlisted for the Commonwealth Writers' Prize), and *The Last Gift*. He is a Professor of English at the University of Kent, and was a Man Booker Prize judge in 2016. He lives in Canterbury.

GRAVEL HEART

ABDULRAZAK GURNAH

BLOOMSBURY PUBLISHING
LONDON · OXFORD · NEW YORK · NEW DELHI · SYDNEY

BLOOMSBURY PUBLISHING
Bloomsbury Publishing Plc
50 Bedford Square, London, WC1B 3DP, UK
1385 Broadway New York NY 10018 USA
29 Earlsfort Terrace, Dublin 2, Ireland

BLOOMSBURY, BLOOMSBURY PUBLISHING and the Diana logo are trademarks of
Bloomsbury Publishing Plc

First published in Great Britain 2017
This edition published 2018

A catalogue record for this book is available from the British Library

ISBN: HB: 978-1-4088-8134-7; TPB: 978-1-4088-8133-0;
eBook: 978-1-4088-8131-6; MMPB: 978-1-4088-8130-9; USPB: 978-1-6397-3001-8

2 4 6 8 10 9 7 5 3

Typeset by Integra Software Services Pvt. Ltd.
Printed and bound in Great Britain by CPI Group (UK) Ltd, Croydon CR0 4YY

To find out more about our authors and books visit www.bloomsbury.com
and sign up for our newsletters

'The beginning of love is the recollection of blessings: then it proceeds according to the capacity of the recipient, that is, according to his deserts.'

Abu Said Ahmad ibn Isa-al-Kharraz,
Kitab al-Sidq (The Book of Truthfulness) (899),
trans. Arthur J. Arberry (1937)

PART ONE

1

A STICK OF CANDY FLOSS

My father did not want me. I came to that knowledge when I was quite young, even before I understood what I was being deprived of and a long time before I could guess the reason for it. In some ways not understanding was a mercy. If this knowledge had come to me when I was older, I might have known how to live with it better but that would probably have been by pretending and hating. I might have faked a lack of concern or I might have ranted in angry outrage behind my father's back and blamed him for the way everything had turned out and how it might all have been otherwise. In my bitterness I might have concluded that there was nothing exceptional in having to live without a father's love. It might even be a relief to have to do without it. Fathers are not always easy, especially if they too grew up without their father's love, for then everything they know would make them understand that fathers had to have things their own way, one way or another. Also fathers, just like everyone else, have to deal with the relentless manner in which life conducts its business, and they have their own tremulous selves to salve and sustain, and there must be many times when they hardly have enough strength for that, let alone love to spare for the child that had appeared any old how in their midst.

But I also remembered when it was otherwise, when my father did not shun me with an icy silence as we sat in the same small room, when he laughed with me and tumbled me and fondled me. It was a memory that came without words or sound, a little treasure I hoarded. That time when it was *otherwise* would have had to be when I was very young, a baby, because my father was already the silent man I knew later by the time I could remember him clearly. Babies can remember many things in their podgy sinews, which becomes the problem of later life, but it is not always certain that they remember everything in its place. There were times when I suspected that the fondling memory was an invention to comfort myself and that some of the memories I recollected were not my own. There were times when I suspected they were put there for me by other people, who were dealing kindly with me and were trying to fill in the empty spaces in my life and theirs, people who exaggerated the orderliness and drama of the haphazard tedium of our days, who preferred that what came to be was signalled by what had passed. When I reached this point I began to wonder if I knew anything about myself because it was most likely that I only knew what people told me about how I was as an infant, at times one person saying this and another saying that, forcing me to bow to the more insistent one and occasionally selecting for myself the younger self I preferred.

There were moments when these guilt-ridden thoughts became absurdly insistent, though I thought I could remember sitting in the sun beside my father on the doorstep of our house while he held a stick of pink candy floss into which I was about to sink my face. That was a memory which came to me as an arrested instant without conclusion, a moment without preamble or direction. How could I have invented that? I just was not sure if it had really happened. My father was laughing in that breathless way of his as he looked at me, as if he was never going to be able to stop, his arms squeezed to his ribs, holding himself in. He was saying something to me that I could now no longer hear. Or perhaps he was not speaking to me at all but to someone else who was there. Perhaps he was speaking to my mother in that heaving, laughing way.

I expect I was wearing a tiny vest, which came to just below my navel, and had nothing on below. I was sure of that, most probably. That is, I was sure I was probably not wearing anything below my vest. I have seen a picture of myself in

4

the attire, standing nonchalantly in the street in that standard costume of male tropical infancy. Girls were not allowed to wander around like that, for fear of accidental damage to their chastity and decency, although that did not mean that they were spared what was bound to happen. Yes, I am sure I have seen that photograph once – a fuzzy, incompletely developed print most likely taken with a box camera – of a half-naked native boy of about three or four years old, staring at the camera with a look of pathetic passivity. Most likely I was in a mild panic. I was a fearful child and a camera pointed in my direction perturbed me. Little could be made of my features in the faded photograph and only someone who was already familiar with my appearance could have been sure it was me. The print was too pale to reveal the scabs on my knees or the insect bites on my arms or the snot down my face, but clear enough to show the tiny bunch that swelled between my legs, as yet unscarred and unblemished. I could not have been older than four. After about that age, adult jokes about the little abdalla and how it was soon going to lose its cap begin to hit their mark and make little boys cringe with terror at the forthcoming circumcision, and an old woman squeezing a boy's testicles and shuddering and sneezing with pretend-ecstasy was no longer funny and began to feel like mockery.

In fact, I can be definite that photograph was taken before I was five because some time during that year and before I started Koran school, I went on a taxi ride with my father and my mother. The taxi ride was a rare event, and my mother made much of it, filling me with anticipation of the picnic we would have when we reached our destination: vitumbua, katlesi, sambusa. On the way, the taxi stopped at the hospital – it won't take long, my father said, then we'll be on our way. I took his hand and followed him into the building. Before I knew what was happening, my little abdalla had lost its kofia and the outing had turned into a nightmare of pain and treachery and disappointment. I had been betrayed. For days after that I had to sit with my legs wide apart, exposing my turbaned penis to the healing air while my mother and my father and the neighbours came to look on me with big smiles on their faces. Abdalla kichwa wazi.

I started Koran school soon after the trauma and deceit of that event. Attendance at the school required me to put on a calf-length kanzu and a kofia, and almost certainly a pair of shorts so that my hands did not wander playfully under there as boys' hands tend to do. And once I learnt to cover my nakedness, especially after it had been tricked and mutilated into a kind of prominence, I would not have been able to uncover it with the same freedom as before, and I would not have found myself sitting on our doorstep in a little slip of a vest. So it was certain that I was about four when I sat there in the sun with my father Masud while he fed me candy floss. For years I felt in my flesh the fondness of that moment.

That was the doorstep of the house I was born in, the house I spent all of my childhood in, the house I abandoned because I was left with little choice. In later years, in my banishment, I pictured the house inch by inch. I don't know if it was lying nostalgia or painful proper longing, but I paced its rooms and breathed its smells for years after I left. Just inside the front door was the kitchen area: no power points or fitted cupboards or electric oven or even a sink. It was a simple unmodern kitchen, although it had once been primitive in its gloom, its walls grimy with charcoal fumes. Like the inside of a beast's mouth, my mother told me. Traces of that grime still came through as a grey under-shine on the walls despite several washes of lime. In the corner nearest the door was a water tap for washing dishes and doing the laundry, the floor around it pitted and crumbling from the force of the water on the poor concrete. To the left-hand side of the door was a mat, never quite losing its vegetable smell over the years, and that was where we ate and where my mother received visitors. Male visitors did not come inside the house, at least not while my mother was young, or at least not all male visitors. That was how it was when I was a little boy but later a table and chairs replaced the mat, and many other changes were made to the kitchen to make it clean and modern.

A door closed off this large entrance room from the rest of the house, our deep interior, which consisted of two rooms, a small hallway and a bathroom. The bigger of the two interior rooms was where my parents and I slept. I had a large cot which I loved. One panel slid up and down, and when I was in the cot and the panel was up and the mosquito net was tucked in, I felt as if I was in a craft of some kind, moving invisibly through the air. I have never lost that feeling of safety when I sleep under a mosquito net. Whenever my mother was busy and wanted me out of the way, she put me in the cot because she knew I was content in there. Sometimes I asked to be allowed in it myself, with the side-panel up, and then for hours I pretended I was hidden away in my own secret room, safe from all danger. It was still comfortable enough for me when I was ten years old. Later my sister Munira slept in the same cot.

Uncle Amir, my mother's brother, slept in the other room. A door led from the hallway to the narrow backyard where there was just enough room for a washing line. The backyard wall adjoined the yard of the neighbours who lived behind us, a man living quietly with his mother. They lived so quietly that for a long time I did not know the man's name because no one spoke to him or about him. His mother never went out. I don't know whether it was because she was ill, or whether the habit of seclusion had made her frightened of the outside. They had no electricity in the house and it was so dark in there that when I was sent round with a bowl of plums as a gift – plums were rare in those days – I could hardly make out her features in the gloom. I almost never heard any noise from their yard, just sometimes a man coughing softly or the clang of a pot. If I had to go to the toilet at night I tried if possible not to open my eyes, feeling my way to the bathroom in the dark. I never even looked at the back door at night but I could not help imagining a shadow looming over the wall in the diffused glow of a turned-down oil lamp.

There was no garden or pavement in front of the house, so a visitor stepped off the street straight into the entrance room. On hot days when the door was left open, the slight breeze lifted the door-curtain in a lazy billow into the room. Sitting in the sun on that doorstep with my stick of candy floss meant my father and I would have had our feet on the road, assuming my legs were long enough to reach the ground, and we would have seen life trickling by. It was only a quiet lane, just wide enough for two bicycles to pass each other, with care. The tin roofs of our house and the one opposite almost met overhead to create a quiet twilight chamber which cooled the air and would have intimidated a stranger with its sense of intimacy and enclosure. The sun shone on the house steps for only a brief while in the day, peering in between the overhanging roofs, and that would have been the moment of the candy-floss stick.

No car could come down these lanes nor was ever intended to. These were streets built for the shuffle and slap of human feet, and for bodies to rub shoulders against each other, and for voices to murmur and reverberate their courtesies and curses and outcries. Any freighting that was necessary was done by handcarts and human muscles. Nor was the road straight like a proper road, though it was paved with old flagstones, worn by time and traffic and the water, which ran over them during the rains. Sometimes, late at night, the crack of hard-shod feet on the flags filled the lane with menace. Soon after it passed our house the road turned to the right, and a short while after that to the right again. Aside from the big roads that led out into the country, our roads bent and turned every few metres, fitting themselves to the way people lived their lives. In our part of the town there were no mansions and courtyards and walled gardens, and people lived their lives in a small way. That was how it was when I was a child, when the lanes were quiet and empty, not as crowded and dirty as they became later.

Our front-door neighbours Mahsen and Bi Maryam lived in a house as small as ours, door facing door like its opposite. Everyone called him Mahsen, without any kind of title, and always called her Bi Maryam. Mahsen was a messenger at the Municipal Offices, a short skinny man who would have been a certain target for bullies when he was a child. Messenger was the official and puzzling name for his work, because he did not really carry messages. He was sent on whatever errands the officers and clerks wanted done: fetch a file, escort someone out, buy a cold drink, a cigarette, a bun, go to the market, take a broken fan to the electrician – the interminable busyness of office life.

Some of the officers and clerks were a quarter of his age but Mahsen never complained. He was always mild, soft-spoken and smiling, a man of endless courtesy and impossible piety. He greeted everyone as he walked home from work, anyone who made eye contact with him received a smile or a wave or a handshake, depending on intimacy, gender or age. He asked after this one's health and that one's family and transmitted any news he had picked up on the way. He was up at dawn every morning to go to the mosque for the al-fajiri prayers – not many people did that – and he did not miss a single one of his five prayers every day, devotions which he performed with discretion as if he meant to keep quiet about his doings. If he had not been so modest he would have been mocked as an exhibitionist. He was even polite to children when so many adults spoke to them with belligerence and suspicion, as if they disliked them and suspected them of wickedness and anticipated a challenge from them. Not a shred of evil reputation attached to him although some unkind people wondered aloud if everything was in its place up top.

His wife Bi Maryam did not bother much with discretion, and in many other ways she was unlike Mahsen. She was stout, suspicious and combative. She took every opportunity to draw attention to her husband's piety and generosity, as if anyone doubted it. *A man of faith*, she announced when the moment presented itself, *the beloved of Our Lord, see how He has given him good health and such looks. He will get his due when his master calls him back to Himself, despite your envy.*

She made a living cooking buns and flapjacks for local cafés, and had something to say about almost anything, which she always did and in a robust voice that was meant to be heard by her neighbours and any interested passers-by. She had advice to offer on people's ailments, had views on people's travel plans, on how best to grill fish and on the likely outcome of a rumoured marriage proposal. Children hurried past her door in fear that they might be summoned and sent on an errand. Mahsen and

Bi Maryam had no children of their own. Her greatest fear was to be misunderstood, which people were always deliberately and maliciously determined to do, so it seemed to her. Her voice and opinions did not seem to jar on Mahsen as they did on other people. My father said that Mahsen had probably gone deaf and could no longer hear her, but other people said it was because he was a saint. Some people said she knew medicines and were wary of her but my mother said that was just ignorance. What she feared was Bi Maryam's quarrelsome and ill-natured bullying.

For several years, before things went wrong, my father Masud worked as a junior clerk for the Water Authority in Gulioni. His job there was respectable and secure, a government job. That was before I really remember and I only know that time of his life as a story. When I remember him clearly he worked at a market stall or he did nothing, just sat in his room. For a long time I did not know what had gone wrong and after a while I stopped asking. There was so much I did not know.

*

My father's father was a teacher, Maalim Yahya. I never met him because he left to work in the Gulf before I was born but I have seen a picture of him. Later I went to the same school where he used to teach, and there were several group photographs of the staff in the headmaster's office. There was one taken every year and they covered most of one wall in the office. The practice must have stopped several years before because there were no recent ones. The headmaster did not appear in any of the photographs nor did any of the teachers working in the school when I was a pupil there. It was like a glimpse of a mythical past: unsmiling men in buttoned-down long-sleeved white shirts or kanzus and jackets. Many of them must have passed away since then. Some were killed in the revolution although I would not have been able to point them out from the photographs. We only knew from rumours that some of the teachers were killed at that time. The headmaster himself had been a student in the

10

school and had been taught by Maalim Yahya. He pointed him out to me.

'Your grandfather. He was very stern, most of the time,' the headmaster said. I knew that describing a teacher as stern, or even fierce, was intended as a compliment. Teachers who were not stern were feeble by definition and were appropriately tormented by the children. They called him Maalim Chui behind his back, the headmaster said, because of the way he glared at them and made his hands into claws as if he would tear into them. The clawing threat was so comical that the boys struggled not to laugh but they did not because when their teacher was angry he was frightening. The headmaster demonstrated the glaring and clawing and I could not help laughing. 'But when you had done something wrong and he looked at you in that certain way,' the headmaster said solemnly, demonstrating an expression of ferocity as he attempted to retrieve his authority, 'you felt as if you were about to wet yourself. In those days teachers did not hesitate to hit us, and if you received that look you knew that at the right moment you were going to get a cuff on the back of your head, which actually was not as bad as the way some of the other teachers beat us. You are a spoilt generation compared to us.'

I was in the headmaster's office to be praised for a story I had written about a cycle ride to the country. The topic we were given came from our English Language textbook: What did you do on your holidays? Below the topic question was a drawing, which was intended to give us ideas. It showed two smiling children, a boy and a girl, running after a ball on the beach, free-flowing blond hair streaming behind them, while an adult woman with short blonde hair and a sleeveless blouse looked smilingly on. Another drawing on the same page showed two more children, or perhaps the same ones, this time with hair blowing about their faces, playing in front of a building, with trees and a windmill and a donkey and some chickens in the background. What did we do on our holidays ... as if we were like the children pictured in our school books, whose hair blew about our faces when we ran, and who went to the seaside on our holidays or went to our

11

grandfather's farm during the summer and had adventures in the haunted old house by the mill. Holidays were when the government school was closed, because there was no holiday from Koran school and the word of God, except for the days of Idd and the Maulid, or because of bed-ridden illness. A headache or a gut-ache or even a glistening grazed knee were not enough for a reprieve, although running blood was indisputable. On ordinary days, we went to government school in the morning and Koran school in the afternoon. During school holidays we went to Koran school all day, not to the seaside where our frizzy curly hair did not stream behind us as we ran nor to grandfather's farm where there was no windmill and where our hair did not blow about our faces.

But I had made good progress with the Koran compared to many other boys in my class, and by the time I wrote the story of the cycle ride to the country, I had finished with Koran school. I had escaped, which is to say I had completed reading the Koran twice, from beginning to end, to the satisfaction of my teacher, who had listened to me read every single line of every page over the years, correcting my pronunciation and making me repeat a verse until I could read it without stumbling. By the time I stopped attending Koran school I could read the Koran fluently and with the appropriate intonation without understanding anything much of what I read. I knew the stories, I loved the stories, because there were always occasions for the teachers to re-tell the travails and triumphs of the Prophet. One of the teachers at our Koran school in Msikiti Barza was an expert storyteller. When he stood up on those occasions we were told to put our tablets and volumes away and listen because it was a day that commemorated an important religious event, there was usually no further need to hush the students. He told us about the Prophet's birth, about the miraj, about the entrance to Medina. I loved the story of the angel who came to the young orphan boy herding sheep on the hills of Makka, split open his chest and washed his heart with driven snow. However many times I heard that story in my boyhood, it moved me and thrilled me, a heart made pure with driven snow. The angel must have brought it down with him from snow-laden clouds, because I don't expect he would have been able to find that commodity on a Makkan hillside.

So what did the escaped ex-Koran school youngsters do during the holidays? They did not do anything in particular. They slept late, wandered the streets through the long day, gossiped, played cards or went for a swim, which did not amount to the seaside as it was only a few minutes' walk from home. No one did anything worth writing about, or if anyone did, it was likely to be something forbidden and so could not be written about in a classroom exercise. But I was asked to write about my holiday highlights, not to grumble about the absurdity of the task. So I made up a story about a cycle ride to the country, and named the trees that provided me with shade, and described the boy who pointed me in the right direction when I got lost, and the girl I spoke to but who disappeared before I could find out her name, and the blinding whiteness of the sand when I reached the sea.

My teacher liked it and showed it to the headmaster, who wanted me to make a fair copy in my best handwriting – the school did not have a typewriter – so it could be put on the noticeboard for everyone to admire. That was what I was in his office for, to be praised for what I had done. Then when the headmaster ran out of praise, yet could see that I was still standing patiently in front of him instead of grinning with pleasure and shuffling to be released, he pointed to the photograph in the manner of someone bestowing a parting gift. Take this and go. In the photograph, my father's father, Maalim Yahya, was standing at the end of a line behind a row of seated colleagues, a tall, thin, ascetic-looking man who returned the gaze of the camera with the look of someone suffering an ordeal. Or perhaps he was struggling with a very bad headache as my father sometimes used to do. My mother told me that my father inherited his headaches from his father, who was severely afflicted in that regard. He was wearing a jacket over his kanzu, a gesture towards his government-school role. My father looked nothing like Maalim Yahya, he must have taken after his mother whom I have never met or seen in a photograph.

13

At that time, respectable women did not allow themselves to be photographed for fear of the dishonour to their husbands if other men saw their image. But this fear was not the only reason to refuse as some men were also resistant, and in both cases it was from suspicion that the production of the image would take something of their being and hold it captive. Even when I was a child, although that was later than the time of Maalim Yahya's photograph, if a tourist from the cruise ships wandered the streets with a camera, people watched warily for the moment when the foreigner lifted it to take a shot and then several voices screamed in a frenzy of prohibition, to frighten him or her off. Behind the tourist an argument would start between those who feared for the loss of their souls and those who scoffed at such nonsense. For these kinds of reasons, I had not seen a photograph of my father's mother and so could not tell for certain if he did take after her. After seeing the photograph of Maalim Yahya, though, I thought that I had taken a little bit after him in shape and complexion. The recognition pleased me, it connected me to people and events that my father's silence had cut me off from.

The date on the photograph in the headmaster's office was December 1963, which would have been the end of the school year just before the revolution. Maalim Yahya lost his job soon after that, which was why he went to work in Dubai. The rest of the family, his wife and two daughters, followed but my father stayed behind. None of them ever came back while I was there, not even for a visit, and aside from that school picture I saw in the headmaster's office I had no image of my father's family. When I was very young, it did not occur to me that I should have one. My mother and my father were the world to me, and the snippets of stories I heard as a child sustained me even though the people they told of seemed so distant.

*

I knew more about my mother's family. My mother's name was Saida and her family had once been well off, not wealthy by

14

any means but well-off enough to own a piece of farming land and their own house near the Court House. During her childhood that part of town was occupied by the grandees, by people connected to the sultan's government, who lived in the seclusion of their walled gardens, and by European colonial officials, who lived in huge old Arab houses by the sea, and marked their ceremonial imperial rituals with white linen uniforms adorned with fantasy medals and wore cork helmets festooned with feathers and carried swords in gilt-edged scabbards, like conquerors. They gave themselves tin-god titles and pretended that they were aristocrats. Both varieties of grandees thought themselves gifted by nature, which had created them noble and granted them the right to rule as well as the burden that it brought.

My mother's father, Ahmed Musa Ibrahim, was an educated man, a travelled man, who had no time for these self-deluding patrician airs. He preferred to speak about justice and liberty and the right to self-fulfilment. He would pay for these words in due course. He had spent two years at Makerere College in Uganda and one year at Edinburgh University in Scotland, completing a Diploma in Public Health. In between his studies at those two institutions he spent several weeks in Cairo, visiting a friend who was a student in Education at the American University. Then he travelled through Beirut and stayed in Istanbul for three weeks on his way to London. The years in Kampala and Edinburgh, and his time in those other fabulous cities, gave him an air of incomparable glamour and sophistication, and when he started to speak about one or other of the famous sights encountered on his travels, his audience fell reverently silent. Or that was how my mother told it, that his words were held in such respect. He worked in the laboratories of the Department of Health, a short walk from home. His main work was in the malaria eradication campaign, but he also contributed to the cholera and dysentery control project, analysing samples and participating in seminars. Some people addressed him as Doctor and consulted him about their ailments, but he laughed them off and told them that he worked in the rat-catchers' department and knew nothing about hernias and haemorrhoids and chest pains and fevers.

I have seen a photograph of him too, taken at the back of the Department of Health building, near the gate to the yard where the departmental vehicles were parked. He wore a white linen suit, the middle button of his jacket done up, and a red tarbush at a dashing angle. His head was tilted to one side so the tassel hung a little away from the tarbush. His right calf was crossed over his left, drawing attention to his brown shoes, and his right arm leant against the unmistakable neem tree by the gate. In the distance behind him loomed the giant flamboyant that shaded the road running by the building. He stood in a jaunty, cheery pose in which he was play-acting his modernity, a cosmopolitan traveller to some of the world's great metropolises, Cairo, Beirut and Istanbul on the way to London and Edinburgh. The tarbush may have been abolished as backward in Atatürk's Turkish Republic, and it may have been on its way out in other places in the 1950s (Egypt, Iraq, Tunisia) where it was becoming an emblem of corrupt bashas and beys and the defeated armies of Arab nationalism, but the news had not yet reached my mother's father, at least not when the photograph was taken. To him it was still a sign of sophisticated Islamic modernity, secular and practical in place of the medieval turban. The white linen suit was more ambiguous: that it was a suit was a salute to Europe, as were the brown shoes in a sandal-wearing culture, but the suit was white, which when worn with modesty was the colour of homage and prayer and pilgrimage, the colour of purity and devotion. The photograph was saved from any air of vanity by the exaggerated crossing of the calves and by the uncertain, half-apologetic smile on his round chubby face, as if he was wondering if he had gone too far in his dressing-up.

Ahmed Musa Ibrahim hovered on the fringes of a group of anti-colonial intellectuals, people like him who thought them-selves connected to the world, and who knew about Saad Zaghloul Pasha, the Egyptian statesman (hence the tarbush), and Gandhi and Nehru, and Habib Bourguiba, the Tunisian insurrec-tionist, and Marshal Tito – nationalist leaders who had refused to be cowed and crushed by imperial bullies of different political shades. These anti-colonial intellectuals Saida's father associated with wanted to become modern too, like the nationalists they admired. They wanted to be able to determine the outcome of their lives without the overbearing presence of the British and their self-righteous and sanctimonious display of self-congratulatory restraint. Those who had dealings with them, like Saida's father, knew that that self-deprecatory mannerism really disguised a smug and condescending arrogance towards everyone, and especially towards *over-educated natives* like him, whose proper fate was subservience and ignorance. Yes, he knew them all right. They chuckled over babu stories about their natives and their Emperor-Seth-like aspirations to modernity – Diploma in Public Health (Failed) – and then humbly praised themselves for their long-suffering kindnesses to the charges they had appointed themselves to rule over. What else could they do? When they were confronted with their manipulative and intimidating methods ... well, there were times, inevitably, when one had to be cruel to be kind.

'No one bid the British to come here,' my mother's father said. 'They came because they are covetous and cannot help wanting to fill the world with their presence.'

It was the 1950s in a colonised territory, not the place to speak in this way. The British authorities preferred to forget that they were conquerors who ruled by coercion and punishment, and considered any outspoken comment on this as sedition. The empire was very fond of that word, but it was almost too late for words like that: sedition and legitimate government and constituted authority. It was time for them to go. There were heated debates late into the night; shouted conversations in cafés, rallies where activists spoke with hatred and derision; friends fell out and turned secretive as political lines were re-drawn. They were heady times, exulting times, watching British police officers scowl powerlessly on the fringes of rallies as the crowds roared, knowing that the departure of the mabeberu and their lackeys and stooges was unavoidable.

The times being as they were, it was inevitable that Saida's father became involved in politics. So in the years just before independence, he had to leave his job because he could not work for a colonial government while he was plotting its downfall. The particulars of his appointment explicitly, and quite reasonably, forbade him from doing so and promised to send him to prison if he transgressed. He went to work on his land instead, growing vegetables for the market, or rather giving orders and employing others to do the hardest work while he stood nearby with arms akimbo. It may have looked as if he was doing nothing, he liked to tell his family, but if he were not there the work would immediately stop and those labourers of his would go to sleep under the nearest tree. We have no discipline, that's our biggest problem, he would say.

He became an informal adviser to one of the political parties, was active in the voter-registration drive and in the literacy-classes movement. He donated to the party and gave fund-raising speeches in local meetings and participated in the organisation of the rallies, which simultaneously offered a raucous challenge to the colonial order and taunted political rivals. He was visible to everyone as an activist, and there was street-corner talk already that he was likely to be given a junior ministerial post in the future. When it came to determining the outcome of their lives, things did not work out as he and his intellectual and political friends anticipated, though. He was killed during the revolution because he did all that he did for the wrong political party.

My mother knew all this first-hand because she was fourteen when her father was taken away. When she spoke about him, it was always with a certain solemnity. She hardly ever mentioned the stories he might have told, or something ridiculous that might have happened one holiday, when perhaps he tripped and spilled a bowl of fruit salad over his trousers, or dropped an expensive glass bowl, or reversed his car into a tree. It was only occasionally that I caught a glimpse of the chubby-faced, smiling man in the photograph: how he loved to sing along with Mohammed Abdel Wahab, making his voice gravelly like the great singer; how he played the air-guitar and pretended to be a rock'n'roller when Elvis Presley was played on the radio, swivelling his hips and rolling on the balls of his feet like the King. But more often she spoke of him as a personage: about his political activities, his generosity to people, his crisply ironed cotton jackets, how esteemed he was. Her mourning for him was so profound that it had diminished those other more everyday memories of him and turned him into a figure of tragedy.

She returned to the story of his arrest several times. When news of the uprising reached them, their father's instructions were that if soldiers or gunmen appeared at the house, which they were certain to do as he was such a well-known campaigner for the other party, there was to be no yelling and screaming. Everyone but him was to lock themselves in an inner room because there were rumours of assault and violence and he did not want his wife and his children to be exposed to insult or harm. The people who were doing this had been badly misled but there was no need for hysterics on any account. He would talk to them when they came and then they would all wait for everything to calm down. When they heard the jeep stop outside the house, Saida and her younger brother Amir ran to obey the instructions, urged on by their parents, but their mother refused to leave her husband on his own and there was no time for their father to insist.

They heard the soldiers banging on the door with their gun butts but there was no shouting after that, just a murmur of conversation as their father had promised. Their mother later said that she knew every one of the four soldiers by name, and she called them out one after the other to them so they would remember. My mother said the names to me too, so that I would remember, but I have tried not to do so. The talking did not amount to anything. They did not realise the violence the victors had in mind and how quickly cruelty begets more cruelty. Their father was taken away by the revolutionaries and they never saw him again, nor was his body returned, nor any announcement made of his death. He disappeared. *I cannot describe*, my mother said. When she came to this point in her telling she would have to stop for a while. The family land and the house were confiscated and became state property, to be given away to a zealot or a functionary of the revolution, or to his mistress or cousin. The announcement of the confiscation

19

was made on the radio, with the instruction that all confiscated houses were to be vacated immediately. Their mother was too frightened to resist or to ignore this announcement as some people did. They moved in with their grandmother, leaving everything behind except what they could carry in their bags. Their grandmother was really their mother's aunt, but there was no word for that, only a description, so she became their grandmother, their Bibi.

'You can't imagine what that time was like,' my mother said, trying again to describe it. 'You cannot imagine the terror of it, the arrests, the deaths, the humiliations. People were driving each other mad with rumours of new outrages, new decrees, with news of further sorrows. But yes, you can imagine, you must try. Nothing stands between us and atrocities but words, so there is no choice but to try and imagine.'

In those first weeks it was impossible to believe that life could ever be any different from the panic they lived in at that time, she said. They all did what they could to show the men with guns that they were obedient, harmless, pathetic people without the slightest spark of defiance or rebellion. There was nothing to fear from them. They would not dream of causing their new rulers any annoyance or irritation. It took a while, but their lives became tolerable somehow amidst that terror. They stayed indoors at first, afraid of the dangers of the streets, except for Bibi, who went out to check on neighbours and to go to a shop whose keeper she knew and who had offered her some supplies. Anyone could see that she was a foolish old woman and not worth the trouble of terrorising. When they started to go out more regularly, it was to see how changed and quiet the streets were, how some houses stood empty or had new people staying in them, how armed men in unfamiliar uniforms stood on street corners or wandered into shops to help themselves to what they needed. They learnt to avoid eye contact, to avoid provocation, to avoid looking at the acts of malice performed in plain sight.

'After a while,' my mother told me, 'it becomes as if these things did not really happen like that, as if you're exaggerating if you speak of them. So you stop speaking and they recede even further away, become even more unreal, become even less possible to imagine, and you tell yourself it is time to move on, let them go, it is not worth the bother of remembering. But they do not let you go.

'Our Bibi lived in Kikwajuni. Her house had an entrance room that was also the kitchen, just like ours has, but it was small and dark like a cave. She made sesame bread to sell and she cooked with firewood because that was what she had always done. The wood smoke made the walls black, and she herself had a shrunken, smudged look, as if the smoke had blackened her and dried her out. Her bread was famous, and perhaps the wood-smoke had something to do with that. Her customers were boys and girls on errands from their mothers, who came to the house throughout the afternoon and early evening because that was when she did her cooking. They were regular customers and she knew everybody who came and asked about their mothers and brothers and sisters. She did business in the old-fashioned way, accepting the coins without counting, refusing to raise prices, under-charging on a good order, throwing in a bread or two as a gift because a child was ill at home, and somehow she made enough for all of us to live on.

'The house had one room beyond the kitchen where we all slept. The washroom was in the small walled yard at the back, where Bibi also kept her supply of firewood stacked on a platform a foot above the ground because she was afraid scorpions would hide in it otherwise – as if scorpions were afraid of heights. She was so afraid of scorpions! She had only ever encountered one as a child and then just briefly as it fell out of a cloth she picked up off the ground and immediately disappeared into a crack in the wall. For the rest of her life, she was on the lookout for scorpions to which she granted magical powers of hurt.

'When we went to her after they took Baba away, she took us in without grumbling and comforted us as well as she could. We were her only relatives in the world, she said, not once but repeatedly. By that time she had been a widow for over thirteen years and had outlived her only son by a decade. My mother was her

21

younger sister's daughter, and in her sister's absence she was Bibi's daughter too. She said these things repeatedly, not forcefully, not insistently, and somehow it was reassuring and comforting. My mother said she was blessed. Wallahi, she would say, that woman is an angel. There was no room for complaint over the blows that had befallen us one after the other, Bibi told us. Someone wiser than us knew what it all meant. We were to say alhamdu-lillah and do what we could. She cried silently while we sobbed, warmed water for us to bathe with, and gave us her bed while she slept on the floor. The coir in the mattress was lumpy and old, and the room was small and stuffy, but it was all she could offer and it was not nothing. When my mother protested about how much work she was doing for us, Bibi scolded her sharply and told her it was none of her business. A child should not begrudge a mother's love. She went to the market every morning to buy what was needed for our meals and get supplies for her business, a gaunt, shrivelled, tireless old woman who lived as if the world was a kinder place than it was, and who could not walk a few feet without someone greeting her by name and wishing her well.

'After a while, my mother fretted that we were a burden to Bibi. My mother was not used to being this dependent, she who had always lived her life surrounded by family and laughter, waited upon by servants, beloved by her husband, made plump by contentment and affection. She who had slept in a comfortable upstairs room where a breeze blew through the open window all night long now lived an overcrowded life where she could not keep herself or her children clean. It was not what she was used to. She slept on a rope bed whose coir mattress was infested with vicious bedbugs which bulged with our blood. When we crushed the bedbugs they smelt like festering wounds, like decomposing meat. The room we slept in reeked of sweat and smoke and some nights my mother could not sleep at all because of our restlessness and Bibi's snores on the floor beside her. But her greatest ordeal was using the unlit and cockroach-infested bathroom and latrine. She whispered to us about how revolted she was by everything in it but we were not to say anything to Bibi. She tried to make things better but could not manage it. Her helplessness made her feel useless. She did what she could to help in the kitchen, but it was not work she was used to and she often seemed to get in Bibi's way, disrupting her customary preparations with questions and suggestions. The smoke was too much for her, and she did not have Bibi's endurance or her touch for bread-making.

'Then at last we had word from a freed detainee to confirm the rumour of our father's death. The man stopped Bibi in a lane and told her in a whisper that he had heard it from a witness, who swore in the name of God that he had seen the act with his own eyes. We did not know if the man who witnessed our father's death said *the act* or if he described what was done to him, but that was what Bibi said and we did not ask for more details because the news made my mother break into a wail of despair. She sobbed for hours on end, clinging to us as we sobbed with her and then stopped and started each other off, again and again, until we were exhausted. For the next few days, my mother sat grieving, weeping silently, shattered and drained, unwilling to believe what she had known for weeks. Then one morning, her eyes swollen and her body sagging in misery and exhaustion, she announced what she planned to do. It was hopeless from the start.

'She was ashamed to have become such a useless victim of events and to know no way of ending them or lessening their tyranny, she said. Her voice was hoarse and thick from crying as she spoke. Everything had always been too easy for her in her life and now she was useless and could not cope, a spineless snivelling wreck. They had all become like that, too ashamed of their puniness to feel anything like indignation or rebellion, to know how to resist these monstrous wrongs, and all they could manage was a subdued, helpless grumbling among themselves. Thousands of people were forced to leave because they had no work or money, and had no choice but to throw themselves on the mercy of a brother or a cousin living in a more fortunate place, further up the coast or across the ocean. Now she would join them, said my mother, to see if she could manage something with the help of relatives or acquaintances who had gone on before to Mombasa or even further afield. It was a time of turmoil, their lives torn apart like that, and they were forced into a kind of callousness in order to survive. She hated abandoning her children …that was what she said and my heart leapt at her words …just the contemplation of the idea made her feel worse than anything she had ever done in her life, but she could not be a burden forever. She would go out there and see what she could manage, and then she would send for them. It would not be for long, just a few months, and then they would be together again. For days she talked like that. Bibi might have said something about the futility of such talk, but she did not. She might have said this is how life finds you, now bear up and do what you can to preserve yourself and your children, but she did not. She murmured, she fed us and warmed the water for our baths.

'But before my mother could carry out her desperate plan, before her preparations to leave had even progressed beyond words and words and endless oaths never to forget her children come what may, she fell suddenly ill. It was like an order issued by a spiteful force outside her. She was sitting on a little stool in the yard, grating a coconut for the lunch-time pot of cassava, one of the kitchen duties she had taken on, when a powerful blow made her lean back and pant for breath. She started to slump to her left and could offer no resistance or even call out. That was how we found her, half-fallen over and panting for breath. I don't think she could have known what felled her because her mind never cleared after that, at least not so far as anyone could tell because she did not say another word we could understand. It was not a fever because she did not have a temperature nor was it anything in her gut because there were no signs, you know, no …'

She gestured behind her but did not say the words.

'There was Bibi and us children and we knew nothing about these things. My mother had lost consciousness and was trembling all over and all we knew to do was to take her to the hospital, Bibi on one side of her in the taxi and Amir and I on the other, between us holding her upright, as if it was important that she should not lurch or slump to one side. It was not far but the taxi was not allowed through the hospital gate and we had to help our mother to walk as best we could, heaving her dead weight without a word spoken between us.

'We went to the accident department first but could not find anyone to speak to. There was one nurse on duty and she strolled past us calmly as Bibi tried to explain what had happened, just walked past as if no one had spoken to her. I don't know how *a nurse* could behave like that. When she did not come back, we joined the dozens of other people in Out Patients, who were waiting for the arrival of the doctor. We sat on a stone bench and said nothing for a while, just like everyone else, holding on to our mother while she trembled and groaned. The room was large and all its doors were wide open but that did not disperse the smell of waste and disease. There were people of all ages there: a fatigued old woman with her eyes closed, leaning against a younger woman who was likely her daughter, a baby wailing without pause in its mother's arms, its eyes clotted with infection, young women in no obvious distress, and men and women in the exhausting grip of one of the many illnesses that befall people like us who live in the poor countries of the world.

'There was a male orderly in attendance and when Bibi approached him to report our presence he waved her away without saying a word. He refused to allow anyone to address him about his or her ailments, cutting off whoever it was with a swipe of the arm and an imperious finger pointed towards the concrete benches where everyone else was waiting. To those who were too persistent to obey immediately, he addressed a few brutal words of warning, which soon sent them wearily away. He then retreated to a glass cubicle, a look of distress on his face, shuffling his papers and hiding from the people he could do nothing for. No doctor had turned up by early afternoon and the orderly told them all to go home, take an aspirin and try again the next day. The Out Patients hours were over and he was locking up. The duty doctor must have been feeling unwell. Go home, nothing to be done now, come back tomorrow. He'll be here tomorrow. I'm locking up now.

'Bibi went to find a taxi and we took our mother home. Throughout the night she struggled more and more to breathe and to say something, but she only managed explosive gasps now and then in which a confused noise that resembled a word could be heard. By the following morning her breathing was such a torment to her that we dare not move her, dare not speak to her in case she attempted a reply, dare not leave her, could not bear to listen to her. A few hours later she died. She could no longer breathe. Her heart burst. I was fourteen and Amir was ten, and I was relieved my mother's agony was over. It may sound terrible to say that but it was a relief when it was over.

'After my mother died, I realised I did not have a photograph of her. We had left so much behind in the old house and were afraid to ask for it back: clothes, furniture, clocks, books, photographs. Then as the days passed I began to fear that I was losing the memory of my mother's face. My eyes could not focus on her and my mother's features became imprecise and shifting. When I moved closer, my mother moved her head slightly, turning her face away, hiding from me. It was because I had not really looked at her when she was alive, had not looked at her as if I intended to remember her face always, had not held her hand while she struggled for breath and had not properly loved her as I should have done. The thought made me feel panicked and ashamed, but as the weeks passed my mother's face slowly came back to me – sometimes a flash of her eyes or the shape of her smile as her face retreated into shadows – but slowly the details emerged and every night, for a while, I called her image to me before I fell asleep in case she tried to hide herself away again. I still call up her face at night sometimes, just to see if she will come.'

2

AFTER BABA LEFT

Saida and Masud, those were their names, my mother and my father. They met at an event organised by the Youth League of the Party when they were both at school. I got that information from pestering my mother about when they first met, pleading with her while she sat in a sullen silence. 'It's just a simple question, Ma,' I persisted. Her reluctance to tell me was part of her general reluctance to talk about my father and herself as they used to be. In the end she told me that it was something organised by the Youth League: they were always nagging us and bullying us in those days, to volunteer on building sites, to sing praise songs to the President every morning, to attend rallies. It was just bullying. But she would not say more about Baba and her and it went on for years like that. If I gave her direct factual questions, sometimes she answered those but not if I wanted details of how it was with them.

I know that he was twenty-one and she was twenty when they married, not too young by our customs. I was born two years later, and just a few days after that Bibi died. After her death, Uncle Amir moved into the house with us too. So at last I was present on the same stage as the main actors in my early life although it would be a while before I had any understanding of the events that I was part of. Uncle Amir was the prince of our kingdom and I grew up adoring him. He made me laugh and brought me little presents and let me play with his transistor radio. When I had a piece of fatty meat on my plate that I could not eat, or a slice of kidney or a lump of yoghurt, he took it away before my mother

27

noticed. But I adored him because my parents did too; I did not stop to think why they did so.

My father was a different man then from the father I knew later but I was too young to form memories of him I can deliver in a lucid narrative. I just remember a kind of gentleness and that heaving laughter and other endless, very clear little fragments: sitting on his lap, a hug, a story, the look in his eyes as he listened to me. I do not remember who took me to my first day in Koran school when I was five. I expect he did because he was very eager I should begin as soon as I was allowed to. I can remember clearly that the first lesson was the letters of the alphabet, which my mother had already taught me. *Aliph, be te, he, khe*. I can see that moment as if I were there now looking on. It was definitely my father who took me to my first day in government school when I was nearly seven, and there our first test was to read the alphabet backwards starting with Z. This was to thwart the cheating ruses of the colonised, just in case we had memorised the sequence of letters without really learning to read them. But my mother had also taught me how to read the Roman alphabet so my first day there was a happy one.

In that year I started government school, where I was happy from the very first day, my mother began work in a government office, and one of Uncle Amir's friends opened a hotel for tourists in Shangani called the Coral Reef Inn and appointed him the manager in charge of social activities. It was the beginning of a tourist invasion which no one had seen anything like before. It took a little while to get going properly but that was when it started. The government relaxed foreign exchange regulations and people from rich countries wanted to come in and take a look at our derelict little island. It was also in that year I was seven that my father left us.

The moment of his leaving passed without my noticing at first. The everyday turmoil in my seven-year-old mind must have been absorbing and profound because it took me some time to understand that something important had happened to our lives. I slept in the same room as my parents and immediately registered my father's absence, but when I asked after him my mother told me that he had gone away for a few days. It was the beginning of a series of important lies which my mother would tell me for the next many years, but when I was seven I had no reason to disbelieve her. It would have seemed to me like the usual comings and goings of the grown-ups, whose affairs were never completely comprehensible to me. I did not understand then that the air of mystery was sometimes fugitive and devious, and sometimes an attempt to disguise anxiety and muddle. Uncle Amir had also been away for a few days but then he came back just before my father went away.

In that confusion I did not realise the meaning of my father's absence, until finally I began to understand that he was not living with us any more. For several days the idea frightened me in a physical, heart-racing way, as if I had lost my grip on my father's hand in a huge crowd of strange people some distance from home, or slipped over the edge of the sea-wall into the black-green water so that my father could not hear my screams. I imagined him distraught that he could not find me and take me home. I was literal in my anxieties at that age and those were my recurring images of abandonment: I was lost in a crowd or sinking soundlessly in the black-green water off the wharf.

When I asked my mother about Baba in the days that followed, she told me again and again that he had gone away for a few days. When the few days were up she said that my father did not want us anymore. She told me that in a way that made me understand she did not wish to speak about it for long. She did not speak with anger but in a voice that was both sharp and resigned at the same time, her eyes bright and glistening, threatening to spark into a rage or fill with tears. It made me reluctant to ask further questions, although I did, again and again, and she did not spark into a rage. She rarely did and I hated it when that happened. She said such ugly things. When I asked if I could go and see Baba wherever he was, she said no. He does not want to see any of us. Perhaps one day. In the end, whenever I asked her why Baba did not want us any more, she sucked in her breath as if I had hit her or else made her hands into fists and turned away, refusing to look at me or give me an answer. I don't know for how long she did that but it seemed a long time. It was at that time that my mother's unhappiness began.

Later I knew that my father moved to a rented room at the back of a shop in Mwembeladu which was owned by a man called Khamis, who was related to him in a distant way on his father's side of the family. My mother took Baba a basket of food every day for years. Day after day, she came home from the Ministry of Constitutional Affairs where she worked, cooked our lunch and took Baba's share to him in Mwembeladu, walking there in the fierce early-afternoon sun. At first Uncle Amir told her to stop but she took no notice and made no reply, only sometimes she pulled a face of pain and disgust at her brother, and once she pleaded angrily for him to leave her alone. They had a shouting argument about it then and at other times too. Later, it would be my chore to take the basket of food every day to the room at the back of the shop. But that was some years later and by then my father had no interest in me. It seemed that when he gave up my mother's love, he lost all desire for everything.

My father no longer worked at the Water Authority in Gulioni. He had been dismissed from there. He was no longer a clerk in a government office. He lived on his share of the takings from the market stall where he worked for several hours every day. He went to the market every morning and returned to the shop just after noon. His hair and beard grew bushy and then both began to show signs of grey, making his face glow darkly in that shaggy tangle. He was then about thirty and the signs of age in his young face made people stare at him, and some of them must have wondered what sadness had befallen him, although many others knew. He did not speak willingly and walked through crowds with his head lowered and his eyes deliberately vacant, not wishing to see. I was ashamed of his abjectness and lethargy because even at the age of seven I knew how to be ashamed. I could not bear the way people looked at him. I wished my father would disappear without trace, forever. Even later, when I delivered his basket of food, he hardly spoke to me and did not ask me anything about what I was doing or how I felt. At times I thought he was unwell. Uncle Amir said he was doing it to himself, there was no need for it. There was absolutely no need for it.

Just after Baba left, Uncle Amir moved jobs, from the Coral Reef Inn to the Ministry of Foreign Affairs, which was what he had always wanted. He had worked at a travel agency for some years before moving to the hotel, and those years were like a preparation which sharpened his hankering for the great world, he said. He wanted to travel, to see the world and then to contribute his experience to the progress of his people. That was his dream. Uncle Amir often talked big like that. Whenever he was around he filled the house with his voice and his laughter and his busyness. He told us about the important people he worked with and how they admired him and his style, about the functions he went to and the new people he met there, about how one day he was going to be a big man, an ambassador, a minister.

In those years, our house was made more comfortable. Uncle Amir would have preferred to move to a larger house in a more comfortable neighbourhood. It's not as if you'll have to pay the rent, he said many times, but my mother always interrupted him and changed the subject. I'm fine here, she said. Sometimes they glanced at me, and I said I was fine there too because I thought that was what they wanted to know. It took me a long time to work out what they were talking about.

The government had straightened many of the roads in the area we lived in, knocking down small houses because they were backward slums, and building modern blocks of flats instead along the widened and brightly-lit new roads. These blocks were painted in various bright colours and built in different parts of town and even in country villages, where they loomed over the weathered village houses like a menace. There were times when there was no electricity, which meant the roads were dark and the pumps did not work so the water did not run because the pressure was too low to deliver it to the upper floors, and the people who lived in the flats complained about the smell of the blocked toilets in the heat. A few streets, including ours, escaped the clearances and lived on in a tangle of lanes. Sometimes I heard my mother and Uncle Amir arguing about where we lived: so noisy here, no privacy

31

from stupid interfering loud-mouthed neighbours, that woman is always bickering with everybody, this house is a slum and every day I have to look at those monstrous ugly flats. Uncle Amir often described our house as a slum. They argued about other things too, about money and about the lunch basket for Baba. Uncle Amir sometimes stormed angrily away, saying mocking words over his shoulder. He said he would move to his own flat at some point soon, but in the meantime they could at least modernise the kitchen. So various people appeared to instal an electric cooker and fit cupboards, a sink, work surfaces, a washing machine, wire-mesh at the window to keep out the bugs, a ceiling fan, a freezer. You can make iced buns and cakes for us now, and steak and chips, Uncle Amir teased my mother, knowing how little she enjoyed cooking. These were foods from his hotel-working days, and he sometimes rhapsodised about steak and chips to annoy my mother when she served green bananas, or rice and curry yet again. Uncle Amir was always joking and making fun.

Both our bedrooms were air-conditioned now, and Uncle Amir had a colour television installed in his room. The television boomed out in our house and could be heard in every room. As soon as Uncle Amir came home he switched the set on just to see that it was still working as it should because there were times when it did not. Then he would get angry with it and fiddle and fiddle until he got it to work, although sometimes it remained blank for days on end. When he did not succeed he said abusive words about the electrician who fixed it for him and went off in search of him. In the end he found another electrician, who told him that the aerial was not properly adjusted, although that did not mean the end of Uncle Amir's anguish over his television. At these times it exasperated him so much he shook his fists in rage at it and promised to kill it, but I think he also did that to make us laugh.

I still slept in a cot in the same room as my mother, but Uncle Amir teased me that I would not be doing so for a great deal longer because he was planning to move to his own flat and then I would have to give up the cot and sleep in a room of my own like a grown-up. He knew that I did not like any of these ideas. I liked sleeping in the cot in the same room as my mother and I loved listening to the stories she told me when she was in the mood. Also, I did not want Uncle Amir to leave.

He was always coming and going, Uncle Amir, always fidgeting, unable to sit still for long, his legs crossing and uncrossing, ankles jittering restlessly. He needed to do things, he said. He could not just sit around staring at a wall. He played music or watched television with his door open, played the guitar and sang at the top of his voice as if he was still playing with the band like he used to when he was younger. He talked about one plan or another, making fun of my mother or of me, laughing and prodding and provoking. So when he went away the following year an unexpected silence descended on our house and us. I was too young to understand precisely where he was going and why, but he explained it all anyway and later explained it again. He was sent on a three-year International Relations course to University College Dublin, intended, he told my mother and me, for future high-flying diplomats. Those words International Relations at University College Dublin stayed with me for years even though I did not know their full meaning.

'It's a very prestigious programme,' he told us, 'very difficult to get into, very generous stipend paid by European governments. Do you know what a stipend is? It's like a salary, only more classy. It's Latin. Do you know what Latin is? It's an ancient language spoken in prestigious universities. Only the very best people are selected for this programme, people like your Uncle Amir. Do you know why they have a programme such as this? It's so that people with personality and style will be fast-tracked to the top.'

Almost no time seemed to pass between the announcement of Uncle Amir's selection and his departure for Ireland, so eager was he to go. He liked to do things that way, he said, get on with them. He planned to do a six-month refresher language course, and at the same time get acclimatised to the Irish way of doing things. He did not need the refresher, he said, but it was all covered by the scholarship, so why not, and he would be getting his stipend from the first day.

33

When Uncle Amir left to go to Dublin to study to be a diplomat, I moved out of my mother's room. From time immemorial I had slept in my cot at one end of my parents' large room. It had a curtain strung across the middle of it to give them privacy. Then my father left us, and I shared the room with my mother, and in our unsettled life she did not always bother to draw the curtain between us. When Uncle Amir left, I was moved into his room. My mother threw Uncle Amir's television away because she said it was junk and more trouble than it was worth. Some time afterwards a brand-new set arrived, which she put in her room because she said it was not right for a child to have a television in his. I could go into her room and watch with her sometimes, whenever I wished, but she did not really like to watch the cartoons, and turned the volume down when I watched them, and chased me off to bed at the earliest opportunity. She liked to watch the news and then endless dramas with women in long dresses and men sitting behind huge desks, all of them living in enormous mansions and driving long, gleaming cars. When I said it was boring, she told me not to take it seriously, then it would seem more amusing. When I tried to see the funny side of the dramas I failed because I could not understand what the people were saying and my mother talked over everything, re-telling the story as she wished it to be and chuckling at her own wit. Sometimes she turned the sound off completely and we watched the silent goings-on on the screen while my mother made up comic stories about what was happening.

When I moved into my own room, I did not like to shut the door on myself. I was so alone in there. A small window high on the outside wall overlooked the lane but I did not leave it open at night because then the darkness surged in and filled me with fear. I missed sleeping in the same room as my mother, who sometimes sang softly to herself as we lay in the dark or sometimes spoke about the past times she could bear to talk about. You have to grow up stop crying don't be such a baby you are nine years old, she told me when I made a fuss about being alone. I covered myself from head to toe as soon as I switched off the light so that I would not hear any of the small scurrying night noises, and I never left the safety of the mosquito net until daylight reappeared. I adjusted these arrangements as I grew less fearful, and especially after I learnt to read books from beginning to end, when I stayed awake longer and forgot about being afraid. When I was a little older, I read so late into the night that my mother sometimes knocked on my door and told me to switch off the light, but it took a while to get to that. I did not lose my fear of stealthy night noises, not realising that everyone felt like that.

At about the time when I moved to my own room or soon after, the woman neighbour who lived at the back of our house died and a short while later her son disappeared. He was a fisherman and it was said that one day he went out to sea alone in his outrigger as was his practice and never came back. Their house remained empty for some years and then turned into a ruin. Later, when I went to live in other places, I realised that ours was a house without echoes, its noises muffled by the soft walls.

I began delivering the daily lunch basket when I was eleven years old. My father had been gone for many years then and I had become used to not hurting when I thought of him. The sight of him looking so shaggy and beaten in the streets helped me to do that. I had seen so little of him since he left us, and he was so silent and far away when I greeted him as we passed in the street, that I was not sure he knew who I was any more. What I knew was that he wanted nothing to do with me. I was afraid of him because he seemed like someone who was unpredictable, someone who had lost his mind. So when my mother asked me if I would take the basket of food to him, I could not restrain my shameful tears and said that I did not want to because I was afraid of him. I expected my mother to get angry, to yelp at me with the unexpected fury that occasionally overcame her, but she did not. I saw that she was making an effort to control herself. She made me sit with her and she explained that I should never fear my Baba, because he was the only Baba I would ever have, and that when I had finished crying I was to dry my face and take the food to him and wish him good health. I did not really see how thinking that he was the only Baba I would ever have would make me less afraid but I appreciated the effort she was making and did my best to suppress my anxiety.

The next day I delivered the basket to the shopkeeper Khamis, a silent slow-moving man who said my name softly and smiled as he accepted the basket and said hujambo to me: *Salim, how are you? You have come to see your Baba*. I hoped that my father was not in and I could leave the basket and go, but he was in and Khamis called him to collect it himself and to greet his son. When Baba came out, I could not look him in the eye and could only mumble a greeting. He took the basket from me and thanked me, then handed me yesterday's empty basket for me to take home. It was like taking food to a prisoner. My father was always in when I took his basket to him and he handed me the empty one every day for years. I got used to it after a while, and within a few months I could not believe that I was once afraid of him in whose eyes, as I learnt to look into them, I saw only detachment and defeat.

In exchange for taking away the television, my mother allowed me to keep one of the boxes of my father's old books in my room. There were several of them. She did not care much for reading but thought it was good for me. There is nothing more important than reading, she told me, although later when I became an avid reader she counselled moderation. When she woke up in the night to use the bathroom and saw that my light was still on in the early hours on a school day, she banged on my door and shouted for me to go to sleep. I was about ten when I learnt to read a whole book, all words and no pictures, and I remember it was a book called *The Tempest Tribes*, found in one of my father's boxes, about people who lived in jungles and mountains and caves and who rebelled against their tyrannical jungle king because a kind stranger from England came and explained to them how unjust and backward their jungle king was. On reflection I think the story must have happened somewhere in Asia because there was a beautiful princess in it, and there was no story with a beautiful princess set in an African jungle. I did not understand all of it, sometimes because the words were new and long, and sometimes because I could not work out what was going on, but I read every page regardless. After that I started on another book and another one after that. It took me a long time to read through the whole box and I did not read everything in it. I found it easier to read the mysteries and Westerns and the alfu-leila-uleila stories. Then I went to my mother for another box and it went on like that until I had all five of them in my room.

One day I put one of the books in the basket for my father, and slowly over the months and years that followed I delivered more of the books with his lunch, after I had read them to my own satisfaction. Some of them I re-read several times before I parted with them, especially the mysteries and the Westerns. I read *Riders of the Purple Sage* six times before I handed it over to him, and even then I was not certain I was doing the right thing. Some of the books I did not part with at all because I never tired of them: Lamb's *Tales from Shakespeare*, Ferdowsi's *Shahnameh*, and the Arabian Nights stories. The story of the humble wood-cutter who stumbled on the young bride imprisoned in a cellar by a jinn haunted me for many years: how he fell in love with her and tried to help her escape and how the jinn took his revenge. When eventually I delivered the basket directly to my father's room at the back of the shop, and he allowed me in there to sit with him for a while, I found the books lined spine upward in an old fruit crate, like objects he cherished.

In the meantime Uncle Amir came back from Dublin in triumph. He returned with his girlfriend, Auntie Asha, who had herself been doing her A-levels at a boarding school in Suffolk. She was the daughter of the former vice-president, and had been Uncle Amir's girlfriend even before he went to Dublin. She visited him there several times, and during the vacations they travelled to London and Paris and Madrid. They were now betrothed. His living arrangements were all in hand, or in his future wife's hands, my mother said. A flat was rented for him even before he returned, because apparently there was no room for him and his belongings in the old house.

'His new relatives are big people,' my mother said sarcastically, although it was true.

The wedding was imminent and there was no question of the newly-weds moving into an old slum. That was how my mother mimicked the way the powerful relatives talked about us, though I had not heard anyone except Uncle Amir use that word for our house. They would only live in the flat for a short while because he was due to take up a diplomatic posting soon after the wedding. He came to see us every few days, once driving Auntie Asha's new white Toyota Corolla. He did not stay for long that time, because he had to leave the new car some distance away and was not sure how safe it was there. 'Who would dare touch a car with government plates? He just wanted to tell us that he was driving a new car,' my mother said afterwards.

It was as if his time in Europe had anointed Uncle Amir with even more glamour, and vigorously polished his halo of personality and style. Perhaps it was my mother's sarcasm about his new relatives that started me off but I found myself resisting Uncle Amir's seduction in a way I had not done before. Or perhaps I was getting older (I was nearly thirteen!). He moved in a different way. The jerky restless movements were more restrained. His manner was unhurried, like someone who knew that admiring and envious eyes were always on him. He laughed differently, in a more controlled manner, giving a demonstration of how to laugh with restraint. Now and then the old joker broke out, and then Uncle Amir would grin mischievously at us, as if he had used strong language but did not want us to take offence. But I did not completely resist seduction. I cherished the gifts he brought me, among them a short-sleeved jersey with UCD written in big letters across the back, which I wore whenever it was clean so that it was faded and threadbare in a matter of months. I loved the photographs of their travels in Europe that Uncle Amir displayed when he was in the mood: sitting at a table in a pavement café in Brussels, Auntie Asha and him in front of the Eiffel Tower, both of them standing by stone lions in a park in Madrid, strolling round Regent's Park Zoo, leaning against a parapet by the Thames. Uncle Amir's and Auntie Asha's presence made those places more real to me and less like fantasy cityscapes on TV.

The wedding was a grand affair attended by ministers and ambassadors and army uniforms and their wives, the guests swaggering in their suits and stroking their jewels. The celebrations were held in a marquee erected in the private gardens of the house of the former vice-president, Auntie Asha's father. My mother was persuaded to sit on a podium with the dignitaries while the speeches were made, and I was required by Uncle Amir to wear black trousers and a tie. Afterwards I wandered the grounds and gaped at their extent and their serenity and the labour that had gone into creating that atmosphere of tranquillity out of such shrill air. Soon after his wedding to Auntie Asha, Uncle Amir was posted to the consulate in Bombay for a three-year mission. Before he left for India he bought me a bicycle as a gift, which changed my doubts about him to shamed gratitude.

I was in my second year in secondary school when my sister Munira was born. By this time I had a better understanding of the situation we were in. My mother had never said anything to me about what was going on in her life and nor had Uncle Amir. No one outside had said anything to me either, not even in mockery, except once, but bits and pieces had drifted into view and I had added them up. I had understood that something shameful was connected to my father, which was why it was a matter not to be spoken about. I had acquiesced to this prohibition because I too felt the shame for my father and my mother regardless of the cause. I was surrounded by silences and it did not seem strange that I was not to ask questions about unspoken events in the past. It had taken me a long time to add things up because I was an inept and unworldly child with eyes only for books. Nobody taught me to see the vileness of things and I saw like an idiot, understanding nothing.

I saw my father every day when I cycled to Mwembeladu with his basket of food. I did that as soon as I came home from school and then went back for my own lunch. I no longer waited at the front of the shop for him to come out but went right to the back, greeting Khamis's wife before going to my father's little room. My father did not go out very much apart from in the morning to sit at his stall in the market, although he did not do much selling, helping out if he was required and sometimes leaving early to return to his room. I took him clean clothes every Saturday, and clean bedding which I changed while he ate his food. If he let me.

Sometimes he asked me to leave the bed alone and I would have to wait until the following day or the day after that to change the sheets. My daily visit did not take long, often I was in a hurry to get back for my own lunch. I put the basket of food on the small table that my father kept clear and where sometimes he read, or did his sewing repairs, or just sat still with his hands folded together, staring out of the window with far-gazing eyes. Then I picked up the basket with the empty dishes and asked if he was well and if there was anything he needed. I waited a moment to see if he would speak to me, which sometimes he did and sometimes he did not. Sometimes he said, I am content, alhamdulillah. Then I walked through to the front of the shop, said goodbye to Khamis, mounted my bicycle and rode home. That was what I did every day.

I was fourteen years old then and a person can feel old and wise at that age even when he really had no idea, and what he took for wisdom was only a precocious intuition arrived at without humility, just a little shit working things out for himself. I thought my father was a spineless and defeated man who had allowed himself to be humiliated into silence and craziness, that he had lost his mind or had lost his nerve, and I thought I had an idea why he had turned out like that although no one had told me. I thought my father was shameful, the owner of a shameful, useless body, and had shamed himself as well as me. I also knew that when my mother went out some afternoons, it was to see a man, and sometimes a car dropped her off two streets away in the evening. I thought she was ashamed of those visits and that they were something to do with the sadness in her life. When she came back from those outings sometimes she did not speak to me for hours.

Once I began to understand what was going on, which was perhaps a year before Munira arrived, I expected to be mocked at school and in the streets, and could not imagine that boys of my age could restrain themselves from the malice. But it happened on one occasion only, when a boy made fun of a pair of shoes my mother had given me, whisperingly asking if they were a gift from my mama's friend. It had never occurred to me that the gift was from this man. The boy who said this was very big, almost an adult, and he said those words to me with a taunting grin, looking to goad me into a reaction so he could beat me up. I turned my back on him and pretended I had not heard the whisper, ignoring the jeering laughter that lashed across my shoulders. Like father like son, I too turned away meekly from shame. I never wore those shoes again. My mother did not mention the man's name or even his existence until just before my sister Munira came, when her body was beginning to swell and grow hard, and by then I did not need to be told.

'His name is Hakim,' she said, with her hand on her belly. 'The baby's father. He is Asha's brother. Do you know who I mean? You see him on television sometimes.'

I did not speak. I could not bear the smile on her face as she said his name. I had seen the same smile when we saw him on the TV news and it was then I guessed for the first time that he was the man she went to see. I looked away when his face came on the TV after that. When she said his name to me, images of that hard-headed man passed through my mind. Did she say *habibi* to him when he touched her?

'Do you know who I mean? You met him at Asha and Amir's wedding,' she said.

I nodded. I saw him, I did not meet him. I could see the look of pain on my mother's face because of my silence. I nodded to reassure her, to make conversation. I saw the man sitting dead-pan on the podium reserved for the bride and groom and their important guests. My mother sat up there too, looking beautiful. She had pleaded hard to be excused but Uncle Amir would not have it. I did not know about that man and my mother then. I was busy breathing in the aroma of brute power all around me.

'His Excellency the Minister,' I said, and my mother chose to smile, to make light of my sarcasm, to pretend I was teasing.

'He is the father,' she said again, touching herself on the bulge, smiling unawares again, pleased with what seemed to me her grotesque disfigurement. 'I would like you to meet him, to show him courtesy.'

41

I did not know what to say then. She looked suddenly so help-less, so unhappy.

'He has asked me to marry him,' she said after a long silence.

'Why does he want to marry you? Isn't he already married?' I asked.

'To be his second wife. He wants me to be his second wife,' she said.

'Why does he want a second wife?' I asked.

'It's not that strange. He wants to be able to see the baby. He wants the baby to have a father,' she said. 'But I said no, I'm already married.'

'Then why are you having his baby?' I asked.

My mother shook her head and looked away. We were both being stupid because she could not speak openly to me and I could not restrain my bitterness. I saw she was annoyed with the way I took her words but I did not know what else she could have expected of me.

'What did he say when you told him that you were already married?' I asked. 'It probably wasn't news to him.'

She shrugged, refusing to placate me. 'I can't talk to you when you are like this,' she said.

'Did he say, we can soon take care of that? He is a big man, why hasn't he already taken care of that?' I asked. 'Why hasn't he taken care of it in all this time?'

She shrugged again, and closed her eyes as if my questions were a matter of great tedium to her.

'What happened between you and Baba?' I asked.

My mother opened her eyes to look at me. I had never asked that question before, not exactly like that, with that directness, with that degree of dislike, with that intensity of blame. He had left when I was so young and my mother and I had found a way of speaking about his absence that avoided conflict. Whenever I asked for details she deflected or ignored me and I did not persist for fear of causing her pain or making her angry. I had always blamed my father for his absence, suspected he was guilty of something that made him cringe in shame as he did. So I had never asked the question in that way before, forcing the issue, demanding of her. She appeared to give thought to it for a moment and then just shook her head. I knew she was not going to tell me anything. Somehow I knew that she did not have the words to tell me what I needed to be told. 'I don't know how to tell you. It is too bad. I caused him grief, and he has made it into a kind of piety,' she said. 'I cannot put right what I've done.'

'Was this man part of what you did to cause him grief?' I asked.

'Don't say this man. Yes, he was,' my mother said.

'Was it because of this man that Baba left us?' I asked.

My mother shook her head again, and was silent. 'It was because of what I did that he left,' she said at long last, and I saw that she was reluctant to continue, that she would refuse to talk even if I pressed, that the wretchedness of it was too much, that she would walk away and lock herself in her room and sob, as she had at other times when I had insisted to be told. I could not bear to hear her do that. 'I cannot undo what I have done. I did not know he would ruin his life,' she said.

'Is Baba so sad because he still loves you?' I asked.

My mother glanced at me and smiled, no doubt amused by my naivety about the human capacity for hatred. 'You ask so many questions. I don't think so. Perhaps he is sad because he is disappointed and ashamed of what he thought he loved. Do you know what I mean? Then he chose to ruin his life.'

I shivered because I was listening to a half-truth. It happened when she lied to me or told me an incomplete story about her absences. 'Why did you do it?' I asked, and then watched as my mother wiped a hand across her brow and turned her face away from me.

After Munira's arrival, I became disobedient and difficult. I did not always respond when my mother called me, and I walked away from her when she rebuked me. There were times when I found her repulsive and could not bear to be near her. I did not hide my disdain from her. I shut myself away in my room whenever I was home and kept out of her way, doing schoolwork or reading. When she sent me on an errand I took hours and sometimes deliberately bought the wrong thing or sometimes bought nothing, just put the money back in her hand without explanation and walked away as she shouted with rage. Once she sent me out to buy a tin of powdered milk for Munira's feed and I returned with a can of fly-spray. I suppose that was the limit. She was not producing enough milk and Munira was yelling at her and I played that prank on her. She shouted at me then with such ferocity that Munira began to scream, and I turned round without a word and went to get the milk.

It did not stop me, though, and I intensified my disobedience with adolescent perversity and malice. The next time she asked me to buy bread from the café, I came back forty minutes later with a box of buttons that I had gone all the way to Darajani for. In the house, I carried out various acts of sabotage. I destroyed the fridge, cut the aerial wire for the new TV, and stole or hid anything else that I thought was a gift from my mother's lover. I intended to smash all the expensive toys that were bought for Munira because I knew their source, but I found myself unable to do so. To my surprise, because I had hardened myself to this mission of destruction, I found that I liked having her with us when I had thought I would not. I liked holding her and feeling her compact completeness and her plump helplessness. So I only sacrificed the odd toy I thought too ugly to survive.

My mother was surprised at first by the campaign of destruction, and pleaded with me to be sensible, but later she said nothing when every few weeks something else was broken or disappeared. When once the man planned to visit, and my mother told me about it, I stayed away all day, walking for miles out of town and returning home exhausted in the dark. I could not tell her, but I grieved for the air of barely perceptible melancholy she carried around her all the time, and I was made sad by the thought of the hard-faced man exchanging intimacies with her and mocking my poor Baba. She never let that man visit the house again, at least not that I knew.

A few months after Munira came my mother installed a telephone in her room. I guessed it was so that the man who was her lover could ring her to ask about the baby. I bided my time for the opportunity to cut the wires and crush the mechanism as I was sure I would do sooner or later. Then I found out that I could hear the shrill ringing of the phone clearly in some parts of my room even with the door shut. Sometimes I could even hear Munira crying and my mother's voice soothing her. We had lived so quietly before that I had not noticed the way sound travelled between the rooms. I would have heard the television except that she hardly ever watched on her own, and when she did often turned the volume down low.

It did not take me long to work it out. The sound came from behind a framed print of a Bombay skyline, which dated back to the days when Uncle Amir worked for the travel agency. I left it on the wall because it was the only framed picture I had in the room and because I loved the sweep of the bay in the foreground. On the floor below the print was an old pencil stub I had not seen before. When I removed the print, I found a hole in the wall about one centimetre in diameter, and guessed that the pencil stub had fallen out of it. It looked as if the hole might once have been where an electric wire came out of the wall to the light switch. The pencil stub fitted into it perfectly. When I took it out again and put my eye to the hole, I found out that my mother's bed was directly in my eyeline. She was not in the room at the time, so I put the pencil plug back and hung the picture in front of it again. I understood immediately that through this hole Uncle Amir had spied on my parents.

When I was a child and Uncle Amir lived with us, I adored him. He had been there from the earliest days of my life, always teasing and laughing and saying outrageous things about people. He never told me that I should *not* do anything, not in those young days, and sometimes he winked at me behind my mother's back when she told me off. He knew what was going on in the world, knew about songs and films and football stars, knew about what to like and not to like. To me as a child Uncle Amir seemed fearless and smart. Afterwards when he left to study, and then to travel everywhere as a diplomat, he became a figure of legend and glamour to me. He always came back with something for me, a token of one of the exotic places he visited: a shirt from Miami, a digital clock from Stockholm, a mug with the Union Jack from London. There were times when I wished Uncle Amir was my father, rather than the silently sorrowful and bedraggled man to whom I took a basketful of food every day. It was a wish that made me feel treacherous and unworthy, a sleazy and muddled little boy, a betrayer, but I did think it more than once.

Later I grew less in awe of him without losing the feeling entirely, but finding the hole in the wall was perhaps when I first began to have doubts about my uncle. It seemed such an ugly, sly thing to do. I thought I should tell my mother about the existence of the hole, in case it should be discovered one day and thought to be my handiwork, but I did not. I never dared to look through the hole, but every now and then, when I was in the mood for their company at night, I switched my light off and took the wooden plug out so I could hear Munira and my mother in the other room, just voices and scratchings. I did not try to listen. That was how I learnt about my uncle's plan for me.

Uncle Amir, after a sensational few years, had become a senior diplomat in the London embassy. He and Auntie Asha had two children now and the whole family were back for one of their periodic visits. Uncle Amir had put on weight, and his manner had become more deliberate, as was appropriate in a man of his eminence. There was at times something menacing in his manner, a hardness he had obscured with his high spirits and bubbling laughter. He was not as restless as formerly. He used to cross and uncross his legs repeatedly, and his dangling foot would waggle as if it had a life of its own, but now his legs were still for long moments, only breaking into a twitching frenzy for a few wild seconds now and then.

They stayed with Auntie Asha's family when they came home but Uncle Amir had used his connections to get the old family house back. His Excellency the Minister would certainly have had something to do with it too. It was now being repaired and redecorated so next time they came they would stay there, Uncle Amir said. My mother asked if any of their things were still in the house and Uncle Amir looked pityingly at her and told her there was only junk and old rubbish there. Still, our parents would have been happy, my mother said.

Uncle Amir visited us every few days and sometimes Auntie Asha came too, but not often. When she came her talk was mostly about her children and their lives in London, how precocious were the former and how complicated and stylish the latter, how hectic and brilliant and expensive. She talked all the time when she visited, as if she knew that we wanted to hear about these things, that we were eager for them, our eyes round with admiration for their sophisticated lives. There was nowhere to sit in comfort in our house except in the bedrooms or round the dining table in the entrance room, and we sat there while Auntie Asha leant back in the chair, talking cheerfully as her bangled arm swept the air.

One evening Uncle Amir came on his own to have a talk with his sister. He announced this as soon as he arrived, glancing briefly and, it seemed, involuntarily towards me, frowning with the importance of the business he had come to discuss. That look was such an obvious clue the talk was going to be about me that while Uncle Amir was sipping his welcome tea, I went to my room, and with unaccustomed decisiveness turned off the light, put my ear to the hole in the wall and waited to eavesdrop. I guessed that if they wanted to talk hush-hush they would go to my mother's room rather than sit in the outer room, in case I came out again.

I did not hear everything. Uncle Amir's voice came through strongly but I could not catch very much of what my mother said. Her pitch was too low and some of what she said was mumbled or perhaps would have been completed by a gesture, but I heard enough to work out the rest. Uncle Amir said he would take me to London. I was a hard-working and clever boy, he said, and it would be a pity to waste that talent. But he would not tell me about the plan until after I had completed school and passed my examinations. He did not want me to stop working and think that the future was all mapped out for me. My mother said she was grateful but was he sure he could afford it? It would not be fair to take me so far away and then leave me to manage for myself.

'Of course he will have to manage for himself to some extent,' said my uncle. 'That is the point. To learn to look after himself in the big world. What do you think everyone else has to do? What do you think I had to do to get to where I am? When I was in Dublin, I had to take summer jobs on building sites and factories and eat chips and cheap mince night after night. But no, I don't intend to abandon the brat there without assistance. We have room in our house, and the embassy subsidy will easily absorb one more mouth to feed. When our eldest was born, I set up a trust, an insurance policy into which I have been paying money for our children's education, and recently I added more contributions so it will cover some of his education expenses as well. He will have to get a part-time job, this is not going to be a holiday. He'll probably not have enough money to visit home for a while either, so if you let him go, you have to be prepared not to see him for some time.'

After what seemed a long silence, when maybe they were talking softly, Uncle Amir's voice came through again. 'No, no, not like that. And anyway, it's my way of paying you back for what you did for me all those years ago. Although you haven't done too badly yourself, after all.' He laughed loudly after he said that. I did not hear my mother's reply. 'It's OK, I'll take him to London with me. I know he's becoming a nuisance here, causing trouble at home and getting bored, and sooner or later he is bound to turn bad. It will also be good to get him away from that feeble-minded man and give him a new start. I don't like the way he goes to see him every day.'

She said, 'Thank you for thinking of him. He will be grateful to you forever, as I will be.'

My first thoughts were not ones of excitement but disquiet. Uncle Amir's and Auntie Asha's affectations about living in London made them seem silly to me and the idea of going there to live with them was unattractive. *How unbearably hot it is back here, is the water safe to drink, this chicken is so tough, I can't eat this bread, oh all these flies, we don't have flies like these in London.* It was mostly Auntie Asha who talked like that, but Uncle Amir sat beside her and looked quite comfortable with her tone of voice, and now and then added something sneering and condescending to advance her case. Then also I had not heard

Uncle Amir mention Baba in that way before, feeble-minded man, although I knew that was how most people must think of him. I had never heard that tone of open contempt used about him, although somehow it did not surprise me. It was what I would have expected a man so full of worldliness as Uncle Amir to think of someone as uncertain as my broken Baba.

I did not know why I had to be taken away from him. My father had no desire for me, and hardly anything to do with me. I took him his lunch and carried away his empty dishes, and I sat with him at times while he silently darned his ragged clothes and talked to him about whatever I pleased. It did not seem to matter what I said, my father rarely asked me anything or remarked on what I said. Sometimes he looked at me for a moment longer than I expected as if untangling a detail in what I was saying, and sometimes, unaccountably, he smiled at me with a kind of relish that confused me, and sometimes he exclaimed words that I did not fully understand. I thought his head must fill up with air sometimes. When we passed each other in the streets, we did not always speak.

When Uncle Amir mentioned my father in conversation, which only occurred very rarely, he called him Masud and never said anything cruel. What I overheard him say through that hole in the wall was spoken with the freedom of a familiar thought, and it made me understand that this was Uncle Amir's suppressed opinion of my father and I found that I minded and wanted to defend him from such disregard, even though it was something he had brought upon himself with such dedicated self-neglect.

When I finished school and the offer to go to London was passed on by my mother, I asked her why Uncle Amir was doing this, and she said because you are like a son to him. I did not ask what she had done for him that he wanted to pay her back for. I was not supposed to know Uncle Amir had said that. I found that when the invitation came, all my doubts evaporated and I could not resist the opportunity to go and see what was out there, could not resist the glamour of living in London. After that, preparations for my departure overtook all other feelings and concerns for a while.

I knew that my mother was considering a move to a flat her lover had rented for her. Munira was then three, and her father wanted to see more of her and was insistent that they should move to more spacious accommodation. He did not want his daughter growing up in a hut, I said, to wound my mother. She was hesitating because of me. She knew I wanted nothing to do with *that man* whose name I never spoke, and that I would make a fuss about moving. I had given up my campaign of sabotage by then but had not relented in my hostility to her lover, and perhaps she feared I might renew the campaign and come up with another atrocity in the new flat. In short, I knew I would be in the way, and when the London offer came up, I was happy to go to that fabled city and see what I could make of myself there. What harm could it do?

It was the last Friday in July when I went to see my father for the final time. He was only forty years old but he looked older, aged. I told him that I was leaving that afternoon, and my father sat very still for a moment and then turned to look at me. It was a long, considering look, towards the end of which I thought I saw something like a gleam in his eyes. What did it mean? Was it amusement? Had he arrived at a new understanding in that long moment? It was unsettling. What was going through the old Baba's mind? It never occurred to me that it could be distress. I had told him about going to London before, but he had not appeared to take any notice. It was when I said, today, this afternoon that he turned that long, considering look on me.

'I'm going to London to live with Uncle Amir and his family,' I told him, ignoring the feeling of unease this gave me. 'He asked for me and he'll send me to school. They both asked for me to join them. London, can you imagine?'

My father nodded slowly, as if thinking about what I had said or maybe whether he needed to say anything. Our eyes briefly touched as they glided past each other, and I shivered slightly at the intensity of the contact. His eyes looked dejected. 'You won't come back,' he said. Then he sighed and looked down and spoke firmly but softly, as if to himself. 'Listen to me. Open your eyes in the dark and recollect your blessings. Don't fear the dark places in your mind, otherwise rage will blacken your sight.'

'What do you mean?' I asked him. My father sometimes spoke incomprehensible words, like an inchoate poetry, and it took me a long time to realise that these were often quotations from something he had read. He had taken to reading his father's old texts and papers, which he had asked me to fetch for him from the trunk where he had stored them. I wondered if this little gem was from there. 'Where does that come from?' I asked again when he did not reply.

'It doesn't come from anywhere. It's just a thought,' he finally said. 'Recollect your blessings, that is the beginning of love. That is from Abu Said Ahmad ibn Isa-al-Kharraz.'

I was not sure if this was a real quotation or something my father made up. When he came up with his Ahmed ibn Khalas al Khalas al-Aduwi or whoever, I sometimes wondered if there really had been such a person or if my father was showing off in learned epigrams, doing his mayaani yaani.

'Can you say it again?' I asked, and he looked up and repeated what he had said. Recollect your blessings, that is the beginning of love. Asking him to repeat it was a mean trick to see if it would come out differently the second time, but it did not. Repetition did not make the meaning of the words any clearer though.

'It was one of my old father's nutmegs,' he continued. 'Listen to me: I have been nowhere, but as you travel keep your ear close to your heart.'

This was a conversation by our standards, but I was not sure what my father meant. Was it a warning about what was to come or just a general reminder not to forget where I came from? Was it wisdom? Was it a test or was he rambling? Should I just forget it? I smiled non-committally, allowing my expression to mean whatever he would like it to mean, and watched as my father glanced back at me and shook his head, his smile broadening. That shake of the head meant that he knew I had not understood him but he was not going to explain. It was at moments like these that I was convinced of his lucidity, and wanted to say to him stop this, stop acting so defeated, let us be up and doing and talk about hopeful things. What has got into you to allow yourself to be crushed like this? Tell me about the dreams of your youth. Come, Baba, let's go for a walk with a heart for any fate. The breeze under the casuarina trees will be sweetest at this time of day. But I did not, because my father's sadness had hardened over the years and his silence was impenetrable, and I was too young and did not have the self-assurance to break it. In a way, I was awed by his misery, by his lethargy, by his self-neglect, and I imagined how deep his disappointment at the loss of my mother's love must have been for him to live like that with such resigned dedication. Then even as I watched, my father dropped his eyes and retreated to his hiding place. As I rose to go he rose too and somewhat hesitantly touched my shoulder.

Before I left the shop, I went to say goodbye to Khamis's wife, who reached forward and kissed me on the cheek. I had not had much to do with her in my coming and going and that kiss took me by surprise.

'Look after yourself and we'll look after him until you come back, inshaallah,' she said, 'he won't be any trouble.'

I shook Khamis's hand and waved as I cycled away, farewell to feeding the prisoner. I did not know who was going to bring his basket for him after I left. As I rode home with a feeling of relief that the episode was over, the anxieties and excitement of the imminent journey reappeared, and I went through the list of all that I had to make sure not to forget and the hazards that I had to avoid. Like Baba, I had never travelled out of the country.

Before we parted, my mother said to me, 'You'll come back, I know that, only don't keep me waiting forever. You'll write to me often, won't you?'

'I'll write to you every day,' I said, and watched her smile at my exaggeration.

That afternoon I boarded a flight to London via Addis Ababa and later remembered very little of the journey. I was so over-whelmed by the strangeness of everything – the inside of the aircraft cabin, the land spread out below, the very idea of being above the clouds. I was so anxious not to do anything stupid. I felt that I was on the brink of something momentous and had no idea that I was just another innocent about to be put through the mill.

Two years after I left, my father's father whom I had never met, Maalim Yahya, came back. He was then seventy years old and living in Kuala Lumpur where he had moved to after Dubai. The old scholar came to collect his only son whom rumour announced to have lost his mind. My father made no protest as his father arranged the travel and flight documents, found a barber who came to the shop to give Baba a trim, bought him some new clothes, and, on the appointed day, arrived in a taxi and took him away from that room where for endless years he had lived a life of squalid loneliness and resigned dejection because of love. I imagined that as they boarded their flight to Kuala Lumpur, there would have been tears in my father's eyes as there were in mine.

PART TWO

3

I Will Write to You Every Day

When I went to live with Uncle Amir in London, it was his wish that I should study for a career in business. Medicine was beyond my abilities and qualifications, he said, and required brilliance and a sense of vocation I did not have, although it would have been pleasing to have a doctor in the family. We would all have felt smarter somehow. Uncle Amir said this with a grin on his face intended to mean he was just making a joke.

'In any case, I will not be able to support you through the long period of training that profession requires,' he said. 'Too much money. How about law? Although that too will take a long time before you are a properly qualified practising lawyer. You don't just leave college and become one, you know. And I cannot get over a prejudice that lawyers sometimes cause needless fitna just for a fee. It's old-fashioned of me but you have to draw a line somewhere. But Business Studies! Business Studies is respectable and flexible, and you can study and work, adding to your qualifications as you gain experience, and make plenty of money besides. In your circumstances, it is the perfect option and it will allow you to work anywhere in the world, because the language of business is the same everywhere. Make money! Think of the outcomes: accountancy, management, consultancy, and at the end of it all plenty of money in the bank. Are we agreed?'

It would have sounded cowardly to tell him that I should have preferred to study literature, and perhaps I did not know how much I did at the time. By the time I left for London, I had worked my way through most of my father's books, had made good progress through the school library shelves, had borrowed and exchanged books with friends, and I thought of myself as someone with proven credentials as a future student of literature. I could quote lines from 'Ode on a Grecian Urn' (*Heard melodies are sweet, but those unheard are sweeter*), from *Leaves of Grass* and 'A Dream Deferred' (*What happens to a dream deferred?/ Does it dry up/Like a raisin in the sun?*). In addition to scores of mysteries and adventure stories I had read *David Copperfield, Anna Karenina, Another Country, Things Fall Apart, The Mystic Masseur* and so on. When I came to London I realised how unimpressive my credentials were, how much there was to read, how much there was to work through. I did not find this a discouraging discovery. It did not matter, anyway, because by the time I came to this realisation, events had already moved on and my opinion was no longer required. Uncle Amir had different plans for me and I did not have the courage to say anything about how I might have preferred to proceed with my life. He had brought me to London and it seemed right that he should also be able to select my future for me. It would have been ungrateful of me to prevent him.

I was moved by the pleasure they took in my arrival. They both beamed smiles at me and Auntie Asha spoke to me as if I was a diffident younger brother who needed to be brought out of himself. This is your new home now, she said. I was too flustered to take in everything immediately, but I noticed the amplitude of space and the expensive furnishings and felt a mean kind of content. Not everyone lived in a house like this even if it did belong to the embassy. When Auntie Asha took me upstairs to show me my room, she gave me a quick hug of welcome, smiling at me as if we shared a secret. The room was luxurious: a large bed, a dark wardrobe the depth of a coffin, a wide desk, a chest of drawers, a bookshelf, a comfortable reading chair, and still left enough space in the middle for a rug. A whole family lived in a room of this size where I had come from. I made a mental note of that as a line I would put in my first letter to my mother. My suitcase, which I had bought new just before I left, looked cheap and flimsy and tiny on that rug, like a cardboard box. I sat on the bed when I was left alone, looking around the room, gazing out of the darkened window then at the clean bare desk with its angled lamp, and I smiled. That is the desk where I will sit and write to you about the wonders I encounter, Mama, and I won't allow the thought of my ignorance to discourage me. I allowed this resolution to overcome the slight feeling of panic I sensed at the edge of my mind. What was I doing here?

The following morning, which was a Sunday, Uncle Amir rang my mother and passed the phone to me so that I could speak to her. He made the gesture casually, but I could see he was exuberant with excitement. After listening to my self-conscious mumblings for a moment or two – I had no previous experience of speaking on the phone and felt an instant discomfort with the disembodied voice – he took the receiver from me and gave my mother a full account of my arrival, piling on the clichés and laughing at my provincial awkwardnesses at the airport. After the phone call he asked me if my room was comfortable and watched me intently as I babbled my gratitude. That evening I had my first-ever encounter with a knife-and-fork. I gave everyone a start so I could follow their example but they were wise to me. Uncle Amir laughed out loud at my clumsiness while Auntie Asha suppressed her smiles. Even the children joined in with their giggles, Ahmed who was eight and was called Eddie and Khadija who was seven and was called Kady. I smiled too because even I knew about the unavoidable comedy of the knife-and-fork moment that initiated someone like me into the life of Europe.

'Do you understand what it means to eat with a knife and fork?' Uncle Amir elaborated after he had his chuckle. 'It's not about becoming a European stooge and giving up your culture. Some of the old folks used to think that using a spoon was a first step towards becoming a Christian. No, it's not about losing anything. It is to begin thinking about food as a pleasure, as a refinement.' Uncle Amir nodded vehemently after he said this, and waited until I nodded back in agreement.

I understood quite quickly – within days – that Uncle Amir's laughter and teasing were now accompanied by a tone that required obedience and a ready smile, and that he could effortlessly turn from raucous jokes to frowns when anything checked his wishes. In those moments, even Auntie Asha's air of unguarded sophistication became watchful and her cheerfulness subsided. *What's up, mister?* she would say, and if Uncle Amir wished to be cajoled out of his petulance he would offer a small smile and make a tiny joke to indicate the beginning of a return to benign times, but if he was not ready yet, he would make an exasperated gesture, waving her away, and continue with his glum looks until whatever had provoked him was put right and his equanimity was stroked into place. It was a manner calculated to intimidate and I duly lowered my head whenever I made eye contact.

Having completed my studying arrangements to his satisfaction, Uncle Amir took me to Debenhams to select my wardrobe for me, reluctantly accompanied by Auntie Asha, who favoured Marks & Spencer. The clothes I had brought with me were quite unsuitable for the cold, Uncle Amir told me. Thin cotton shirts and Terylene trousers, what was I thinking of? You'll freeze your balls off! Uncle Amir preferred that I understood little of what I saw in London, that I needed everything explained and decisions made for me. My opinion was not required on any issue. They bought me a thick light blue sweater, which came up to my chin and wrapped round my neck like a brace, and a navy blue raincoat made of thick raspy canvas-like material. It was two sizes too big to accommodate the woollies I would have on underneath. They bought two long-sleeved blue shirts, which looked shiny and cheap and felt slippery. They finished off with a pair of thick light-blue gloves, blue socks and scarf, and dark underpants. Auntie Asha liked blue. As they walked around the store, Uncle Amir and Auntie Asha discussed the clothes, held them against me, debated the colours and then chose blue, and explained all their decisions to me carefully if briefly.

For the first few months, every day when I left for college Auntie Asha examined me to see that I had my full kit on, whatever the weather. I wasn't used to the cold, Auntie Asha told me during the inspection, and if I did not take care I would end up with a bad chill, and then who was going to look after me? This was London and they were a working family. For the first few months I had no choice but to dress as if I was on an expedition. The sweater was too hot, the coat was too big and made me feel as if I was wearing something discarded by one of the giant Englishmen I passed on the pavements. I took off the gloves and scarf as soon as I left the house and stuffed them in my bag. I was a relation they were paying to educate and clothe, so it was only reasonable that they should be able to choose the clothes they were willing to buy for me. I was surprised, though, by the bluntness with which they did this. I realised that I had anticipated something like it but had not understood the deference and compliance that would be expected of me. I was grateful for their welcome and did not find their sense of entitlement to dictate to me unbearable to begin with but I wished they had allowed me to choose less embarrassing clothes. I knew that I would not be able to replace or wear out that raincoat for years, not so long as I was Auntie Asha's and Uncle Amir's poor relation. It felt like a badge of my neediness. Maybe any clothes would have embarrassed me at that time because the embarrassment lay deeper than what I wore, it was more to do with the overbearing shrillness of the strange air around me.

In the third week in September, three weeks after my arrival in London and fully kitted out, I started college. I made my way there in fear and trembling, London terrified me so much. The streets confused me. I could not make them out from each other. The buses and taxis and cars roared past and churned up my gut. The rush of people and vehicles muddled my sense of direction and panicked me. It humbled me that I recoiled with so much anxiety. I felt as if the city despised me, as if I were a tiresome and timorous child who had wandered unwelcome out of the dust and rubble of his puny island shanty into this place where boldness and greed and swagger were required for survival.

*

Uncle Amir's and Auntie Asha's fabled London life turned out to be frantic and I had to play my part in it and bustle about just like everyone else. It made me think of the way I had lived with my mother for all those years, how quietly we went about our days and nights. Homesickness probably made the memory of it seem even calmer. We hardly ever spoke crossly to each other, or not until the later years when I turned saboteur to make plain my feelings about her lover, and even that we resolved somehow. She hid or locked away whatever she thought I would destroy, if she could, and I did not have the spitefulness to carry the matter through, and reprieved necessary household objects from my rage. In any case I could not sustain the anger and after a while I felt I was being perverse, punishing her for her betrayals and lies. As I shared the anxious, frantic lives of Uncle Amir and Auntie Asha, I thought back to the accommodating way my mother lived with me and I missed her.

Dear Mama,

Salamu na baada ya salamu, I hope you are well and sister Munira is well. I hope you received the letter I sent you several days ago. I am enclosing a picture of Hyde Park, which I cut out of a magazine. I haven't been there yet, but I hear it's not far and we'll go there one of these days. This is how it looks when it's warm, so that's something to look forward to.

It is now October and I started college last week. Everything is going perfectly except that it is getting so cold. This morning I was woken by cramp in my calves and when I am outside I cannot prevent my teeth from chattering. I used to think it was a joke that your teeth would do that, but it's true, they do, and there is nothing you can do about it. Chatter, chatter, chatter, whatever you do.

London is full of people from everywhere in the world. I just had not expected to see that, Indians, Arabs, Africans, Chinese, and I don't know where all the European people come from but they are not all English. That is only from what I've seen in the few streets I have walked through and this is a huge city. When a double-decker bus goes by and you see the faces through the window, it is like a glimpse of a page in an illustrated children's encyclopaedia under the title People of the World. Everywhere you go, you have to push your way through crowds and hold on to your possessions. Maybe not in Hyde Park because it looks so roomy, but more or less everywhere else.

I walk to college almost every day. I make myself do that so I will lose my fear of the streets but also because I prefer it. It takes me about forty minutes to get there, but it's better than struggling with all those people on the buses or the underground. To be honest, I think I'm scared of that press of people. It gets so crowded on the underground that I feel as if I can't breathe. Trains that travel under the ground! We are so backward! It is not really far and the walk is more peaceful. You just cannot imagine how enormous this city is. Remember how it used to take me ten minutes to ride to school. Don't worry, I'm not going to turn into you-know-who, talking about London as if it is a place of magic. Uncle Amir and Auntie Asha send their regards. They are looking after me very well and have made me feel as if I am at home. I think of you and Baba. Who is taking his lunch basket to him?

Love,
Salim

I tried not to mind their impatience. At first Auntie Asha treated me like a guest and took my side against Uncle Amir or the children. That only lasted for a few weeks. Afterwards I could not be sure how she would be with me. When she called for me by shouting my name as she sometimes did, I had to drop whatever I was doing and run to her, to avoid her accusing me of disrespect. I was not used to that tone or to the raised voices and the hectoring words and being blamed for so much that was not my doing. Do you think you have a servant in this house? she would say when I had not been quick enough to carry out an instruction. Sometimes she talked to me with confiding affection, as if I were a younger brother. At other times she spoke to me as if I were a lazy servant, or rebuked me for a mishap to the children as she would an inattentive ayah. Then for a while she would not speak to me at all, as if in the grip of a deep resentment.

Perhaps my presence disturbed the balance of my uncle's and aunt's lives, intruded into their ease. Both of them had a wounded way of speaking as if the whole world was against them whenever the smallest thing went wrong. But they weren't like that all the time, and I tried to fit in as required. I reminded myself to be grateful. I went to college every day and attended all my classes. I looked after the children when required, gave them milk and biscuits when I was told to, and sat with them when their parents went out. They were sophisticated children, who knew already that their lives were going to turn out eventful and fulfilling.

One sunny weekend day we walked to Hyde Park, which was even closer to where we lived than I realised. I chased about with the children while Auntie Asha looked on, smiling and applauding our antics, and Uncle Amir took photographs. He got me to sit for some quieter shots to send home to my mama: here is the young man having family fun in the famous Hyde Park in London where everything is the most famous in the world. When he got the photographs back a few days later Uncle Amir frowned at the quiet ones he had taken of me. I was grinning widely in every one of them

'That grin has obliterated any sign of personality or style,' he told me. 'You look like a buffoon. Why are you grinning like that?'

'I don't know. I think cameras make me nervous,' I said.

Uncle Amir looked at me with astonishment. 'Stop talking like a child,' he said.

'Whenever anyone points a camera at me, I smile like that,' I said.

'That is not a smile, that's a grin,' Uncle Amir said. 'Next time I take a photograph of you, I want you to compose yourself so that your personality comes through, not your teeth.'

Another sunny day was not long in coming and I was instructed to fetch my books and spread them out on the patio table, then seat myself there unsmiling and hard at work. That was how Uncle Amir wanted me to look. That was what he wanted my mother to see he had brought about.

After several weeks I found evening work in a supermarket and discovered unexpected satisfaction in stacking shelves and mopping floors. I did not at first understand that it was because it offered an undemanding escape from the stifling atmosphere in the house. I did not know the uses of all the products I stacked on the shelves. Everything was new and sometimes surprising, but the strangeness was also familiar in an unanticipated way. What a good idea, I would think, as I learnt the use of this or that. I had to take myself to the store and bring myself back late in the evening, working out the way, catching the bus, learning to live. When I received my first pay, I briefly forgot how tiring the work was. To have money I had worked for! It was such a delicious feeling of freedom, so ridiculous, as if I now had a life of my own. During vacations I worked in a warehouse as well and later in a launderette, turning myself into a migrant helot to show Uncle Amir and Auntie Asha that I deserved the good fortune they had granted me.

In December it snowed.

Dear Mama,

I stood on ice today. I woke up in the morning to a deep hush, and went to the window to look out at the back garden, and everything was changed. All the neighbouring roofs were covered with snow and everywhere looked so clean. It made me think of the angel on the Makkan hillside, cleansing the shepherd boy's heart with driven snow. The pavements were covered too, which was beautiful to walk on at first, crunchy and almost silent, but the snow soon became dirty and perilous from so many feet and from the wash of cars driving by. But that first moment when I stood on ice, I will never forget that. The crisp air made breathing easier. I think today was the happiest day I have had here.

I did not send that letter because I did not know how to continue after those few lines, and when I returned to it the mood was gone. Uncle Amir took a photograph of me in the snow in the back garden, and I sent her that and wrote on the back: *I stood on ice*. I had bought myself a fat spiral-bound notebook with thin pages that were perforated along the margin. It was my letter-writing pad, which I kept hidden in a drawer. I abandoned several letters because I had lost the thread of my thoughts or had been too frank or homesick and unhappy. I left the unsent letters in the notebook so it also became a place where I captured solitary and gloomy reflections, sometimes deliberately. One day Uncle Amir came into my room as I was in the middle of writing, and in my surprise I was slow to close the notebook. He playfully snatched it from me and started to read aloud in a mock-confiding voice. He must have realised that he was reading something intimate because he stopped and gave the book back to me. 'It's not wise to write things down,' he said, scowling disapprovingly. 'You can never unwrite them.'

I learnt to live in London, to avoid being intimidated by crowds and by rudeness, to avoid curiosity, not to feel desolate at hostile stares and to walk purposefully wherever I went. I learnt to live with the cold and the dirt, and to evade the angry students at college with their swagger and their sense of grievance and their expectations of failure. I learnt to live with the chaotic languages of London, which did not speak to each other, and to cope with English that was broken and wrong, missing articles or in the wrong tense. I tried but could not join in the city's human carnival. I feared the silent empty streets at night, and always hurried home when I left work, crossing the street as soon as I glimpsed a group of people on the pavement ahead. I made unexpected friends: Reshat whose parents were from Cyprus, who made me laugh with his endlessly dirty talk, and Mahmood from Sierra Leone, whom we called Mood for short, who never seemed to run out of smiles and goodwill. They were my college friends. My time after college and work belonged to Uncle Amir and Auntie Asha. My college friends teased me about that, saying that my father was an ambassador and he lived in Holland Park and would not allow me to play with the poor of the Third World. I told them Uncle Amir was not my father and he was not an ambassador, but they took no notice. Reshat clowned around as the self-important ambassador, stomping up and down, shouting obscenities about immigrant riff-raff in London slums.

'I will report the fuckers to the Special Branch if they don't stop trying to turn you into a drug-pusher and a pimp,' he shouted, pushing out his belly and pouting his lips.

I laughed too but I thought there was something unhinged about Reshat. Sometimes Lizard, another of Mood's friends, joined us. He was doing a diploma or something in Quantity Surveying. He did not seem too eager to talk about that or about anything else. His face was often dead-pan, on the brink of a sneer, but even he could not resist Reshat when he was on his manic high-horse. Mood said Lizard had been to juvenile prison for hurting someone in a fight but he was not really as scary as that sounds. I asked why he was called Lizard and Mood said he did not know, but Yorubas were big on lizards. People like Lizard made me realise how sheltered my life had been, and that made me feel as if I had been denied something rather than spared, that I was somehow inadequate.

The newness and the strangeness did not last but nor did they completely go away, and despite the chores and the labours I took on, I could not disguise from myself that I had no interest in what I was studying. I thought I could study without being interested but I had not anticipated the anxieties of living in an alien and hostile city without the company of other students like myself or the nagging persistence of my mother. I had not understood the difficulty of speaking in the company of strangers. Uncle Amir kept me under surveillance but he was busy and often tired and too easily satisfied with my garbled accounts of my progress. At some point during or after dinner he would ask for a report on my day, and seemed to take as much pleasure as I did in every small victory. If we were on our own, he would make a joke about girls at college and whether I had managed to get a phone number out of one of them. I could just imagine the frowns and the glares if I said yes. Is that what you have come here to do, spend your time doing filthy things with English girls?

I did not tell him that so many of the books he saw me carrying around were novels I had borrowed from the college library, not instructive texts on accountancy and management. It was in that library that I had run into Virginia Woolf and Joseph Conrad and

John Dos Passos for the first time, and there was a deep pleasure in the unhurried way I was able to read them and have them lead me to others I knew nothing about.

Sometimes Uncle Amir had to go out in the evenings to attend a diplomatic event, and then he came home and showered and changed into formal clothes, whistling and teasing his children as he looked forward to the function. He looked glamorous in his dinner jacket and bow tie, like a ballad singer on a Saturday Night special on TV. He was so very pleased with himself that I imagined him able to walk into a room and just not see anybody without even trying, having eyes only for himself. Auntie Asha went with him sometimes, but she did not look forward to these events as he did. He had no time to keep an eye on me at such times, so altogether it was not too difficult to evade his scrutiny. Also in the first year I did well, which would have reassured him, but when I returned after the first summer vacation my college life went to pieces. Somehow or other I was able to disguise this decline for several months, and in moments of optimism I was even able to reassure myself that dedicated cramming in the later stages was sure to rescue the situation.

*

I was frequently at home alone with Auntie Asha and the children. If she needed me downstairs she called for me to amuse the children or to help in the kitchen. It pleased her when I asked questions about cooking. Unlike my mother, Auntie Asha was a painstaking cook, trying new recipes that she had read about or meals that they had eaten when they were out, and I sometimes stood in the kitchen watching and listening as she went about her work. My mother, on the other hand, hardly ever varied her menu, and cooked the same meals week after week, only changing her routine if there was a shortage. The sameness was sometimes wearying.

Auntie Asha had her favourite subjects, which were mostly herself or the children. She talked to me about her youth, about the boarding school in Suffolk – the best time of her life – about her vacations in Dublin and Paris, and, when she was in the mood, about how in love Amir and she were in those days. She spoke about her father, who was no longer in the government and whom I had never met but had seen often on TV. She mentioned her brother Hakim whom I had never met either and whom I loathed with calm detachment. He is practically your step-father, she said, and I did my best not to react. She talked about Uncle Amir and my mother, approaching and retreating, hiding something, the stories varying as she circled events and narrated them in their best light. Oh once we almost got into trouble, she said, but she collected herself and said no more and I wondered what it was she was struggling with and whether it was to do with me. Sometimes she paused in what she was saying and looked at me wonderingly, and then I tried hard to look as harmless as possible and for a while I played the fool. I learnt to ask questions, not wanting to know too much, not caring if the same story was told again and again, flattering her when I was required to and slowly I gathered together tantalising fragments of a story that still did not come into focus.

I did not think she always told me the truth, and was convinced from her tone at times that she was lying. I did not know if there was any reason to lie or if she was doing it out of habit. I thought she trusted me because I was obedient and spent so much time with the children, the royal infants as I thought of them, whose glittering futures in glamorous professions were already assured if their parents had anything to do with it.

The last traces of the awe I once felt for Uncle Amir were gone, and I had learnt to beware his compulsion to dictate and control, and to escape the suffocating family life he required me to be part of. He probably knew he had lost me. It is impossible to disguise such treachery. I was now quite familiar and secure in London streets and did things with friends at the weekend, mostly playing a football game or going to central London for the afternoon or else West to nowhere in particular, or sitting tight in my room reading or listening to music. I was missing most of my classes and had exhausted my dutiful labour at the material and now only felt resentful and inadequate as I struggled to learn things I had no interest in. When I was scheduled for my most unbearable classes, I found a secluded corner in the college library and buried my head in novels. At some point I knew I was adrift and I understood that what I was doing would take me years to put right but I could not do anything about it. I hid this knowledge from everyone including myself. I ignored the pathetic teenager inside me who was sinking into paralysis. When Uncle Amir questioned me, I lied. I rarely attended classes and no longer completed assignments, and in the end the teachers stopped bothering me.

One Sunday afternoon in March, a few months before the examinations were due to take place, when I had made myself completely wretched for weeks with my derelictions, when I was beginning to feel nauseous with anxiety and self-hatred, I decided to come clean. I did not really decide there and then, it took me several days of silent debate before I was able to speak out. It was a warm afternoon. Uncle Amir and I were sitting on the patio after lunch while Auntie Asha was on the lawn with the children, building a tent out of some old sheets.

He turned in my direction at some point and I blurted out: 'I can't take the examinations. I don't want to do Business Studies. It was a mistake. I have no ability for the work.'

He looked at me in surprise and did not say anything for a moment. I was afraid I was going to burst into tears or something stupid like that. 'Come inside,' he said, getting to his feet. I followed him into his office and shut the door behind me. There was no need for the world to hear him abusing me. Uncle Amir examined me for a moment longer, frowning, as if he would be able to understand what I said better from my appearance. 'What does this mean? You were doing well. What's happened?'

'I struggle constantly with these subjects. I have no interest in them and I don't have the talent. I find the work so difficult to understand, so boring,' I said, hearing the whine in my voice but feeling too miserable to suppress it. *So boring*, just like a child. 'I don't see how I can go on to study this sort of thing for the next three years. I don't have the skills for it. What is the point of struggling for the next two months to pass examinations that will be of no use to me?'

Uncle Amir stared at me as I spoke, a look of pained surprise on his face. He spoke to me, reasoned with me: don't give up, unexpected things happen all the time, don't think they don't. He tried to cajole me into continuing, flattering my talents and my capacity for work, and then impatience overcame him and he exploded. 'Don't be such an idiot,' he shouted. 'Of course you'll take the exams. Do you think life is easy? You don't have the talent! What is all this talent rubbish? The only talent you need is hard work. We'll talk about alternative careers later. For now you just stop this whimpering and get your arse in gear. You can't give up after all this time, after all this expense, after all I've done to bring you here and to look after you.' The room quivered with his indignation. His mouth was opening and closing as if he was gasping for air, as if his rage had taken him unawares. I could not prevent my lips from trembling. It was not from fear of pain but from the tension his rage provoked in me.

'I won't pass the exams,' I said carefully, to disguise the quivering of my lips. Uncle Amir stiffened, restraining himself. 'I can't study this material,' I continued slowly. 'I've been missing classes all term. I haven't completed assignments for a long time. It's pointless.'

Uncle Amir looked at me without speaking for a moment, his face slowly swelling. Then when it seemed as if he would start shouting again, he took a deep breath and turned his back on me. They must train them to do that in diplomat school. After a few seconds he turned round and, in a calm hard-edged voice, said, 'You impudent little shit, you will do as I say, and you will go back to class and revise every day and pass your exams or I will crack your head open. Who do you think you are? You must have inherited some idiot genes from your father. Go up to your room and get started on your revision now ... go!'

I went, of course, because the alternative was to leave the house and I had not thought what I would do if it came to that. I had hoped he would listen and get angry with me because that was his way and because I deserved it, and afterwards say to me, all right, let's see how we can move on with this. For the next several days he did not speak to me at all except to ask me in a bark if I had attended classes, while Auntie Asha encouraged me with little lectures and admonitions. I did as I was told because I had no option. He was my guarantor and my financier and could have had me expelled from the country at will, so I went back to classes and did the assignments as best I could. Auntie Asha asked me questions about my college tasks and must have sent back good reports because after a while Uncle Amir offered me haughty words of encouragement: Keep it up, my boy.

Auntie Asha said to me: 'Your uncle is doing this as much for your mother as for you, you must remember that. It isn't only yourself you have to think of.' When she saw how well her encouragement was working and how dutifully I sat at my desk in those miserable weeks, some of her trust in me returned and she spoke more gently, took pity on me and even brought me a cup of tea now and then. I must have found the self-abasement satisfying in some way because there were times when I offered additional gratuitous cringing when it was not even required. I said one day that I did not deserve this kindness that they were showing to me and Auntie Asha glowed with righteousness. 'Well, I told you, it's for your mother as well as for you,' she said.

I was sitting at the kitchen table, my notes and books in front of me, and Auntie Asha was putting pots and pans away and wiping down the kitchen surfaces while dinner was cooking. It was like an invitation and I could not resist. 'But you don't owe her anything,' I said.

I expected her to see through my probing ruse and change the subject, but after a long considering silence, she made a decision. She came over to the table and said, 'Well, in a way, your uncle does owe her, I suppose. Do you remember, I told you about that time when we were almost in trouble, when we first got together?'

'Yes, I remember,' I said.

'Well, I don't think I told you that your uncle was detained for several days, did I?'

'No! You mean detained in jail? I've never heard that,' I said with overstated horror, although I really did not know that Uncle Amir had been detained. But this was the story coming, I thought.

'Yes, in jail,' Auntie Asha said. 'Your mother helped him then when he was in trouble. Do you know why he was held? It was to do with us, the two of us. We had just met then, and my brother Hakim, your uncle Hakim, did not approve of us being together.'

She paused there and looked at me in a teasingly tantalising way, as if she was considering withholding the rest of her story after all. I thought she was enjoying the telling of it, and, despite myself, I smiled. She smiled too, and then continued. 'Well, it was worse than that. I mean it was worse than disapproving. It was a complete misunderstanding. Hakim just got it wrong. He got angry with Amir, very very very VERY angry, and you probably know what he's like when he loses his temper. He …' she paused for a moment as she looked for the right words but then she changed direction '… so he had Amir arrested. It was a mistake, Hakim just got it wrong. He thought our family had been insulted. He lost his temper and decided to be nasty, that's all. But –' she laughed, and waved her brother's rage away with a sweep of her bangled arm '– when he saw your mother he fell in love with her, and your uncle Amir was released from jail and we are now living happily ever after. So that's what he owes your mother.'

The words sat in my mouth for a few minutes before I spoke, filling it up until I could not keep them in any more. 'Did she have a choice?' I asked, eyes lowered, trying to avoid a challenge.

'What!' said Auntie Asha sharply, retreating from the table, but then she spoke more calmly. 'What did you mean by that?'

The words had been sitting in my mouth for months, but I had not dared to let them out because the question seemed so wild. I had seen that man on television, the Minister of State for Something, with his shaved head and powerful stubborn neck, and when I thought back to that face I thought to myself: he forced her. Why not? A lot of wives and daughters had been forced to make themselves available to the powerful. I did not know about Uncle Amir's detention then.

When I did not reply, Auntie Asha said, 'What did you say just now?' Her voice crackled with the beginnings of outrage, and I took heed and did not speak. 'Nobody forced her, do you understand? You can ask her yourself. How can you say such a thing about your mother? You have no respect. You don't even know what you are talking about. How can you say such a thing? How can you even think such a thing? You are an enemy, you are a snake. And what does that make your uncle Amir? How dare you! How dare you!' Auntie Asha said, her voice trembling with rage now. 'You are a despicable, dirty insect. You are an ungrateful, filthy boy. How can you live in the man's house and say such a thing? He has been like a father to you. How can you eat the food we put in front of you and think this?'

Because I am feeble and shameless, and have taught myself to eat shit, I thought but did not say, could not say. Because I have been fed deference and defeat in my mother's milk. Because my mother wanted this for me and she has seen enough sadness. Now I am here like a vagabond at your mercy.

'Don't you dare say a word about this to your uncle, do you understand?' Auntie Asha said and then left the kitchen.

I rose to my feet as well, collected the books that I now carried with me around the house as a sign of my intent to obey, and went upstairs to my room. I will write to my mother, I will demand to know, I told myself, but I knew I could not do that. The meaning of Auntie Asha's rage must be that something bad happened, and it had something to do with my father leaving.

I expected that when Auntie Asha reported what I had said and put whatever inflection she chose to on my words, Uncle Amir would come hurrying upstairs to rage at me, but no feet pounded up the stairs. When dinner was ready Eddie was sent up to call me, and I went down and ate without a word being addressed to me – no instructional lecture tonight – while Uncle Amir and Auntie Asha talked to their children. In the days that followed Uncle Amir did not speak to me at all, and did not even look my way. He spoke to Auntie Asha and the children in his normal way, as if I was not there.

All my penitent studying amounted to little. I knew after each of my examinations that I had failed. I just could not work up the urgency and did not have the knowledge. I could only complete one answer and dabble at the other two in each of the papers, despite the genuine effort I had made in those last weeks. I decided to speak to my uncle, to negotiate my exit before Uncle Amir formulated a decree. I had been in England for two years by then, and I thought I knew enough to be able to fumble my own way around, but to stay on at all I needed Uncle Amir's cooperation. So during the weekend after the results came out, when he was in his study doing paperwork, I knocked on his door.

'I made a mistake with this course,' I said. 'It was my own fault, I should have spoken sooner, I should not have lied to you. I should've explained to you what I really wanted to study and persuaded you to support me. I am sorry that I have been unable to repay your generosity by turning out to be a successful student. I had thought that with application and perseverance I would be able to succeed even in a subject that I had little enthusiasm for, but I could not after all. I am sorry for all the trouble I have caused you.

'I now want to study literature and I will re-enrol at the college to do that. I will have to re-enrol as a full-time student because otherwise I will not get a visa. I will then find unregistered work and support myself. But I will need to show financial means of looking after myself while studying. Will you agree to provide the guarantee? You will not need to give me any money. The alternative is for me to disappear but I don't know if I will still be able to study after that. If you are unable to offer the guarantee, the best thing will be for me to go back.'

Uncle Amir looked at me thoughtfully and did not say anything for a long while nor did I attempt to add to what I had already said. Then he nodded and said: 'You have put your case simply and clearly. I have been wondering what you were going to come up with now that you have made such a mess of this opportunity. You are a stupid, ungrateful boy. It is a side of you I was unaware of before but which I have seen more and more of as you have been living with us. If I had known, I would not have wasted our money and brought you here to live with us. It would have saved us all a lot of stress and we would have been spared the pointless anxiety of trying to get you to study when you had no intention of doing so. In addition to that it appears there is something malicious and rotten in your spirit and that you are itching to cause mischief. Asha told me what you said to her about your mother. Nothing could be further from the truth. I will tell your mother about your ingratitude, both to her and to us. I think she had higher hopes of you.

'I don't know why you want to study literature. I don't know where this idea came from. It's a pointless subject, of no practical use to anybody. What will you do with it afterwards? It will neither feed you nor teach you any skills nor allow you to make anything of your life, but that's your business. I tried to help you but all I got back was vileness and ignorance. I have enquired at your college but they tell me they cannot give me any information about what went wrong. This country and its stupid rules! I expect you got mixed up with drug addicts and criminals, this city is full of them. Now you can join them and be a proper cheating unemployed immigrant. I tried to give you something more worthwhile than that. We tried to give you an opportunity and a home, but that was not good enough for you. You preferred to spend your time with those immigrant loafers. You are my sister's son and I cannot give up my responsibility to you, but I want you out of my sight. In the meantime, I will arrange the financial guarantee, as you ask, but I will not support you. I don't want you here any more. I would like you to make sure you move out into your own accommodation before we go away on vacation. Then after that you can go to hell. If you require anything else from me, write me a note.'

4

THE OAU HOUSE

I moved to a room in Guinea Lane in Camberwell, in a house I shared with three other men all of whom were African. It was a long way from the embassy house in Holland Park, a long way in luxury but also in many other respects. The traffic roared by in both directions on Camberwell Road, and the ramshackle chaos and littered pavements of Peckham Road were just a few minutes away. I heard about the room from Mood, who knew about it from his cousin who lived in the house. The landlord, Mr Mgeni, lived next door. Camberwell was not a part of London I had been to before, and in my imagination the Borough of Southwark was a landscape of dark houses that were crusted with soot on the outside and smears of dried human fluids on the inside. It must have been something I read but I imagined it as a place of ancient pain. I had not been south of the river that much altogether: a tube ride to Brixton Market with Mood, an afternoon in Greenwich with a group of friends, a museum trip organised by our Liberal Studies teacher at the college. It was not a famous museum and most of the exhibits were textiles from poor and oppressed places in the world, so at least part of the point of the visit was to show us *ethnic art*, to teach us not to despise the clumsy efforts of backward people. It was in this spirit of adventure that I set off to view the room.

Mr Mgeni was a neat, friendly-looking man in his sixties, with a good-natured smile and a carefully modulated voice and cheering manner. He was skinny and short with a peppery moustache and tight-knit hair. His movements were jaunty and a little overstated as if he was constantly making an effort. He swayed slightly as he walked, hands in the pockets of his short jacket, his whole body in motion as if gently keeping time to a beat only he could hear. I thought he had a teacherly look about him, but I also saw something spiky and world-weary in those alert eyes. I liked him at once and grew to like him a great deal more as I came to know him. He gave me a long look and broke into a huge smile when I greeted him in Kiswahili.

'Aha, I thought so,' he said. 'Jamaa, mswahili mwenzangu. One look at you and I knew. Mswahili huyu. That's what I said to myself. We're related.'

I had guessed from his name, then when I saw him I was certain. Mr Mgeni asked me where I came from and explained that he himself was from Malindi in Kenya. He had left so many years ago that he could hardly remember anything about it. No, that was not true, but he could not be sure if anything still looked as he remembered it. Had I ever been to Malindi? It must look very different now, with all these package holidays you see advertised. He could not imagine the Malindi he knew being a package-holiday destination. Had I seen the brochures? Probably all filthy criminal money from somewhere, money laundering whatever that is. The hotels in those brochures are like fantasies. Tourists wouldn't go there if they couldn't stay in palaces, of course, as if that was how they lived in their own homes. Did I want to see the room? Please understand these are bachelors' quarters, rough and ready and cheaply furnished, just right for a jaluta like you. A week in advance and a handshake was enough for him. Of course the room was mine if I wanted it. It was a little small but it was empty, so I could move in straight away if I liked.

When I got back from Camberwell, I told Auntie Asha that I would be leaving the next morning. My announcement probably sounded like insolence and discourtesy but it was meant as a small gesture of independence. My belongings still fitted comfortably into the cheap cardboard suitcase I had brought from home. I woke early, washed and dressed and waited on my bed for the house to wake up. I looked round the room I had lived in for two years and I shivered. It was a sunny Sunday morning and no one was in a hurry, because while I was upstairs pretending to pack last night, they had all stayed up late to watch the musical *Aladdin*, ignoring me and refusing to make a ceremony out of my disgraced departure. It suddenly seemed sad to be leaving in such a petulant silence. When I could hear that everyone was about, I went downstairs to say goodbye. I kissed Kady on both cheeks and waited while she kissed me back. I shook hands with Eddie, who was ten and did not take kindly to kisses any more. I thanked Auntie Asha and then kissed her hand. She slapped me playfully on the shoulder and said that she wasn't a grandmother to have her hand kissed by a grown man. Then suddenly she reached out for me and held me for a moment. 'Look after yourself and don't lose touch,' she whispered. I don't know what that was about.

Uncle Amir was in his study and I had to go in there to say goodbye. When I made to speak, my uncle raised his hand to silence me. It was a haughty gesture, meant to stop me from wheedling for mercy. His face was grim but no longer had the power to menace and intimidate that it had while I lived with him. We shook hands, and then Uncle Amir transferred a roll of notes from his left hand to his right, which he extended towards me, the money lying in his palm for me to pick up. For a moment I was paralysed by the condescension, then I shook my head and uttered my thanks. 'Take it, don't be stupid,' Uncle Amir said, and thrust the notes into my shirt pocket with his fingers.

As I walked along the pavement with my suitcase and backpack, headed for the bus stop, I felt like a character at the end of a novel on his way to adventure and fulfilment. In real life, I was on my way to Guinea Lane, and more likely on the way to heartache and struggle, and as I thought this, I could not prevent my eyes from smarting with regret and self-pity that I should find myself alone where I was, and where I did not want to be.

*

Dear Mama,

Salamu na baada ya salamu. London streets are huge – not all of them but many. They couldn't always have been like that. They must have had to knock down a lot of buildings to make the roads so wide. Whereas I think of our place as a town built piecemeal, one building at a time, and each house is kept standing by one ingenuity or another, because ruins are a kind of death.

I have disheartening news to give you. Forgive me. It has been a hard few months and I have made a mess. It is September again and I have now been here for two years. I think of September as a terrible month; it was when I first came here and became a vagrant, when I lost so much. At first I thought my real life would begin after I reached London, that I would do things differently from then on. I thought everything would change for me here in the land of luxury and freedom and opportunity, that nothing could possibly thwart me. I promised myself that. But it turned out to be untrue. It was a lie I was forcing on myself because I had no choice. It seemed I did not have the strength and hardness for it. I have now left Uncle Amir and Auntie Asha's home. They have asked me to leave, which was also what I wished. I could not be as they wanted me to be. I could not bear them in the end, and they could not bear me. Uncle Amir expelled me with unnecessary hard-heartedness but it did not come as a complete surprise.

I abandoned that page and started a fresh one.

Dear Mama,

Salamu na baada ya salamu. I hope you are well and that Baba is well, and that you have news of him. It is September again, and I have now been here for two years. If we are lucky, September can be the most beautiful month of the year, with everything still

82

green or just beginning to turn gold. The leaves change colour as the cold begins. I knew that from geography classes at school but I did not really understand what it meant before I saw it. You cannot imagine what the trees look like as they turn. The movement of the leaves is rhythmic and slow and it is like listening to music played over a period of days. I am struggling to explain. Then the strong winds come and whip all the leaves off in a few hours.

I am also writing to send you my new address. As you probably already know, I am no longer living with Uncle Amir and Auntie Asha. I moved to this address a few days ago. I am grateful that they have looked after me so far. I did not do well in my examinations and I have decided not to continue with Business Studies but to change to studying literature. That is what I wanted to do from the beginning but did not say so when I came here. I talked myself out of it because it seemed an indulgence. They provided an opportunity for me to study and I thought I should use it to learn something useful, which would earn me a lot of money. What is the point of literature? I think that the person who asks that question will not find my answer convincing anyway. I will try again, I don't know if there is anything else I can say. I will find work and I will continue with my studies as best I can. I will try to write to you more frequently, I promise. Could you please reply to this when you have a moment, so that I know the letter reached you, and that you have this new address?

With my love,
Salim

When my mother replied several weeks later, she told me that Maalim Yahya had come back and taken my father away to Kuala Lumpur. As I read that, I saw again the man in the photograph the headmaster showed me all those years ago, and for the first time I thought of him as my grandfather. And I saw my Baba leaving when for so long he had refused to go.

My mother wrote: Your Baba will be there with his family now, with his mother and his sisters and their children. They will look after him and make him happy. I am saddened to hear that your studies have not succeeded so far, but you must not think it's because you are incapable. You are young, and it is not always easy to go so far from your home and succeed at what you try. But you must not give up. I know you will not stop trying, and after you have completed your work, you will return to us. I was also saddened to hear that you have said unkind things about me to your uncle. I don't know what I have done to you to deserve that. Alhamdulillah, but I have an obligation to care for you whatever you say, and you have an obligation to me. In addition you must always remember to be courteous to everyone, and you most certainly should always remember to be grateful for what your uncle has done and is willing to do for you. You can have no understanding of how much he wanted to be of help to you. I have the highest expectations of you. Call me when you have time. I would like to hear your voice.

Your mother

I wrote: Dear Mama, he lied. I did not say anything unkind about you. I asked if that man forced you.

I left that page in my notebook.

*

Mine was the smallest room in the house, big enough for a bed, a narrow hinged shelf under the dormer window and some floor space in between. I could reach everything from my mattress. The wallpaper was clean and the window opened easily so that was something. The room overlooked a small paved yard, which had some pots of struggling plants or maybe weeds, and an abandoned and rusted barbecue. The window of the house opposite squarely faced mine, about a dozen feet away. I would have to get a curtain to add to the venetian blind, if only to keep the early-morning light out. The shower and toilet were downstairs, not gleaming marble but not disgusting either.

Mr Mgeni called it the OAU house, the Organisation of African Unity, because all the tenants were Africans, Alex from Nigeria, Mannie from Sierra Leone, who was Mood's cousin, and Peter from South Africa. Mr Mgeni introduced me to them that Sunday morning when I arrived. Peter was the most outrageously disrespectful of them and the most worldly, and it was to him that the others addressed questions. After Mr Mgeni made his joke about the OAU house, Peter said: 'To me the OAU has the sound of a sleazy loan company, or a money-laundering bank.'

'What is money laundering?' Mr Mgeni asked.

'Money laundering is making criminal loot legal,' Peter said, and explained to them about over-invoicing, off-shore bank deposits, over-valuing property deals, the cash economy, and endless variations of those scams. 'All international criminals, including our OAU heroes, have to know about that kind of stuff, or they have to hire someone who does, or make it part of the deal they cut with the big global companies when they negotiate their kickbacks, otherwise they can only hide their dirty money under the bed because of the risk of criminal charges when they try to spend it outside their own filthy yards.'

'How do you know such things?' Mr Mgeni asked admiringly.

In time, I came to understand that all four of us were living lives in some disarray, working long hours, struggling with debt and fantasies of making good. I did not think that when I first met them. They seemed composed and at ease to me, people used to living in the city whereas I still felt like a stranger from a small town, anxious about destinations and directions although I did my best to disguise this.

Alex worked as a security officer at the National Gallery. He was slim and stylish, and strutted as he walked. Sometimes he mouthed a song or mutely broke into unexpected dance steps in the middle of a conversation. I imagined him doing that in the galleries when there were no visitors around, astonishing the solemn burghers who hung on the walls. Alex had personality in abundance, but I did not think Uncle Amir would approve of

85

his style. He loved to wear jeans and leather jackets and shirts with two different blocks of colour, which made him look like an incompetent conman in a slum market, but he carried off this costume because he made it seem that he was doing it for fun and that he expected you to smile at the audacity of his taste. I knew he would be able to carry off a leopard-skin mantle and a penis sheath if he so wished.

Mood's cousin Mannie worked for an office-cleaning firm, and was out until the early hours of the morning vacuuming and polishing London's towers in the City. He had a thoughtful and silent manner that made him seem serious, someone I felt I could trust, although that may have been because he was Mood's cousin. It made a difference knowing someone who was related to someone else when so many of us were bumping into each other so casually in the middle of nowhere.

Peter was the wit of the house, a cynical mocker of what he called bullshit, which was whatever he felt like mocking: newscasters on TV, politicians of all complexions, Muslim fanatics, Afrocentric gurus, the international community – especially the international community, bankers, generals, faith-healers ... liars, liars and bullshitters, all of them. He worked as an advertising salesman for the local free newspaper. He rang up businesses and tried to persuade them to advertise, and in the meantime, whenever an opportunity arose, he wrote a little piece for the paper. His latest was: *Pensioner Puts Out Fire in Corner Shop*. It was all experience for the day apartheid would be over – which will be any day now, my bro, and then he could return to Cape Town to work on a proper newspaper. In unguarded moments his silences were deep and troubled.

Uncle Amir would have described them as losers and paupers, people without talent, immigrants, none of them going anywhere. For me this was the first time in my life when I could choose how to spend each moment: to study, to sleep, to eat, to sit all day long in front of the TV. The scope for lounging was limited by the need to go to classes and to work but in between I could still believe in that fantasy of choice. In the evenings I worked in the supermarket for a few hours, my legal work, moving stock and mopping floors as usual. I did illegal work in a clothes sweat-shop in New Cross and when Mr Mgeni needed help on a job, he asked me along and paid me in cash. I think he understood my situation from the beginning and found me work whenever he could.

Mr Mgeni was a self-employed builder, who was nearly retired now. He advertised in Peter's paper and chose what jobs he wanted to take on. When he needed an extra pair of hands, as he put it, he took me with him, to mix the mortar or to carry materials up the stairs or to hold a plank or to sweep up afterwards, or for someone to listen while he talked about his life and his travels. He loved telling stories and I loved listening to them. I had never met anyone with such openness. His wife Marjorie was Jamaican but Mr Mgeni had never been there even though they had been together for seventeen years. Whenever Marjorie felt like going home she went with their daughter, Frederica. Mr Mgeni told me this and many other things as we worked together on his jobs, dwelling on details because I was so attentive. When he got tired of talking he played tapes of Nat 'King' Cole on an ancient cassette player crusted with flecks of plaster and tiny lumps of concrete, and sang along with the King. *Rambling rose, rambling rose, why I want you, heaven knows.*

'Nor have I gone back to Malindi for a long time, for much longer than seventeen years,' he said. 'Why not? That's another story and perhaps you'll find out the answer yourself one day. But anyway, it means that Marjorie has not seen my home either. I am tired of travelling and restlessness and now I am quite happy here in Camberwell. For many years I worked as a sailor and travelled the world. I've seen the estuary of the Amazon river in South America, or I should say I have been in it because you can't see it. It's like being at sea. I've watched the sun set on the Sargasso Sea in the Caribbean and seen miles and miles of the seaweed drifting on the water like an island, and I have danced in the surf on the West African coast with the youth and fishermen. Those were wonderful unforgettable experiences, worth the hardship of that work. I've even gone as far north as the Baltic ports and back, which I would not recommend to you. Then when I tired of sailing I became a welder, a carpenter, and finally a builder. I was injured on a job ... that was how I met Marjorie, who was a nurse at St Thomas' Hospital. I did not let her get away after that. Her fate was sealed the moment I saw her. What a magnificent hospital St Thomas' is!'

Mr Mgeni was prone to sudden changes of direction in his stories and I nodded to see where we were now heading. 'I haven't noticed its magnificence before,' I said. 'You don't mean the buildings?'

'I don't mean magnificent to look at so much as the idea behind it, a place where the sick could be cured. You'd think, isn't that what hospitals do, cure the sick? Yes, but did you know that it was first opened a thousand years ago? I'm not joking,' Mr Mgeni said when I laughed at this unexpected switch. 'What would your grandfather and mine have done when they fell sick a thousand years ago? Laid on their beds and groaned, probably, and called for a sheikh to come and read prayers over them while they waited for Azraeel to come and do his work, God forgive any disrespect. These people were building hospitals for their own sick, although they probably learnt to do that from Muslims in Persia and Egypt.'

Mr Mgeni spoke to me in Kiswahili and I think that was part of the pleasure he took in telling me his stories. 'I don't have anyone I can speak to like this any more, not someone who will understand the language properly, without mangling it with Somali and Kikuyu, and slang and shang and who knows what words. It makes me so happy, to speak the old language and to use the big words with their flourishes and their yaanis and their graces.'

Mr Mgeni came round to our house every day to say hello and sit with us for a while. Sometimes when he came during the day and saw dirty dishes in the sink, he did the washing up. Sometimes he brought fruit or a cake Marjorie had made for *the boys*. In the evenings he came in for a few minutes, listened to the talk and the teasing and then went back to his house. It was as if he had come to see that we were all getting along together. No one seemed to mind his frequent presence.

Peter's girlfriend Fran was also a regular visitor. I had become friends with Peter and sometimes the two of them included me in their plans. Fran was attractive and soft-spoken, a tall well-built woman with a bronze complexion and pulled-back dark hair. Her temperament was smiling and subdued, quite unlike the edgy frenzy of Peter's wit and conversation. She was fussy about clothes, dressing in elegant combinations that had obviously been selected with care. The expensive clothes and her groomed appearance made her seem out of place in the cheerless décor of our house. She was in her twenties and despite her demure airs had an aura of restrained sexual energy, or so at least it seemed to me in my innocence. She worked in the finance department of a large department store in central London, from where she was able to buy clothes and accessories at a huge discount. Peter often made fun of what he called her middle-class disguise.

'I think her mother chooses her clothes, don't you?' he said to me in front of Fran. 'Her mother's English and does not want her daughter to forget it.' Her father was a Rwandan theology student who went home after he completed his studies and did not keep in touch. I knew this from Peter who brought up his girlfriend's story every now and then. I sometimes thought he was ashamed of her and treated her slightingly to punish her and himself. It might start in a light-hearted way, with Fran doing something unlike her usual fastidious self, perhaps licking her knife or picking a gherkin out of the dish with her fingers.

'Hey, what would your English mother say about that?' Peter would pounce and then repeat the gist of the story of her mother's abandonment. 'And to think your father was a priest.'

Fran put up with these cruelties and did not defend herself, which seemed oddly forbearing. It was as if she knew something I did not, and knew what Peter really meant. It was difficult to be fond of him at such moments. I wondered if his mockery was to do with his own unspoken shame, and to forestall any suggestion that he had strong feelings for Fran, or that he did anything more than tolerate her. We did not talk to each other about intimate pains. We managed those kinds of things on our own. If I was the only other person in the house, Peter and Fran stayed to watch the TV for a while, and I saw them murmuring to each other on the sofa and saw the way Peter clung to her. If the others were all there, the two of them went upstairs to Peter's room and sometimes Fran stayed the night. I thought she was uncomfortable with the others, perhaps because Peter played up the teasing and banter when they were around. Fran treated me like a younger brother although there were no more than two or three years between us and we were the same height. So many young women treated me like a younger brother. It was disheartening.

Alex and Mannie never invited their girlfriends to the house, or at least they did not come, so I never met them. Once Alex showed me a photograph of a woman looking over her shoulder at the camera in a familiar glamour pose. Her body was half turned away and her head was bent slightly forward as if she had been looking down and had just lifted her eyes at the photographer's request. Strands of her auburn wig partly concealed her left eye. She was wearing a white running top, which was tight across her breasts, and the top six inches of her white track pants were visible in the half-body pose. Her glistening black midriff was bare. 'Beautiful, huh? Her name is Christina and one day she'll be my bride,' he said before returning the photograph to his wallet.

Alex loved talking about the huge appetites of Nigerian politicians for stolen wealth. When it came to pilfering public money, they were *definitely* the worst in the world. He said *definitely* with an unusual emphasis, as if with awed respect. Nobody else came close to Nigerian corruption. Travel allowance, community allowance, hardship allowance, constituency allowance, contingency fund, seedcorn fund … you name it, they voted it for themselves. And all that besides the secret numbered accounts and the hidden commissions. He named improbable figures of stolen money, and the absurd carelessness in the handling of it. How assistants and family members travelled with thousands of dollars in their hand luggage, which they then left in a taxi or the departure lounge. He described these carryings on with a perverse pride, beaming at the audacity and the nonchalance of his country's legislators, laughing so hard that he staggered from the force of his mirth. 'Nobody in the world is as corrupt and greedy as us.'

Every Saturday Alex washed and shampooed and creamed and perfumed himself until he gleamed, and then he put on his multi-coloured shirt and leather jacket and headed off to Tottenham to see his girlfriend and to join the congregation of the Church of Resurrected Souls of Bethany. He did not return until Sunday evening.

Mannie's girlfriend lived in Coventry. He said nothing about her, except that he was going away to Coventry for a few days and when he returned he was visibly happier. I learnt about her from Mood. He had never met her but he knew that she came from Martinique and was a Catholic. Mannie's father was a Sunni imam back in Sierra Leone and would be upset to know about her and Mannie.

'Everyone knows how tolerant Sierra Leoneans are about religion,' Mood said.

'Yes, everyone says that about themself,' I said.

'But it's true,' Mood said, with such anguish that I laughed and conceded. 'But I think Mannie is afraid his family will be very angry with him, because in addition to everything else, his girlfriend is still married and has one child by her husband and another one by Mannie, and her husband refuses to divorce her. It will be too much for Mannie's father, who is as devout an imam as you can find anywhere, a proper pious alhaji, closed off to the world. I don't know what is going to happen to them, except maybe they will just continue like this. That's why Mannie doesn't talk about his girlfriend ... too much guilt. He is afraid his family will find out and tell his father. I don't know why people make such impossible choices for themselves.'

I did not have a girlfriend and the others pestered me and kept suggesting candidates. Even Fran joined in, telling me, as she would have done a younger brother, how handsome I was and how all the girls at college were probably waiting for me to ask them out. Peter frowned slightly when she said how handsome I was, but it inflamed my secret lust for her.

I could not tell them that I felt alienated by the idea of being alone with a woman – or that was what I believed, despite my physical longings. It was not that I did not have desires and cravings, and I did what was necessary to satisfy those, but when I imagined intimacies with a woman, I felt a kind of nausea and anxiety, and had to suppress memories of the defeated silence that surrounded my father, and refuse glimpses of my mother's coercion and that man's hard hands on her. The idea of sexual intimacy seemed to me like a submission to an ugly and shaming force and filled me with a kind of terror.

Dear Mama,

Salamu na baada ya salamu. I think of you often even though many months pass and I am silent. Even as time passes I find I cannot forget and that I miss everything so much. I miss the sight of familiar faces and old buildings and streets. I can shut my eyes and feel myself walking this or that street, leaning a little to the left as I turn into the Post Office Road or hear bicycle tyres squelching on the wet road behind me as I walk the lanes behind the market. I miss the sights and the smells that I know without knowing that I do. There are sights I don't remember seeing which come back to me in full recall, and make me ache with their absence. I don't know why I cannot shake off this feeling of painful longing. Why can't one place be as good as another? I know there is a thought I have been keeping at bay, which is that you are a betrayer, that you sent me here to be with Uncle Amir to get me out of your way, that you could think of no further use for me.

I started again.

Dear Mama,

Several months have passed since I have been here in Guinea Lane and I have been working in my various jobs and attending my classes and saving a little bit of money. In this way

I have had glimpses of many different worlds, for which I have no immediate use but which complicate my understanding of what I thought I knew. The winter is almost over, but sometimes it drags its feet into the months of spring, as late as May and June even. Then it seems that the cold will never go away and life will never change and I will never get away from here.

It will be three years in September since I came here and it feels like a lifetime of standing still while debris builds up around me. I have worked hard and learnt a great deal, especially this year, about myself and about other people, many of whom have been kind to me. I do not know why I have been offered these kind-nesses, by Mr Mgeni in particular. I have done nothing to deserve them, nor do they come to me through any virtue of mine. I had not understood how fear and trouble can co-exist with such generosity, and how complicated people are. Mr Mgeni invites me to eat with his family and he helps me with work and things like that. I wish I was more daring and could take everything on and succeed. Instead I have learnt that I am timid and cautious, afraid to cause offence.

I think of you and Baba and I try to understand. Do you think Baba likes it in Kuala Lumpur? Have you had any word? Salamu Munira.

Love,
Salim

*

In addition to telling me stories on our job outings, Mr Mgeni took to asking me a lot of questions. Sometimes they were ques-tions about college and then he listened patiently while I held forth on the book we were studying, about the opening scene of *The Rainbow* or the slave-ship allusions in 'The Rime of the Ancient Mariner' or something else that he had not the slightest interest in but which none the less I delivered to him without mercy. At times he asked probing questions about me. I resisted at first but

93

he persisted and in the end I succumbed even if I told myself that I had no choice.

'What brought you here?' he asked me one day as we were decorating an upstairs flat in Old Kent Road. We were scraping off old wallpaper in the stairwell when he paused to ask that. I often asked myself that question when I was weary: what am I doing here? Hearing it from someone else made it sound such a pointless and obvious question that I did not answer for a moment. Because that's how things worked out. He must have thought I had not understood because he elaborated: 'What brought you here to London?'

'My uncle brought me,' I said.

Mr Mgeni waited a moment and then prompted me: 'Yes, OK, very funny, he brought you here. To do what?'

'He sent me to college to do Business Studies but I failed so he told me to go,' I said.

We went back to scraping while Mr Mgeni processed this information. 'Does your uncle live in London?' he asked.

'Yes,' I said, scraping diligently and even turning slightly away from Mr Mgeni.

'Shall we go and find him and plead with him?' he asked, and without turning to look at him I could hear the smile in his voice. He did not mean it. 'Is he your real uncle?'

'My mother's brother,' I said.

'And he threw you away like that,' Mr Mgeni said, and then we did not speak for another short while. 'You did not do anything bad that you're not telling me?'

I shook my head. 'I said something he did not like. He did not think I was grateful for what he had done.'

'Is he a man full of anger?'

I thought for a moment. 'I think he likes to be feared.'

'It's your luck,' Mr Mgeni said. 'You can't do anything about that. What does your uncle do in London?'

'He is a diplomat.'

'Ah, a big man. Are your mother and father still living?'

'Yes, but not together.'

'They cannot help you?' said Mr Mgeni.

It was a question so I said, 'No.' I did not tell him that my mother was the one who sent me here and that something broke in my father's life a long time ago and I was the debris of their disordered lives. He asked many other questions until he knew the matter in detail though he did not ask again about my mother and father. He knew that Uncle Amir had agreed to give me a financial guarantee for the moment, but that he was angry with me and spiteful, and he was unlikely to help me in that way for long. It was more likely that in the next year or two I would have to leave or disappear. Mr Mgeni returned to the matter several times until he knew my circumstances by heart and then he came up with a plan.

'There is someone I know,' he said. 'He is a Sudanese lawyer who is very good at this kind of thing.'

'What does that mean? Is he crooked?' I asked.

'He has his ways,' Mr Mgeni said and then paused to see if I wanted him to continue. Of course I wanted him to continue and nodded several times to show him my eagerness. 'I have done business with him before. He specialises in cases of dependants who require papers to join their families. His clients are mostly Somalis and Eritreans and his fee is very big but I knew his brother many years ago when we lived in the same house in Toxteth, a whole bunch of us crowded on top of one another, understanding nothing. He will take care of this, I'm sure.'

The solicitor's chambers were in a former Junior School in Walthamstow. I saw from the nameplates by the door that in addition to Jafar Mustafa Hilal, Solicitors, there were other respectable businesses operating out of the building: a litho and digital print service, a textile designer and an accountancy firm. A handsome young assistant showed us into the solicitor's office and shut the door on us. There was no one else in the room or so it seemed. Mr Mgeni sat on one of the chairs facing the desk and I sat on the other. After a moment I heard the noise of running water and realised that the room was not empty after all, and that someone was washing behind the partition in the corner. In a moment a man came out from behind the screen, wiping his hands on a towel. Jafar Mustafa Hilal was somewhere in his fifties, tall and dark and heavily built. His face was round and clean-shaven and his lips were thick and bulging. His hair was close-cropped. He smiled as he walked towards Mr Mgeni with outstretched hand, but that did nothing to soften his menacing appearance.

'Ahlan wa sahlan, my old friend,' he said. He gripped Mr Mgeni's hand briefly and then reached out for mine. 'And this is our young man. Welcome, my son,' he said, crushing my hand in his right while still gripping Mr Mgeni's hand with his left. He released both of us and waved us back into our chairs. When we were all settled Mr Mgeni began to speak, to explain my situation, but I did not get the impression that Jafar Mustafa Hilal was paying careful attention. His eyes were on me, curious, smiling, and I thought predatory.

'Yes, yes,' he said when Mr Mgeni paused in his brief recital of my wretchedness. 'He will do very well as your dependant, very becoming. We will see what we can do.'

He leant back, elbows on the arms of his office chair, eyes almost closed as he contemplated illegalities with what seemed like deep contentment. 'We will have to get him a complete set of papers. It will take a while and there will be a cost, but I will do my best to make it manageable. There is no accounting between us, as you know, my brother, and the only cost will be to pay the witnesses and the providers of certificates.'

He nodded after he said this and Mr Mgeni nodded back and smiled and then leant forward slightly to express his gratitude. Mr Mgeni must have done something big for his brother. I was looking forward to the story of Toxteth. Jafar Mustafa Hilal then turned towards me. 'This will take a little time but it is not impossible,' he said, and I wondered if those bulging lips made it hard for him to form words, if they required greater effort to manoeuvre. 'We will take down a few details and then you can leave this to me. You just concentrate on your studies. There is nothing more important than learning. You will be Mr Mgeni's nephew and he will be your last remaining relative. We will also have to lower your age to strengthen your case for dependence.

It will take a little time to send for the papers but once we have those we'll get the residence issue sorted out. I will be in touch. Maasalama ya habibi,' he said, his eyes softening with the endearment.

'What's the Toxteth story?' I asked Mr Mgeni later.

'I made a promise not to tell anyone,' he said, but I saw the mischief in his eyes and knew that he would.

'I'm your nephew,' I said.

'It is an unpleasant story,' Mr Mgeni said, without any sign of reluctance. 'Did I ever tell you about my brother? I had one brother and three sisters, all younger than me. My brother was the baby of the family. Then my father married a much younger woman than my mother. This new family and the way the young wife treated my mother became intolerable to me. I was sixteen then, already working at sea on the coast trade, and the insolence of this woman with whom my father spent every night was unbearable, so I signed up for a cargo ship and went sailing around the world. I moved around the earth like the sun until after a while I no longer knew the way back.

'I wrote to my brother from Liverpool and told him I was living there. I had just learnt to write in evening classes, and that was the first letter I wrote. My brother wrote back after several weeks ... I mean he got someone to write the letter for him because he still did not know how to write. He begged me to send money for him to join me, *begged* me, because he said life there in the old house was intolerable. I saved up enough and sent it to him and he came to live with me.

'I lived in Toxteth as I told you, in a house I shared with other men, all of them Muslim, one of them Jafar Mustafa's brother Sadiq, most of us hard-working and all of us poor ... black men away from their homes. My brother turned out to be a violent and lazy young man. He did not stay long in any job. He just wanted jokes and dole and women and drugs, and in Sadiq he found a perfect partner. They were just the way the English want all of us to be. They roamed the streets and visited women and went to the pub. Then one day they killed a woman. Yes, they killed a prostitute in a violent sexual game of some kind. They hurried home and told me. I gave them all the money I had and they escaped. Neither of them had papers and we would all have got into trouble if they had been arrested. It was a terrible thing to do, helping those two to escape, but there is an obligation … The police came, of course, and asked a lot of questions. We said none of us knew anything. But we found out that the woman did not die after all, and she was a black woman, so the police were not interested for long. That is the story of Toxteth. That is why lawyer Jafar Mustafa Hilal is so obliging.'

'Do you know what happened to them?' I asked.

Mr Mgeni shrugged. 'They're somewhere in the world doing the same dirty business,' he said. 'Perhaps lawyer Jafar knows but I don't.'

*

In the meantime I fell in love with Mr Mgeni's daughter Frederica. She was sixteen and perfectly beautiful and I could not help myself. Whenever I went round there to have dinner with the family or to wait for Mr Mgeni before we went to do a job, or when I went to collect my pay – Mr Mgeni preferred to pay me out of sight of the others – I hoped that she would be there too. My sexual innocence was a burden to me in a country where provocation was intense and constant and I felt diminished and inadequate about it. Frederica's manner told me that she knew more about these matters than I did, despite her parents' watchfulness. I was sure she knew about my secret adoration and had no interest in it, but still rewarded me with smiles and occasional flattery as if she was the elder of the two of us. It must sound ridiculous, but I was *profoundly* in love with Frederica for several months and the anguish her lack of interest caused me is impossible to describe. If I knew how to do so I would have written a poem or a song. It was exhilarating in its way. I am sure Mr Mgeni and Marjorie knew what was going on and were amused by it. It couldn't be helped.

My anguish needed cooperation to sustain its intensity and since Frederica was not willing to provide it, it dissipated and leaked away, but I knew it was something real, something truthful, not something imagined or misconstrued, genuine like the pain I felt when loneliness and homesickness overcame me. Homesickness sounds like a silly adolescent condition to be in, but there were times when it consumed me and paralysed me with sorrow and then I locked myself in my room and wept for hours. That too must sound ridiculous but it was real and unarguable. My misery was so deep it was tragic, but that could not be helped either and after a time I had to open my door and get back out. I was having to learn so much so quickly, and I was so busy with so much work, that I did not have a proper sense of what I knew any more.

The work at college was reassuring, but I suspected my grades were inflated to encourage me. Most of us were students who had failed before and were trying again, which was not to say that some were not able and clever, but perhaps our teachers feared we were short on confidence. When I felt doubt or was wearied of the task I had been set, I reminded myself of what it would make possible for me. I would be a student in a university and participate in the life of the mind, among people who valued that pursuit above everything.

That year in the OAU house raced past for me. I had worked hard, learnt to be independent, studied materials I enjoyed, and fallen in unrequited love.

Dear Mama,

You banished me to this place in the name of love. You said you wanted the best for me but really you let him take me away so you could live your life in peace. Sometimes I panic when I think I will never see you again and that this is what you want, but then the panic passes and I return to my labours because there is nothing else I can do. Sometimes I hear your voice in the dark. I know it's you, your voice slightly hoarse as if you've just woken up from a nap, but I know it's you.

The tenants changed during my second year at the OAU house. Alex returned to Nigeria to marry and the man who replaced him was another Nigerian. His name was Amos, a quarrelsome battler who by sheer force of ill will imposed himself on the house and poisoned its atmosphere, changing its routine to suit himself. He brooded silently when Peter and I laughed or looked as if we were enjoying ourselves and then burst out at us with mocking sarcasm and jeers. He was a short, round man of impressive energy, and he looked strong enough to overcome any of us. It was as if he loved to speak only in dispute and disagreement, as if he needed to do that for his own well-being. Amos even cowed Mr Mgeni, who gave up coming round unless he knew that Amos was out. The television blasted the news as soon as Amos came in, the fridge was taken over by his various packages and pots. He disapproved of music and demanded its silencing, and he was revolted by alcohol, screwing up his face if anyone opened a can of beer in his vicinity. He was a diligent church-goer and had a phobia about Muslims. Whenever something about Islam came up on the news and I happened to be there, he turned to me as if I were the only Muslim in London and in some way responsible for what he disliked.

'Muslims are fanatics, imperialists, racists,' he said, eyes bulging with rage. 'They came to Africa and destroyed our culture. They made us subservient to them and stole our knowledge and inventions and made us into slaves.'

I was not sure why I deserved Amos's outrage any more than Mannie, who was a Muslim too and whose father was a devout imam, or Mr Mgeni, or several million other Africans who could also have shared the blame. Peter, though, refused to be cowed, and the two of them spent several evenings arguing and shouting at each other as if they would come to blows.

'What inventions did they come and steal from you? What inventions are you talking about?' Peter said. 'The only thing Africans ever invented was the assegai, and *we* did that. What were you lot doing up there all the time? Selling each other for trinkets.'

'You South Africans have no sense of history,' Amos sneered. 'The white man ate your brains generations ago.'

'You are right, we are full of bullshit,' Peter said. 'But at least we know it instead of inventing a history that did not exist.'

'You are just a self-hating kaffir, my friend,' Amos said.

'Who's your friend? I don't make friends with bigots.'

Amos took off his belt and waved the buckle threateningly in front of him, but he kept his distance and Peter ignored him. I found Amos's bluster and noise so disagreeable that often they drove me away to my room, which perhaps was just as well for my studies.

I had not been to see Uncle Amir and Auntie Asha since I left the house in Holland Park, nor had I sent them the Guinea Lane address. I forwarded my financial guarantee renewal papers to the embassy. At first it was because I could not face seeing them after my expulsion, and could not rid myself of the memory of the hard words my uncle had to say to me in farewell. But as time passed, my reasons for staying away multiplied: I was ashamed of my failure, I was angry with them for bringing me here, I despised their self-importance, I did not owe them a thing. So I was surprised when around Christmas of that year, I received a letter on embassy paper from Rome. They must have got my address from my mother.

Uncle Amir's name was on the letter-head as His Excellency the Ambassador, so he had become a big man at last as he had promised to do many years ago. The letter was hand-written by Uncle Amir, and it wished me well in my studies or whatever I was doing, and advised me of his current address. Rome! I wished I could go to Rome. I wished I could go anywhere, I wished I could liberate myself from the drudgery of my life in London. If I had been obedient to my uncle and aunt I would have been spending the Christmas vacation in Rome this year. I sent my uncle a postcard of London Bridge, congratulated him on his appointment and asked him to convey my best wishes to Auntie Asha and the children. What else could I do?

I took my examinations in the summer of that year and passed. When Mannie heard the news he hugged me without a word and kissed me lightly on both cheeks. Peter grinned and grinned and then dragged me off to a Turkish café for a celebration meal and the first of many hours of advice about the life of a student. I wrote to Uncle Amir to tell him that I had passed my examinations and was going to start at university in two months. It was several weeks before I received his reply on embassy paper from Rome. I thought I knew what the letter would say. I held it in my hand for a while without opening it, contemplating the uncle I had once loved. I could not get over how he had taken me away from my home and discarded me to a life of such sterility. *Dear Salim*, his letter read, *I am relieved to hear the news of your success and I wish you luck in your career as a university student. I expect you are telling me about it because you want me to pay your fees but I'm afraid I can't do that. The trust I have been paying into has collapsed along with so many others, and I cannot afford to support you. I have received no word of thanks from you for anything I have ever done for you, and until your note arrived I had no idea what progress you were making with your life. You never sent us any news of yourself and did not even send us a greetings card now and then. I have learnt to accept this ingratitude even if it comes from a member of my family that I had once considered like my own son. But now, under these financial difficulties everyone is going through, and which seem to be getting worse each time they come round again, I have to look after the future of my own children and you have to learn to look after yourself. Your Auntie Asha and the children send regards.*

I had been expecting that letter for a long time as a final act of spite from him, an expression of outrage for my ingratitude. I often wondered what had made Uncle Amir bring me to England. I did not believe it was a way of paying my mother back for something she had done for him. Or if it was, then that was only a small part of it. Uncle Amir would not have wanted to dwell too long on his part in messy events,

102

whatever they were, and seeing my face in front of him every day would require him to do just that. I think it was to show that he was a man of substance with a sense of responsibility towards his family and the means to fulfil it. He swaggered into my life and plucked me out and brought me all the way to fabled London, but instead of giving grateful deference and eager obedience to his every command I proved obstinate and without talent, and harboured inexplicable grievances. To Uncle Amir and Auntie Asha, who would have long ago forgiven themselves for whatever chaos they brought to my life, I would have seemed quite the most ungrateful little shit imaginable. So I had been expecting all along, once I failed to play my part as the cringing dependent nephew, that sooner or later they would fling me away as they did.

But by the time Uncle Amir's letter arrived from Rome, the solicitor Jafar Mustafa Hilal had produced the required papers and Mr Mgeni had helped me to arrange a student loan, and in September I moved to Brighton. *Keep your money, Uncle Abhorréd.* I could not resist the thought that everything was going to be different now.

I found a job in a café in Hove, Café Galileo, and took a room on campus. My room was small, painted white and blue, and had an aura of freedom. I went back to Camberwell for a weekend day trip and visited Mr Mgeni and Marjorie and Frederica. I wanted to see them and for them to see me in my transformed self, to say to me: haven't you done well? We are proud of you. Mr Mgeni patted my knee every now and then and smiled in muted congratulation for the plot we had successfully hatched. Later I went next door to say hello and they welcomed me back with laughter and warmth. Even Amos seemed pleased to see me, and asked me to recite Shakespeare to them to prove that I was really a literary scholar at the university. Seeing Mr Mgeni and everyone there at the house was like going home and I laughed hard and genuinely but I could not wait to get back to Brighton.

I loved it there by the sea. I took bus rides further along the coast and walked on the cliffs, bracing myself against the cold breeze and listening to the waves crashing repeatedly against the rocky shore. Sometimes I sat on the shore and watched as the line of foam ran silently up the beach. Although I spent so much time alone, I did not feel lonely. It made me think of my father whom I had not thought about as much as I should have done. Those solitary walks made me think about his friendless retreats. I wrote an imaginary letter to him to tell him that.

Dear Baba,

I thought it would be something you would know about, how it feels to be silent and alone. Perhaps you don't have time for that any more in Kuala Lumpur with all your family around you. I think you would have loved the cliffs and the restless sea and taking a walk in the rain. When the sun is on them, the cliffs look as if they are made of snow. Have you seen snow, Baba? I don't think there's snow in Kuala Lumpur. I have stood on ice. Can you imagine that? When you told me to keep my ear close to my heart, I think it was to warn me against hard-heartedness. I think I have understood now. Or were you just babbling? I hope you have found peace there in Kuala Lumpur. I have become a vagrant like you. Sometimes the darkness is hard and fills me with a kind of terror as it did when I was a child, and then I realise that everything lives on, that very little fades and imagination retrieves what does. I realise that I have forgotten nothing and probably never will.

Yours
Salim

Dear Mama,

I am sorry to have been so long in writing to you, despite my promise to be good. You must get tired of my apologies when I do nothing to put things right but I do mean to write more often, it's just, well, I don't know. Sometimes you seem so far away and the way I live seems unreal, like someone else's life. Still, it is wrong of me to be so neglectful. I will write more regularly from now on. I have moved again and now live in Brighton where I am studying at the university. I love it here. It is a town by the sea, although it is nothing like our sea. I am sending you my new address.

Love,
Salim

5

THE LITTLE UTOPIA

I had coveted the life of a student, the scholarly community, living on campus, attending seminars, but I found myself on the edges of this university life and hardly said a word in class. When I spoke it sounded wrong: not the grammar and the arrangement of words but something deeper, as if I was making things up and my stumbling efforts were evident to everyone. I did not have the self-possession of the other students and I felt uncomfortable among them.

I was surprised by how many causes and injustices they were passionate about: liberation politics in South America, paedophile operations in South Asia, the persecution of Roma people in central Europe, gay rights in the Caribbean, the war in Chechnya, animal rights, genital cutting, NATO in Bosnia, the ozone layer, reparations for colonial plunder. I had told my mother that there were people from everywhere in the world in London but that was not how I had lived my life there. I never spoke to any of its world-citizenry about the realities of the lives they had left behind. Even in the OAU house, we picked up bits of information about each other but did not probe. I did not know anything about Peter's family until Amos, in his confrontational way, asked him how he would be classified in South Africa – this was towards the end of the apartheid days – and Peter reluctantly replied that he would be classified as Coloured. Amos, it turned out, had been a child soldier in the Biafra war, but we could not ask him anything about it because his eyes filled with tears the moment he blurted the words out and then he rushed out of the room.

Everything is complicated and questions simplify what is only comprehensible through intimacy and experience. Nor are people's lives free from blame and guilt and wrong-doing, and what might be intended as simple curiosity may feel like a demand for a confession. You don't know what you might release by asking a stupid question. It was best to leave people to their silences. That was how it seemed to me but it was not how it seemed to my fellow students. If the posters and the campaigns and demonstrations were a guide, any injustice in the world seemed to be theirs to claim, accompanied by frivolities that were like a celebration of disorder. They were fortunate people who desired to own even the suffering of others. It seemed that after all that going around the world their ancestors did and their descendants continue to do – all the effort and the carelessly inflicted misery – people in England now wanted to live a good life, to observe the decencies, to abhor hatred and violence, to give all that up and respect everyone's humanity.

I started work at the Café Galileo at the beginning of term. The café's owner, Mark, did not smile much and was watchful at all times like a herdsman with his flock. His eyes roved over everything and he was everywhere – supervising in the kitchen, helping out with preparation of food, serving at tables, sitting behind the till – and when regular customers he liked came in and it was not too busy, he would take coffee with them and relax in conversation. He was a serious man, and even this relaxing had a working air about it, heads bent close together, talking or listening with small frowns of concentration and occasionally bursting out into raucous ribald laughter, which I knew must have been prompted by a dirty joke. Mark was not English. He and his regulars spoke Arabic. Their bodies moved differently as they spoke: the shrugs, the hand gestures, the shape their lips made as they spoke, the way they laughed and the frequency of Libnan and Beyrut in their conversation made it clear where they were from.

Then one Sunday morning I found out for sure. A dishevelled-looking and hung-over Mark sat silently sipping a strong coffee, looking exhausted. Then he said to me, speaking wearily: 'Salim. Where are you from with a name like that?'

I poured him another coffee and said, 'Zanzibar.'

Mark whistled in a way that was meant to show surprise and appreciation. 'That's a long way away in Africa, isn't it? Way down there below the equator, the other side of the world.' I nodded and waited for what I thought was coming next. The dark continent. 'Darkest darkest Africa,' he said obligingly. 'Zinjibar,' he continued, using its old Arabic name. 'We read about that as children in Lebanon.' His real name was Mousa, he said, but for business purposes he called himself Mark. It made customers feel more comfortable.

'I thought you were West Indian when you came to ask for a job,' Mark said. 'Until you said your name.'

'Don't they have any Salims in the West Indies?'

He shrugged. 'Not that I've heard of. I don't like West Indians,' he said.

'Why not?' I asked him.

'I have my reasons,' he said.

*

The café closed on Christmas Day and I stayed in my blue and white room on a campus that was silent and almost empty and wrote a long letter to my mother. In it I told her about my new life, about the studies and my struggles with them, about Mark and the café, about the foods we served there and how they were prepared. I did not expect her to care about that last bit, it was only a way of saying to her that I was living such a different life from the one we were used to. I wish I could like it more here but I like some of it, I told her. I described how in winter it gets dark by three in the afternoon but in midsummer it stays light until ten at night. I told her about things I found striking, about the little tangles I got into, about mishaps that had befallen me, and I made myself sound ridiculous and at odds with my circumstances, making myself into a joke, stumbling about in this new life I had worked so hard to arrive at. It made me happy to write in that tone, and I hoped it would make my mother smile as she read it, her silly son blundering about clumsily in the big world. I did not ask her anything about her life. This was just a frivolous little Christmas gift. I followed up the letter with my first post-card to Munira, who would be ten years old now, I realised. So much time had passed.

My routine settled into such a pleasing pattern that I started to feel happy. I was required to read books that opened up the world for me and made me see how much roomier it was than I had imagined. I read books which gave me courage and helped me to see, and I imagined that I bore my chalice safely through a throng of foes. But there were also moments when I wondered if I was in the right place, studying for the right degree. Salim Masud Yahya, what are you doing here? Perhaps everyone had moments like that. Some of the material I was asked to read estranged me with its showiness and its relentless knowingness and its pointlessness, as it seemed to me. Some I found humblingly incomprehensible despite my best efforts, and I was caught between admiration and contempt for people who spent a lifetime composing and disseminating artefacts of such over-wrought ugliness. Then when I came to write, I found that I had understood something after all and that there was a way through it, which I was beginning to discern. Take heart, take heart!

*

That summer I moved in with a friend I had met at the café. His name was Basil, an Economics student from Greece. He had just completed his degree and was due to start on an MA in September. He rented a flat with his girlfriend, who was also an Economics student from Greece and whose name was Sophie. Basil was tall, elegantly dishevelled and unhurried, serving customers with such graceful tranquillity that even Mark, who preferred an appearance of speed, did not bother to shout at him. At the end of his shift, Basil tossed a thin scarf over his shoulder with a careless flick of his palm before he went out into the street.

Sophie's father was born in Arusha. 'It was his talk about his life in Arusha that made me pay attention rather than just think of Africa as one large dark and troubled land,' she said. 'It made me see it in detail, so to speak, and that's probably why I want to work in development studies. I feel there's a connection somehow.'

Sophie had glowing dark eyes and short unruly dark hair and so I fell secretly in love with her in no time at all. My virginity was becoming an intolerable burden to me. Sophie hung a hammock in the bay of the living-room window and lay swinging in it in the evening, reading, making notes, writing letters, while Basil listened to music through headphones as he read his professional journals or pored over his computer. They made love almost every night, which I could not help being aware of because Sophie came noisily to her climax. I heard them stifling their laughter and giggles afterwards, and then heard Sophie's soft footfall as she went to the bathroom. I liked to imagine that she walked there naked from her bed. Some nights I waited for her tormented groans before trying to go to sleep myself. Sophie told me that I was too modest and must learn to assert myself. I thought she was being flirtatious in a way I was familiar with. You are such an innocent, she said when she wished to make fun of me. Such a proper Indian Ocean boy.

One weekend Peter came down, and Basil hired a car and drove all of us to Beachy Head where we spent two nights in a rented cottage, walking, cooking, drinking, playing absurd card games late into the night. I did not know that I was not to see Peter again after that weekend. I remember on our last night together he said to me, You like the feeling of sadness, don't you? It's an immaturity on your part. Later I wondered if he was also speaking about himself. Some months later he sent me a postcard from Cape Town to say that he was back home now that his country was free. *Let's not lose touch, brother*, he wrote, but we did.

*

I auditioned for a part in a production of *The Winter's Tale*. The director, Dr Hobson, was our Shakespeare tutor, a soft-fleshed, overweight man who smelt of old sweat. He always wore a greyish-green tweed jacket over a dark jersey, and although he changed regularly, all his clothes smelt. When I went up for my

111

audition, Dr Hobson asked what experience I had in drama and I mentioned the three one-act plays I had appeared in at school, one of them in Kiswahili. Dr Hobson did not react when I mentioned the titles of the plays. One was by Chekhov, because our teacher admired his work for reasons none of us could understand. All the characters were quivering, nervous aristo-crats who seemed about to collapse from sheer terror of life. Another was by Rabindranath Tagore, which the same teacher chose for us to give us a sense of the arts of the world. Theatre isn't all Shakespeare and George Bernard Shaw and the rest of that exhausted crew of imperialists, he told us. The Kiswahili play was written by one of our teachers. It was called *Msitiri Mwenzako*, which I translated for Dr Hobson as *Save Your Friend from Shame*. That one had comedy and treachery and intrigue and a scene of explosive screaming rage. Dr Hobson made a note on his pad and then said thank you and offered me a part in the stage manager's team.

Dr Hobson did not want me in his play. I had heard that he was a BNP sympathiser and even wrote material for their campaigns, so I turned up for rehearsal whenever I could and watched everything that went on, sitting there silently while our director became irritated. I was also an admirer of one of the actors, whose name was Marina and who was in one of the liter-ature classes I took where I first came across Herman Melville: *There go flukes!* I was a distant admirer of Marina, which did not stop me from being secretly in love with her too.

In the three years I had been in England until then, I had kissed some girls at parties when words were not required – snogged some girls at parties when it was dark and the music was loud and everyone had had a few drinks. To be honest, I *was snogged* by three girls at three separate parties when I had done little to deserve their attentions. One of them told me, as she was pulling my shirt out and reaching into my jeans, that she would have gone to bed with me if I weren't black, but since I was, she wouldn't. I asked if she would do it if I were Chinese. She thought for a moment and said she would. She went back to snogging me after that and I made no effort to resist even though honour required that I should repel her and walk haughtily away.

Marina only had eyes for handsome Robbie, who was easily the best actor in the cast. It did not make any difference. She was too beautiful for me and I was content to admire from a distance. She had thick black hair and bright brown eyes with a slatey glitter in them when she turned her head suddenly towards the light. While I was slouching in the wings at some point on the evening of the final dress rehearsal, Marina came gently up to me and without saying anything embraced me, fully and deeply. At that moment, as she held me close, her whole body pressed against mine, I guessed that she knew why I had gone to all those rehearsals. Then she lightly kissed my neck. After a moment she pulled back and I saw Robbie watching us, standing only a metre or so away. His eyes were venomous in that half-light, and I felt Marina start in my arms before she disengaged herself. That night Robbie played his part like a pimp in a rage and there was a scene after the performance. Marina avoided eye contact with me afterwards, and I slunk away to my guttersnipe place in the shadows without further protest. There was only one performance, to a parochial audience who knew the actors personally and sometimes laughed for the wrong reasons.

I dreamt longingly about that embrace and the suspended kiss that I think was about to follow. I knew I would always remember the moment and I fell even more deeply in love with Marina. Maybe I should have been braver, should have sought her out afterwards. Our doubts are traitors. There was a clue I was missing, some way of being that would allow me to carry out audacious acts without hesitation.

Basil and Sophie left that summer. We promised to write to each other, and I had to swear repeatedly that I would go and stay with them in Athens the following summer. As we parted, Sophie embraced me and said: I'll never forget you, and I said: I'll never forget you either. We remained in contact for a while after they returned to Greece, but then the postcards became irregular and slowly dried up.

*

I moved to a large house in Fiveways that I shared with five others, all foreign students. I heard about the room from another student who was working in Mark's café. It was a dirty house and I thought it would be cold in the winter. The windows were loose and rattled in the wind. The carpets and rugs were thread-bare scraps that were impossible to clean but which produced fibres and dust that gave all of us allergies, probably for life. The woodwork was damp and the whole house was enveloped in a powerful stench of rot that hit me like a diseased miasma when I entered, and I knew it was not good for any of us. But it could not be helped.

*

The café was busy, the pavement tables always full in the beautiful late-summer weather. Mark took on a new waiter because of the extra business, but he also said the café needed another young woman on the staff. It would be more reassuring and pleasing for the tourists to see another female waiter. That was when Annie came to work with us and put an end to my torment. To me she seemed a perfect Mark recruit. She was quick, always polite and helpful to the customers, chatty in the kitchen and never late. It was work she had done before and she was confident and relaxed about it. Mark put her on the pavement area, and Annie performed out there as if it was a stage, slipping between the tables and smiling at passers-by as they hesitated about coming in. By the end of her second day Mark smiled whenever he looked at her, even when she was not looking back.

Annie was slim, had a slightly round face, short brown hair, was of medium height, and was at that age when all of these features were in some kind of balance that was perfectly pleasing. But what made her even more attractive was the self-possession with which she moved around the café, never falter-ing or mishandling, her every movement certain, or so it seemed to me. Mark paid her warm attention, but that was his way with women when they started at the café. He flirted with them for a while as if he was practising his courtship skills, and when they knew they were loved, he turned down the volume without quite giving up the chat and left them to get on with their work. Business is business.

In any case, Annie had already made her own choice, and to my astonishment she had chosen me. She flashed me friendly smiles and came to me if she had a problem or a question she could not deal with. Once she put her hand on my arm as she spoke to me, and another time she leant against me briefly during a quiet moment. On the Saturday at the end of her first week, in the lull after the lunch crowd, she asked me what I was doing that evening.

I shrugged. 'Nothing,' I said. 'What about you?'

'I am going home and I'm going to make myself a carbonara,' she said, her eyes open and frank and smiling. 'Do you want to come and share it with me?'

'I love carbonara,' I said, laughing at how easy she made it for me.

It had been a long hot day but as we left the café a cool breeze blew in from the sea. I caught Mark's eye as we left and there was a smile in it. We walked from the café because it was a nice evening and she only lived in Fountain Road, about twenty minutes away. Her face glowed with dried sweat, and her eyes were shiny with laughter and excitement. I don't know what I looked like. Some short while into the walk she took my hand, and as we turned into Fountain Road she stopped on the pavement and kissed me, swelling her lips and opening them for my tongue. Her flat was on the third floor, and she opened her arms in a sweeping gesture, welcoming me in. It was still bright outside and a large window let in light on the living area. The bed was in an alcove around the corner, and she went there and I followed. She did not make a carbonara that night, instead we made love for hours. It did not feel like the first time, intuition telling me what to do when I would not have known before. In any case, she knew what she wanted and guided my mouth and my hands to what she desired. Later, she held on to me for a long time as we lay beside each other, our lips touching in long languid kisses. Yallah, I should have known it would be like this.

I lost all sense of time when the light went from the sky but it did not seem as if either of us wanted to sleep, and I found myself talking between caresses with a freedom I had not known before. Perhaps it's always like that the first time. I don't know if everything I said was true but it flowed sweetly from me. She ran her hands over my body and said again and again, You are so beautiful. Me? We must have fallen asleep at some point because I woke up suddenly in the very early light and remembered where I was. Annie was fast asleep beside me, lying on her side facing me, breathing lightly. I smiled with incredulous pleasure at my memories of the night, and I thought I saw a small smile on her lips too.

I must have fallen asleep again because I woke up much later when Annie put her hand on the side of my face. It was past eight and I was already late for the café. I splashed myself in her tiny shower, regretting that I had agreed to work every available day, and rushed down the stairs after a hurried kiss. Come straight back after work, she said. We'll have the carbonara. I was an hour late and the café was buzzing, everyone at full stretch with Sunday morning breakfasts and pavement customers lingering over their newspapers and espressos. Mark did not make eye contact and in my elation I hardly cared. His eyes roved with satisfaction over the crowd of people in his café. When it was time for him to notice me he looked very deliberately at his watch and said, Fucking is fucking and business is business.

The café only opened in the morning on Sundays, and after work I took a detour through Church Road, looking for a toothbrush, and found myself delaying my return to Fountain Road. Something niggled. It was a sense of having neglected something, of being in the wrong. As I walked on Church Road that Sunday morning I felt a stab of grief, a pang of guilt for my Mama and my Baba and the sorrow of their lives. The night with Annie had been a lavish joy and it was a self-indulgence I had no right to. I pushed the thought away and took the next turning towards her flat. She let me in as soon as I began to speak in the door phone. The carbonara was ready in a matter of minutes and we sat eating under the big open window, with our plates on our laps.

We went back to bed for the afternoon and for a while it felt as if these languorous pleasures could go on endlessly, but we could not, of course, and afterwards Annie explained how things were. She was not apologetic or sentimental about what she had to say, a confident woman who knew how to take care of herself.

'My boyfriend works on the ferries. David. He's doing Portsmouth to Santander, so he's due back on Monday morning. Before that he was on the Portsmouth to Caen route, an overnight trip coming back the next day. That was where we met when I worked in the ferry restaurant. It was good on the ferries for a while, different and exciting, glamorous, working odd hours, meeting crowds of new people every day, but it was not for me in the end. I could not cope with the long hours into the night, and when I got tired the sea made me ill. Anyway, when I started at the café on Monday...'

'Was it only a week ago? It feels as if I've known you longer,' I said, and the interruption earnt me a few extra caresses.

'Anyway, I knew David was going to be away all weekend,' she continued, smiling in anticipation, 'and I fancied a fling while he was away. I love doing that every now and then, when I get the chance. Did you not notice how much I fancied you? Was I too obvious?'

'I thought you were very discreet,' I said.

'Do you know what I really like about you apart from your beautiful body? That you speak so softly and hold me as if I would slip out of your hands if you were careless,' she said. 'I love that. But you won't be able to stay tonight. I need time to clean out the place and wash the sheets and make the place as it was before David comes back on Monday. I need to get your smell out of my hair.'

I smiled to myself as I walked home, soft-spoken beautiful body, you proper Indian Ocean boy. It was absurd, even flies do

117

it – was it Romeo or Mercutio who said that? – but I still felt as if I had done something brave and daring.

Annie did not think it was anything permanent between David and her, maybe or maybe not, but she was living in his flat and he paid the rent, so she had to respect that. Maybe we could have another weekend like that some other time when he was away. Annie stayed at the café until the end of August, and I went to Fountain Road on three other nights in that time. At work she did not touch me, or only briefly, but blew me kisses if she thought no one was looking. She was at the café for just over a month, but it seemed like a full season to me and filled my days with excitement and an unfamiliar anxiety. Annie banished the memory of my longing for Marina and, for a time, the memory of everything else: one fire puts out another's burning, one pain is lessened by another's anguish. At the beginning of September she moved to Portsmouth with her boyfriend. That had been the plan all along but in the end she was not so sure. What was there in Portsmouth?

'Then there's you,' she said. 'It was on the tip of my tongue to tell him about you and just stay on in Brighton, but where would I stay? I'll end up being broke all the time and living in a slum. I did not fancy that but it will be unbearable to leave you. I think I've fallen in love with you a little bit. Do you think you'll miss me?'

After she left, the weeks she had spent at the café seemed like a fantasy to me at times, and the memory of her lived in my body for years. Later I knew that she would have been too much for me, and her life of pleasure would have looked different when viewed from the other side. I remembered how in repose after pleasure her face was slack-jawed with satiety. I thought that despite what she said about David, they were likely to be more permanent than she made their lives together sound. Perhaps it was not at all strange for people to choose to live on the edge of crisis like that. I wanted to tell someone about her but I could not think who that would be.

At the beginning of my final year I moved to a one-bedroomed upstairs flat with an annoying leaking cistern the landlord's plumber could not fix. There would be silence for some weeks, then in the early hours of the night I would hear the unhurried whisper of water escaping and the gentle gurgle of the cistern running into the toilet bowl. At times I thought I could put a face to the leak. I had a dread that the toilet bowl would overflow and bring the ceiling down on the downstairs flat. I could not sleep once I started to think like that and could not make the dread go away.

In my early years in London, I could not always hold off vivid visions of my father's lonely decrepitude. Had he begged in the streets? I am sure he never did that but I saw him approaching people with outstretched hand, a vivid image that I dreaded recalling and could not dismiss. And I woke up in the middle of the night to the echo of a cry that had escaped me because I feared the self-hurt my mother would inflict on herself in her silent guilt. *I must die – because I have done wrong and cannot put it right.*

An elderly Chinese couple lived in the downstairs flat, mostly in silence it seemed to me except for the hiss of frying when it was warm enough for them to open the kitchen window. On some weekend days, a young Chinese woman visited them and brought them their shopping. Sometimes she cleaned up in the little garden, weeding and refreshing the pots with supermarket bedding plants, and every now and then, when it was dry, she hung out their bedding to air. I guessed she was their daughter, and while she was there I could hear her voice, raised and querulous, as if she was hectoring them in their gentle lives. But perhaps words spoken by an unfamiliar voice in an unknown language sounded aggressive to an ignorant ear. Perhaps she was only telling them stories of her working week. The old couple never went into the garden themselves, and I had only ever seen them outside twice, both times walking unspeaking, one behind the other, towards the main road, wrinkled and shrunken with age.

He was wearing an old, baggy suit that had perhaps fitted better once, and she was wearing what seemed like layers of blouses and jackets. They looked as if they were heading to an event: a reunion, or a funeral, or a visit to a hospital. I raised my arm in greeting but they ignored me.

Dear Mama,

Salamu na baada ya salamu, here's another new address for you. Thank you for your last letter, which I almost did not get because I had moved during the summer. I am sorry to hear that you had to go to the hospital in Dar for checks. You did not say for what. I hope the results were OK. I had a bit of a scare myself a few days ago. I was reading in my room, when suddenly I felt cold and shivery and began to sweat. Shetani anapita, as we used to say. But the cold sweat did not pass for several minutes. I thought I was having some kind of an attack, my heart, my lungs, my spleen, what could it be?

The next morning I went to the clinic at the university, expecting the worst, but the doctor could find nothing wrong. It was the first time I had a proper detailed medical check-up: heart, lungs, blood pressure, blood sugar, everything in good shape. The doctor was laughing by the end, telling me I did not know how lucky I was to be so well. I felt so good afterwards.

You ask me to come and visit and I will do that when I can afford it, and thank you for the telephone number. I will know how to get in touch if something urgent comes up. Love to Munira and tell her I wish her luck in secondary school.

Love,
Salim

I wrote to my father too, not letters, sometimes a few lines in my notebook or a paragraph that I allowed to roam back and forth in my head. I composed brief bewildering apothegms in the voice of al Biruni or Alhaj Ahmed ibn Khalas al Khalas al-Aduwi or whoever, and imagined my father reading them, sitting in a low-slung chair under a tree in Kuala Lumpur: *In abeyance I faced the wood and saw a dazzling glimmer of the garden of the knowing, who willed the arbitration of the affairs of the beloved.*

Dear Baba,

I live with a sense of dissembling. I do not know how to speak about the things that sadden me, about the feeling of loss that is with me at all times, the sense of wrong-doing. And perhaps no one knows how to ask. Even those who might have done, don't know how to enquire into what troubles someone like me. Is that how it was for you? Perhaps no one knows another well enough to care, or does not want to presume, or cannot see any troubling thing to ask about. In any case, if anyone does ask I would not know where to begin: with my mother and what befell her, with you, with Uncle Amir, with my journey into this wilderness, with how much I loathe this life, this place, this cringing?

If anyone asks I think I will smile and let the moment pass. It is something I try to teach myself. It would be easier to lie or to evade, to tell a story about a holiday house on the beach, or the walk to school, or to speak about the big rains. I used to love the big rains with a dread I could not explain even to myself: the ancient light, the water-logged land about to slide off the edge of the world, the croaking of beasts in the shadows. I expect you have monster rains there in Kuala Lumpur.

Yours,
Salim

*

After graduation I stayed on in Brighton. It was too far to return home, and I had not earnt the right because I had achieved nothing in the years I had been away. If I returned penniless and empty-handed I would be at the mercy of the man with the unspeakable name who was my mother's lover, who would find a job for me and take me in hand and quarter me in his stables. I could return to London but I had come to dislike the bustle and chaos and dirt of the city since going to live in Brighton. Maybe I would stay here a little longer before bowing to the inevitable.

Over the years I had become a secret miser. I pretended not to be one but I counted every penny and put away what I could. I bought cheap clothes and wore them until they were threadbare. I denied myself whatever I could resist and saved what I earnt with stubborn determination. There was pleasure in the self-denial. Moving into the one-bedroomed flat on my own was a struggle but I could no longer bear the dirt and the tumult of the shared house in Fiveways. At the beginning it had been my idea that I must save enough for a ticket home, in case my life here became intolerable. It was part of the panic I felt when I first arrived to live in London under the protection of Uncle Amir and Auntie Asha. I did not feel safe once I began to understand the wilfulness of my guardians. The price of a ticket home was a sum that seemed beyond possibility at first, but I added pound after pound over the years, watching the numbers grow in my bank statement with a secret gloating, so that by the time I graduated I had saved more than the price of a ticket home.

I wrote to my mother:

Dear Mama,

It's time for a little relief and celebration. It's seven years now that I've been here. Or have you stopped counting? I hope you are enjoying your luxury flat and you find it amusing to mingle with those plunderers of the human spirit. Well, I am learning to stop counting too and will soon become naturalised. That is what happens to people like me in this country. If we are lucky we stop being foreigners and we become naturalised. Everything has changed so much, I feel I have been bleached or emptied of something vital but at last I have managed to complete my degree. What a long time that took, and I am not sure the thing

I've now got in my hands was worth the anguish. If I had listened to Uncle Amir I would have been an accountant or something useful like that by now, instead of which I am working in a café and I don't know what else I can do. Do you have any news of Baba? I imagine him living peacefully in Kuala Lumpur, walking in the Botanical Gardens (there are always Botanical Gardens in places the British have colonised) or lying in the shade of the veranda of his father's house, reciting verses he remembered from his childhood.

I started again:

Dear Mama,

Salamu na baada ya salamu. I hope you are well and that Munira is well. It must be beautiful there now the rains are over and everything is cool and green. I received my results today, and I am writing to tell you the good news that I have passed quite well. I wish I was with you in person to celebrate this news with you, but I think of you whenever anything good befalls me. I am sorry to hear the tests have been inconclusive but that could be good news.

Love,
Salim

After graduating I continued working for Mark full-time while I applied for other jobs. He told me I could stay as long as I wanted but he could not give me a raise. Business is business, my sainted friend, he said, looking shifty and fat. I applied for work everywhere: to the British Airports Authority (Gatwick was only twenty minutes away on the train), local newspapers, estate agents, banks, American Express (their main UK offices were in town), the University of Sussex, the University of Brighton, solicitors, and was tempted by an advertisement recruiting trainee train drivers. Why not? But it all came to nothing.

I went to visit Mr Mgeni in the New Year. 'We thought we had lost you,' he said. He had sold the OAU house to a businessman from Zaire, who was now converting it back to a family home for sale. House prices were soaring in their street. Mannie had moved to Coventry but did not leave an address. Amos had taken a job in Libya and had a bad accident there. A piece of grit entered his eye, which became infected. Mr Mgeni heard that from someone who was a carpenter and who went to Libya with Amos on the same job. 'Someone came to ask for you,' Mr Mgeni said, 'that friend of yours, Mannie's young relative, Mood. I asked him what kind of name Mood was, and he said it was short for Mahmood. Why do you shorten a nice name like that? I didn't say so to him because he did not look well: trembling, sniffing, dirty clothes. He's taking something. He asked me for a pound but I said no, because if you give money to someone doing that kind of thing, he will come back. He wanted to know how he could reach you, but I said I didn't know any more.'

'But I sent you the address,' I said.

'You want him to come all the way to Brighton to find you? Why don't you get a phone?'

I had not seen Mr Mgeni for a few months. His breathing was laboured and his eyes lacked their usual spark. I did not want to interrogate him about his health at our first meeting after so long. Marjorie prepared a small feast and Frederica came to lunch, looking outrageously beautiful in a thin red cotton dress. Mr Mgeni laughed with delight when she arrived, holding her at arm's length to have a good look at her before pulling her briefly into an embrace.

'My child, you look stunning. You have come to woo him, haven't you?' he said, nodding towards me. 'You've decided to give that other one up and come back for your childhood sweetheart.'

Frederica slapped her father on the hand, the playful slap that young women give to an elderly flirt, or that a daughter might teasingly deliver to an ailing father. Marjorie explained that Frederica was now living in Streatham with her partner, Chris, and they planned on getting married soon. I did not know what it meant that Frederica looked so exceptionally beautiful. She was like a miracle. It seemed to me that her beauty must have meaning. If I could grasp what that was, it would be a way of understanding something important.

'You look more beautiful every day,' I said. 'What a lucky man your Chris is.'

Frederica smiled and raised her eyebrows with incredulity at the same time, as if my flattery was only friendly banter.

'He would have come to lunch,' Frederica said. 'I've told him about you, and I know he'd like to meet you. But he's on duty today. He's a physiotherapist in Denmark Hill Hospital, and he just couldn't change his shift.'

Frederica herself worked in the Personnel Department of Lambeth Council based in Brixton, and when I said that I was languishing in a café job in Brighton and thinking of moving back to London, she told me to look out for a Lambeth advert coming out in the next couple of days. She sent me a cutting of it, and although I delayed applying until the last minute, and also applied for several other posts in different offices and businesses, and was almost certain it would all come to nothing, I was offered the Lambeth job and had not the strength to resist. I duly became a local government officer.

6

BILLIE

I found a small studio flat off Brixton Hill above a motorcycle shop. As if that was not noisy enough, my neighbours on the same floor and on the one above were bickerers who argued deep into the night, shouting and banging and throwing things. As soon as I could I moved, to a tiny sublet in Clapham Common and finally to a two-bedroomed flat in Putney. It took over a year to make that journey and in that time I had become reconciled to many things but in particular to the salary that went silently into my bank account in return for my lackadaisical efforts in the office. Rushing around in Café Galileo had tired me and put me on edge, assaulted some part of my senses one way or another, but the work of the Leisure Department was much more orderly and measured.

For a while I was content. I told myself it was a kind of holiday while I was working out what else to do, but as the weeks passed I could not resist the return of my anxieties, and then I thought I was drifting. I feared that word. I feared turning into one of England's helots, becoming accustomed to bondage. Perhaps it was time to go while I had the strength, or maybe in a year or two, especially now I had a residence permit and need not rush my decision for fear of expulsion. I could save money, maybe retrain and then look for work in the Gulf or in South Africa, one of those places where they had jobs to spare for people like me. Or I could go back home and see if there was anything for me to do there. At times I thought I was waiting to return, at others that I never would.

In the meantime I went to work and performed my duties, biting my lip and letting the moment pass until what I did became routine and I no longer needed to suppress a feeling of uselessness as I did what was required of me. Some of my colleagues addressed their duties with a purposefulness I envied and pretended to share. I wondered if they were pretending too. I went out drinking with work-mates, and sometimes to the cricket or to a football match or a motorbike race, for a day-trip to whatever came up and was on everybody's lips, to a music festival, a circus, to Wimbledon, the best tennis tournament in the world. We talked to each other as if we were on the same side, spoke the same language and had grown up with similar experiences and shared similar pleasures. Where I came from no one would dream of saying that anything to do with them was the best in the world. How could one know that without knowing the whole world? Here they have plenty which is the best in the world – the best goalkeeper in the world, the best university in the world, the best hospital in the world, the best newspapers in the world. You had to take that in with your mother's milk to say such words without cringing. When it was necessary to do so I said those words. I was becoming naturalised.

I had many relationships with women. That is, I had more or less brief affairs with women I met and got to know, who also wanted to live a life of uncomplicated encounters. It was not always possible to keep the complications out, and cruelties were sometimes unavoidable, but I became better at sensing the moment when it was necessary for me to slip away. I had spent many years not knowing how to approach women, thinking of sexual intimacy as demeaning and an oppression, which enticed the victim into abjection, but then I found out it required nothing but willing partners. I learnt how to recognise the willing and how to make my availability known to them, and I did not try too hard or become too greedy. It seemed then that matters took care of themselves and one thing led to another without rancour. It was possible for a while to make the pursuit of pleasure the real point of everything. I found excitement in the mutually egotistical brevity of these encounters, which allowed me to suppress the distaste that was sometimes inevitable.

Mr Mgeni was fully retired now. He no longer had the strength for the work, and his blood pressure was dangerously high. The doctor told him he might have had a mild stroke without realising it. Now he needed to avoid exertion or he might harm himself. Mr Mgeni had his doubts about doctors but Marjorie did not. She insisted that her husband took his medication, which he preferred to avoid because it bloated and constipated him, but she did not allow any debate.

'You are a stubborn, ignorant man,' she told him. 'And you have no choice but to take those pills, so better give up sooner then you can have a little peace.'

'I am only sixty-seven,' Mr Mgeni said querulously, refusing to submit to growing feebleness. 'What am I supposed to do with myself? Sit around and get fat? I have only ever worked all my life, since I was a little boy. How am I supposed to stop now?'

'You must be very tired then,' Marjorie said. 'Why don't you take a rest?'

It did not seem likely to me that Mr Mgeni would get fat. If anything, he was losing weight and at the same time swelling around his wrists and his face and perhaps other parts of his body not visible to me. He did not look as if he had the strength to do very much anyway. His hand trembled when he picked up a cup, and he was no longer capable of the unstinting benevolence of years before. He was now more easily irritated, although his tetchiness was often directed at himself and sometimes at Marjorie. He cried very easily. When I saw those tears in his eyes I had to look away for fear they would bring on my own. He looked exhausted and conversation with him was becoming difficult because he was not able to keep his mind from wandering. He said that sometimes he woke up in the morning and did not know where he was. He returned again and again to the hardships of the early years of his life at sea, and then to the decades of his time in England, working in all weathers and living in hostels and cramped lodgings – the life of a beast, he said – until God showered him with blessings and sent him Marjorie. He wandered from story to story, sometimes becoming exasperated with himself because he could not remember a name or a place or a date, or because he tangled up one outcome with another. He spoke about old wrongs that he should have put right while he had the strength. He said nothing when I asked him what those were.

'Are you thinking about your home?' I asked him.

He did not reply for a while and I did not ask again. Then he said, 'This is my home.'

I went round there a few days after I received a letter from my mother telling me that she had to go back to Dar for more tests. He was his old self on this occasion, laughing and telling stories and giving advice. I mentioned my mother's letter to Mr Mgeni because he asked after her.

'Tests for what?' he asked.

'I don't know, she doesn't say,' I said. I had told him that she was having tests but he did not always remember. 'You know how it is, people are discreet about their illnesses.'

'Not with her own son. Call her. You have a telephone in your flat now. Call her like she wants you to,' Mr Mgeni said, bristling uncharacteristically at me, like a proper uncle.

When I lived with Uncle Amir and Auntie Asha they called home regularly, and at some point I was always summoned to exchange a few words with my mother. She hated the phone, I knew that of old, and I hated it too and hated hearing her voice on it. But after I was expelled from that Eden I did not call because the man himself might answer and I had no wish to speak to him.

Yes, I did have a telephone in the flat and I had her number beside it but I still had not been able to bring myself to make the call. It was another one of my anxieties but I did not know what I would say to her. I thought of the phone as an instrument to be used when there was something urgent to say and I had nothing like that to tell her. I had not spoken to her for years and I did not know where I would begin. And then *he* might answer the call. But that weekend evening, stung by guilt and Mr Mgeni's rebuke, I did call home. I dialled the number and after a few rings I was about to put the receiver down with relief when someone picked up. I heard a voice I could not mistake.

'Hello,' he said. It was him. When I did not answer he said, 'Nani huyu? Who is calling? Hello, is this an international call? Can you hear me?'

I put the phone down. His voice was strong and firm as I had imagined from a man with a thick neck and hard hands. I should have spoken and asked for her. I should have spoken like a grown-up person who had learnt to cope with the world and not fled like a child. I tried to put the encounter behind me but could not get over the shame. I could not stop thinking about it for days.

A couple of Sundays later I went round to Mr Mgeni's for lunch and he asked after my mother and if I had spoken to her about the tests. I lied and said that I had called but there was no reply. 'You tried once?' he asked. I did not answer. 'Do you have her number with you? Don't be so stubborn. Go and call her now. Use our phone.'

'I'll call her later,' I said.

'Give me the number,' he said. 'I'll call her and tell her that you are an ungrateful son as well as a worthless nephew.'

'I don't have her number with me. I'll call her later,' I said. He must have believed me because he forgot himself enough to pat my knee some time during the afternoon.

He was almost his old self at Frederica's wedding, beaming at everyone and even stepping out on to the floor for a couple of turns when they put Nat 'King' Cole on for him. I saw Frederica at work sometimes and she always had news of them, speaking to me in a way that had come to her with marriage, a way which was flirtatious but had in it an unguarded confidence, as if she was a grown woman teasing a child. I remembered Peter's girlfriend Fran used to treat me like that years ago. What had happened to Fran? Did she go with Peter? What had happened to him back in the new South Africa?

Mr Mgeni died during my second year in Putney, and I went to the funeral held in the crematorium chapel in Streatham. Marjorie asked me to read something that would remind us of Mr Mgeni's home and the way he grew up, and I read the fatiha followed by al Ikhlas because I did not know any funeral prayers and I did not think Mr Mgeni did either. I wrote to my mother to tell her about Mr Mgeni's death. I had told her about him several times, about how we spoke Kiswahili together and how I used to go on jobs with him and how I was always welcome in his house. After his death, it felt to me as if my mother was someone who knew him and would like to be informed about his departure. I wrote: It might not seem right that there was no one there to say a prayer for him but me, and that all I could manage was the fatiha and the shortest sura in the good book, but I don't think it would have troubled him very much. There was his family there, who were, as he said, the blessing that God had showered on him. That would have mattered more to him than if I had read Yasin for him. He had resigned himself to many losses. As I was writing the letter I thought of what Mr Mgeni would have said to me if he were here. Call her. The thought thrilled me and without further reflection I did so.

'Salam alaikum,' said the destroyer of souls.

I delayed as long as I could before replying, debating whether I should do so or just hang up. In the end I said, 'Alaikum salam. May I speak to my mother?'

'Salim, is that you? Do you know what time it is?' he said, his voice stern. Then he laughed and said, 'Haya, just wait a minute. How are you? Are you all right? Is there a problem?'

'No, there is no problem. I just called,' I said.

'Hello,' she said. Her voice sounded as familiar as if I had spoken to her a short while ago.

'Mama,' I said.

'I knew it was you,' she said gleefully. 'Even before Hakim picked up the phone I knew it was you. Who else would ring after midnight?'

I had forgotten about the time difference. I pictured her face and her eyes and her gesturing hand as I spoke to her. I said I had no reason to call, just to say hello. I asked after her health and she asked after mine. I asked about the tests and she said the doctors were not sure what it was. It could be just early menopause, run-down and headaches and that kind of thing, but they were continuing with the tests. They were not sure what her mother died of. In case it was something hereditary they were doing regular checks on heart and blood pressure and kidneys and so on, but with nothing definite to report. When was I coming to visit?

she asked. I said I would soon. There was, after all, not much to say but I was thrilled to hear her voice.

After a few more predictable exchanges, I said I was going now. I wanted to ask if she had any news of Baba but I did not. 'You must call again,' she said. 'Often. Next time call when Munira will be able to speak to you. Call in the evening and don't forget the time difference. She is always asking after you. She does not even remember how you look.'

'I will,' I said.

To myself I said: I will become one of England's helots like Mr Mgeni if I don't do something about myself, until one day England kills me too. After that call I lay in the darkness of the early hours, looking again at various plans I had considered in the past to extricate myself from my pointless life, then in the morning I dressed for work and fitted myself into the day's events.

After the funeral, Marjorie went back to Jamaica for a holiday. She was to be there for a month, but when that time was over she stayed for another month and then another one after that. St Thomas' Hospital kept her job open for her as long as they could but Marjorie did not return. She stayed on in Jamaica and did not even come back to pack up the house. Frederica and Chris did that. They shipped what they thought she would like to keep and gave away the rest. Then they put the house on the market and banked the proceeds for her retirement fund. I laughed with disbelief when Frederica told me how Marjorie just left everything and went back home. She would have gone years earlier and taken Dad with her, Frederica said, but he was too tired and could not face another move.

*

It was during this time when Mr Mgeni's death forced me into a small crisis of reflection that I met Billie. Her full name was Bindiya but she was called Billie from birth. Her father was English, although he had lived most of his adult life in India, and it was he who insisted that the children should have Indian names, just as he always only used his own version of their

English contractions. So he had familiar English diminutives for her brothers too and only used their given Indian names for ceremonial or disciplinary purposes.

I met her when I went to see a production of *The Cherry Orchard* at the National Theatre. I read about the play in the Sunday newspaper: Trevor Nunn's brilliant production and stunning performances by Corin and Vanessa Redgrave and a cast of stars. I thought it was time to give Chekhov another chance after my disappointing encounter with him as a schoolboy. The play was showing in the Cottesloe, and the theatre was packed and buzzing, but the seat on my left was unoccupied until seconds before the doors were closed and the lights went down. When its owner turned up I was aware that it was a woman, probably more sophisticated and fashionable than the plainly dressed older woman on my right (linen trousers and a thick cardigan) because of the perfume that accompanied her arrival and the stiff swish of her clothes. I suppressed my curiosity about her so I could concentrate on the stage, although it took me a moment or two to do that.

Within the first few minutes I was lost in the play, mesmerised by the pathos of the dialogue and the beautiful staging and lighting. Vanessa Redgrave played Lyubov Andreyevna Ranevskaya and Corin Redgrave was her chatterbox brother Gayev. Brother and sister playing brother and sister, a publicist's cliché, but they were brilliant. When out of nowhere Lyubov Andreyevna declared her anguish: *If only this burden could be taken from me, if only I could forget my past,* I felt my eyes stinging with distress for the middle-aged mother mourning her child. It seemed that human sorrow was always based on regret and pain in the past, and that neither time nor location nor history made much difference. And when later she told the story of her betrayal of her husband and the failure of her love, I wept for her. At the end of the play, as Lopakhin's crew were cutting down the orchard, I knew that the thud of the axes into the cherry trees would always stay with me, as if the blows were a violence on my own body. Three hours went past quickly, and by the end I was on my feet, joining everyone else in enthusiastic applause.

The woman to my left turned to leave and I did too. I had seen during the interval – which I had spent in my seat while she went off somewhere – that she was attractive with a finely drawn face which gave her features an appearance of delicacy even though she was otherwise well-built. As we made our way between the rows of seats, she looked my way and then looked again and smiled. She said hello lightly, and it was apparent she was addressing someone she thought she knew. My mind was still on the play and I must have failed to respond fully enough to her because she smiled and reminded me that we had met at a wedding party some months before.

'Lucy and Morgan ... a boat on the Thames,' she said over her shoulder as we moved slowly out of the auditorium.

Then I remembered a wedding party I had gone to with Theresa, although I knew neither the bride nor the groom and was not invited on my own account. Theresa said they would not mind in the least, and I heard in her voice the expectation of the hospitality that people of her class anticipated and extended to each other. I had met Theresa at a jazz club in Kilburn where I had gone with friends because someone had mentioned it or it was in a listing. We joined tables with another group and I found myself sitting next to her. She had soft dark eyes and a slow smile, but she turned out to be a fast-talking woman with a sarcastic wit and a loud laugh. She worked for a public relations firm and told me that her agency had a big account with a mining company that had African operations. She mentioned the name as if her association with it gave us something in common. At some point in the evening, an African woman who was dressed in a full-length spangly dress and a multi-coloured turban with an ostrich feather stuck in it came out to sing in a language none of us understood. She was the one we had come to see. After that evening I went out with Theresa three times and she told me entertaining stories, that I guessed were well salted, about disreputable goings on in the world of PR. She had no sexual interest in me and I had no other interest in her. The party on the Thames to celebrate the wedding of Lucy and Morgan was the last time we went out together.

In the foyer I had a good look at the woman I had been sitting next to during the play but did not recognise her from the party. I had known no one there, so maybe it was too much to take in after a few drinks. Did she know many people there? She said Lucy and she had been at university together and they kept in touch afterwards.

'We're still in touch,' she said, laughing.

'That's wonderful,' I said, 'because it's so easy to lose contact. Would you like to have a drink?'

The theatre bar was too crowded so we walked out to the promenade and found a wine bar there. That was how I met Billie, or rather, how I met her again. I rang her a few days later and we met for a movie and a meal on Friday night. I suggested a drink afterwards but she said she had to go to work the next morning. She worked for a bank in Liverpool Street, and it was a long way to Acton and then back to the City the following morning. She was planning to move soon but for the moment she still had to trek back and forth. Well, so did everybody else, she said, but it was still tiring. And anyway, she lived with her mother, who worried if she was late. Her elder brother also lived at home, but he could stay out as long as he liked, of course, being a man. Their father was dead, he had died when she was five.

I asked if she would like to meet again, and she said she was not sure, maybe I could call her. I called her later in the week and we met for a drink after work. So things moved slowly for us in this way, a drink after work, sometimes a film or a meal, and several weeks passed, perhaps six or seven. I was not sure if I should press harder or retreat, and whether she was taking her time or was actually reluctant, whether I was bothering her. I could imagine many reasons why she might be reluctant – a half-Indian girl with a mother at home, getting mixed up with a Salim from Zanzibar, just think about it. I would have given up long before this and gone after a more willing partner, but I had fallen out of that routine and now felt a distaste for its predatory relentlessness, and I could not quite give her up.

One evening some two months after I met her in the National, as we sat in a quiet restaurant off Holborn and she was talking

136

about something to which I was evidently not paying full attention, I felt a tenderness for her that I had never felt for any other woman before. I would have to let her know that and make sure she did not choose to walk away from me. We went to Kew on a sunny Saturday in April and when I took her in my arms, she held on to me for a while. I knew this moment, making love to a woman for the first time, the eagerness of it. After walking the gardens we spent the afternoon lying on the grass, our coats spread out beneath us, kissing and fondling and talking, abandoned to the relief of this new knowledge of each other.

'How did your parents meet?' she asked me.

'In a school debate at the Youth League headquarters,' I said.

'Hey, that sounds cool, tell me about it,' she said.

'I don't really know any more. Tell me about yours.'

'They met in Delhi, when he was working there for Canon photocopiers as a sales director,' she said. 'No, he was not a salesman, he was a sales director. An Englishman in India cannot be a salesman. All of us were born in Delhi. Suresh also known as Sol and Anand also known as Andy were both ahead of me. By the time I arrived, my eldest brother was eleven, and my father wanted him to go to secondary school in England. Perhaps it was an ancestral longing but what he said was it would make it easier for Sol, and later for the rest of us, to go to university.

'Our father had not been to university. He had found work more or less immediately after boarding school, through a relative who had Indian connections, and ended up in Delhi working for Canon photocopiers. But it was a different world now and there was not much you could do without a university degree. So we came to London,' Billie said, 'which was something Daddy's company could arrange without any problem. For him it was coming back for good, but for me and my middle brother it was the first time, although I was only a baby and couldn't have cared less. Suresh and my mother had been back with him before, when he took them round like tourists to Bath and Margate and Cambridge and the Norfolk Broads and places like that, staying in B&Bs or with his sister in Wanstead when they were in London. That's our Aunt Holly, still here today aged seventy-one.

'But the move to London did not really suit him. My mother said it was too late for him, his whole body wanted to be in India, his mind, his limbs and especially his heart. She talks like that a lot. At the slightest opportunity she slips into metaphor, especially if it's something to do with sentiment. On special occasions she writes poems in Hindi, all about love and duty and motherhood and sacrifice, devotional poems, more like prayers, I suppose. They're quite good if you like heavy stuff like that.'

'Heavy stuff like what?' I asked.

'Life and joy are born of folly, which opens us to the infinite/I prostrate myself before the wisdom and love of our holy mother. Stuff like that,' Billie said. 'Anyway, whether it was true or not that our father did not want to leave India, his health deteriorated quickly in London, and after two or three years he was not working any more. He was older than our mother, but not yet of retirement age when he stopped working. He was fifty-nine, which is no age to die these days. Look at Aunt Holly, and both my mother's parents are in their eighties.'

'What was he ill with?' I asked.

'His heart. One day, when I was five, he had a stroke while he was working in the garden. I was in the garden too, playing with a toy watering can and plastic cups. I heard him make a noise, and when I looked up he was on his knees. I don't remember what happened after that, I must have cried out or run in to get my mother. I don't know. I remember the several terrible weeks in hospital that followed for him.

'For a long time, that was how I remembered him,' she continued after a silence during which, I imagined, she relived those memories. 'I remember those miserable hospital visits, all of us crying while he lay drugged and unaware. Later other memories came back, but even now I sometimes have to work hard to repel that sight of him in a hospital bed. Do you know what I mean? When an image or a moment comes out of nowhere and overpowers you repeatedly? He called me Billie, and even though I preferred Bindiya, I used the name he called me as a way of being loyal to him. I think I was a sentimental child.'

'Not any more?' I asked. She was close to tears.

'Not as much,' she said. 'Anyway, everybody called me Billie, and I did not think it would be that easy to get them to change. My eldest brother hated his English name and never uses it now, but he lives in Madrid where he is able to train a whole new set of acquaintances to use the name he prefers. He works as a car designer there, did I tell you that?'

'Yes, you did,' I said. 'What does your other brother do?'

'He is a surveyor with a property agency, Hope & Borough. They deal with multi-million-pound properties. Have you heard of them?' Billie asked, looking at me expectantly.

'No, I haven't heard of them,' I said.

'They're famous.'

It was late afternoon when we got to my flat. That was how we spent almost every Saturday that summer, we went somewhere for the day, then back to my flat to make love, and then sometimes we went out for the evening or ate at home. She would not stay the night. 'I love being here with you,' she said. 'I love being with you all day, and I would love to be with you all night. But not yet. While I live at home with my mother I have to return every night. You would understand what I mean if you knew her. I couldn't leave her at home on her own.'

She said: 'My mother was originally from Bombay, as it used to be called, but her father was moved to Delhi on a civil service posting. That was where she met my father several years later. My mother worked for Canon as well.

'The move to London soon after I was born was difficult for her. She was brought up with servants and was used to having them to do the chores. She was used to having relatives and friends around as well as their children, who were company for her own. In London she had to do everything for herself and by herself, and she never really overcame that first recoil she felt from the city and the life it forced on her, especially as it quickly took her husband away. She became depressed and shrill after he died. I am using that word deliberately, shrill,' said Billie, and then paused for me to take this in. 'When I was a child, it shamed me that my mother was so shrill. I thought her voice penetrated the walls of all the houses in the street and that the neighbours laughed at us for being so ridiculous. I did not know that she was depressed and lonely and in a panic.'

'Why did she not return to India?' I asked. Billie looked at me for a long second, and I knew she was thinking: Why didn't you? Why are you still here then? 'I meant, did she think of returning to India.'

Billie shrugged. 'It was complicated,' she said. 'The house in Acton now belonged to her, all her children were at school and settled, as she saw it. Their daddy had chosen Acton because it was not yet a ghetto and its schools were still safe. If she returned to India she would be taking the children away from what their father wanted for them. Also, if she returned to India, she would have to move back in with her parents and she did not want to do that. In the end, it was her duty to be loyal to our daddy's plans for us to go to school here and attend university.

'She became religious after he died. She talked about him so much when I was a child,' Billie said. 'Marathon sessions of daddy-talk which actually did not feel oppressive. It was a way of getting to know him in such detail that he felt real to me, as if he could walk into the room at any minute. It did not feel oppressive until later, when my mother tried to blackmail us at various moments to get us to do what she wanted for us.'

Billie was now the centre of my days. Sometimes we met after work mid-week, but mostly we waited for the weekend. Saturday morning came to have such a magical excitement that I could not contain my happiness as I made ready to meet her. This sense of joy rested on something fragile and insecure. If she was late, my thoughts became cloudy with worry that she was never coming to see me again, or that she was putting off coming as long as possible because she was bored by the predictability of how we spent our time together. She was ashamed of me, of the work I did, of my lack of ambition, of my strangeness, my ordinariness, my blackness, my poverty. Then when she came, and smiled to see me, and held me so tightly and so long that I could not mistake the intensity of her pleasure in me, when she came and held me like that, the darkness evaporated and I cried with happiness. She knew this about me, how tensely and expectantly I waited for her, but she did not know the vulnerability that lay just below it. She took it for the eagerness of my desire and it made her smile to think how avid I was for her.

Towards the end of autumn of that year, when the pavements were covered with wet leaves and the parks were bedraggled and windblown, and we had been together for seven months, Billie stayed with me for the weekend for the first time. She had told her mother that she was going away to stay with a university friend. She also told her mother that she was thinking of leaving home to live in a place of her own, sharing with another woman from work.

'My mother cannot understand this wish, and when I told her she looked bewildered at first then she looked pained as if I had said something ... I don't know ... obscenely unloving,' Billie said. 'I told her just before I left to come here, and hurried out before she could say much in reply. I thought I'd leave it for her to turn over in her mind but I'll have to do a lot more talking when I return.'

In the following months, Billie reported daily heated arguments and pained silences and endless promises she made to her mother. Her brother Anand who was living at home intervened on her side. 'I try to explain to her that's how it is here. Everyone leaves home and sets up on their own. Everybody wants to have their own life and to have control of it. She understands that, of course, but she pretends to find it strange because she cannot bear to be on her own. She would have us all at home if she could. It was the same when my brother Suresh wanted to move to Madrid.'

It did not shock me that her mother was so reluctant to let Billie leave home. I could imagine my mother being just as puzzled by the desire to leave for what to her would seem like no reason at all. Even though we had been seeing each other for several months – I love these sweet English euphemisms, seeing each other – I had still not met any members of her family. This was not a concern to me at first. I had not met any family members of any of the women I had known before. If one asked me to join her for a family occasion I said politely that I would rather not.

141

I did not desire that kind of intimacy. With Billie it was different. She was planning to move in and her mother and her brother would be reassured to know something of who she was moving in with. She made light of the matter whenever I mentioned it. 'We are a long way from any moving yet,' she said. 'But you will, you'll meet them.'

The story she was telling her family was that she was looking to move in with a woman friend from work, and my appearance in their midst would throw some doubt on that. I could not help thinking that the reason she was not allowing the meeting was because she knew they would disapprove of me. I could think of several reasons why they might do so but if Billie was seriously planning to move in, it seemed best to me to come clean and talk them round because she could not hide me forever. She shook her head when I said this and I knew there was trouble ahead.

Despite my apprehension Billie did make the move. One weekend she came with a suitcase as if she was going away for a few days and stayed for the whole week. She went home for the weekend with her empty suitcase and returned on Sunday with some more of her things. In this way she moved herself in slowly without quite moving out of her home. I loved the intimacies of living with her: cutting an extra set of keys, adjusting the central heating times to suit her, hanging her underwear on the drier, shopping together, going to bed with her every night and waking up beside her, making love, sometimes first thing and last thing every day. She browsed my bookshelves but rarely took down a book. I was methodically going through Chekhov at the time and tried to interest her too.

'After all, we met through Chekhov,' I reminded her.

'No, I don't really enjoy reading,' she said. 'I went to see the play because I studied it at school and someone at the bank was raving about the brilliance of the production, and Anand was around one evening when I was talking about it to my mother and he got me a ticket. He likes to do these generous surprises. So I thought I might as well go and see it, and when I did, there he was, my lover, waiting beside me.'

Her mother never asked to visit the flat or meet her flat-mate from the bank, although she apparently issued a vague invitation should Billie wish to invite her. Nevertheless, Billie worked on an emergency procedure that would enable us hurriedly to remove all evidence of my presence in the flat, and somehow or other hide me as well. It made me laugh to see her practising because I always found some giveaway that she missed. 'What's this?' I would ask, holding up the criminal evidence: a size 10 shoe, a belt, underpants and socks in the dirty laundry basket.

'That's cheating,' she said about the laundry basket.

'Why's that? You don't think your mother would check your laundry basket? It's the first place I would go to if I wanted to find out who you were sharing with,' I said.

After several months of subterfuge, I finally met Anand when he dropped Billie off after a visit home. He showed no surprise when we met and must have known all the important facts beforehand. Billie had taken him into her confidence but had still not said anything to her mother. Anand shook hands and smiled non-committally, a soft-spoken, well-built man with a mass of curly auburn hair. I imagined people looked twice when he introduced himself as Anand because he looked so unlike one. His eyes, which were grey, moved quickly round the room when he came into the flat, adding up and calculating like a surveyor and a brother, I supposed. He refused to stop but he gave us a friendly wave as he drove off in his Mercedes.

So I became a secret she shared with her brother, who found the deception difficult, so Billie said. He rarely visited us and arranged to meet Billie in town for lunch when he wanted to see her. Apart from this half-secret matter of where she lived and with whom, everything worked well for us. I loved touching her and I knew that I would never forget the feel of her unblemished skin. Is that how a lover's skin always feels? One night I started to tell her about my mother whom I had neglected in my absorption with Billie, but she fell asleep before I had got past the way she used to talk over glossy American dramas as we watched TV. We had been on a long day out on the coast, and we had wine with our meal, which Billie could not take much of. She remembered the next day: 'You were saying something about your parents and I fell asleep.'

'I was only talking about my mother, how she used to have this annoying habit of talking over what was going on on the TV, kind of rewriting the script,' I said, and tried to leave it at that.

'No,' said Billie. 'Tell me more.'

'When I was seven my Baba left us,' I said, and realised I had never said that to anyone. 'That's all. I don't know why he left.'

'Tell me,' she said, holding me as I made to turn away from her. So I told her, but still not fully, and she tugged and pulled until I told her more and more. I told her all I could, which was still not everything: about my father's silence, about the lunch basket, about my mother's secret visits with her lover, about Uncle Amir, about Munira, about my mother's sadness. 'Her eyes sometimes had a blankness as if they were turned inside out and were gazing inwards, and sometimes suddenly she sucked in her lips as if she had taken a blow to her body. I don't know what memories did this to her and why afterwards she sat in silent despair. But the moment always passed and after it eased away her eyes would quicken again with truculence and anxiety and amusement. When I asked her what it was all about she said things sometimes came back to her.'

'What things came back to her?'

'I don't know,' I said. 'She did not like to talk like that about herself. Something broke in my father after he left us. He did not say much after that, or do much. He lived like a hermit in a room behind a shop. Neither of them wanted to talk much.'

'So *that* is the darkness in you,' said Billie after I was silent for a while. 'I knew there was something you were keeping out of reach.'

I felt humbled in my need, a betrayer, hawking my agony for her sympathy, but she said no, it was a line we had to cross. You have to talk about the things that cause you pain.

At some point in the summer another line came up. Billie's mother decided that she wanted to visit the flat, to see where her daughter lived. Billie went into emergency procedure mode and the following day, which was the one appointed for the visit,

I was sent off for a long walk. It was pointless because I did not see how anyone, let alone a mother, could walk into our flat and think that two women lived there. The second bedroom had boxes and books and a desk and a single bed we had cleverly put in there to fool Billie's mother that a co-tenant lived in it, but it was unmistakably not the bedroom of a woman friend who also worked in the bank. When I returned from my marathon walk I found Billie sitting in front of the TV with the set switched off.

'She wants to meet you,' she said when I asked her how it had gone. 'Tomorrow.'

'It sounds like an order,' I said. She looked at me angrily but did not say a word. 'Was it horrible?' I asked, trying to make amends.

'What do you think?' she said.

Her mother had come with Anand and after a brief tour of the flat had said, He reads a lot of books. In the interrogation that followed Billie was forced into a full confession. It was bound to happen sooner or later, I said. We'll go and see her tomorrow and then work out how we go on from there. I tried to get Billie to tell me what made her so pessimistic but she would not. Don't worry, I said, I'll charm the old biddy, but she snorted and told me I did not understand anything about families. On the way to Acton the next day Billie still looked doubtful and I arrived at their house full of dread. Anand let us in, with a nonchalant smile and a handshake for me and a kiss for his sister, and led us into the living room. Billie's mother was sitting on the sofa, a small smile of welcome on her face, just as one might expect.

'Salim,' Billie said, introducing me, and it sounded as if someone had shouted an obscenity in a sacred place. I stepped forward to shake hands. Billie's mother was around sixty, I guessed, her face a little fleshier than Billie's but the features similar. She was dressed in a sari with lines of brown, saffron and cream and wore large tinted glasses, a friendly elegant woman who showed no sign of turning shrill. She patted the sofa beside her and said Billie's name. In the meantime Anand ushered me to a chair by the window and retreated to another one on the other side of the sofa, deeper into the room. No doubt the plan was to keep me in full view. Billie and Anand did most of the talking, telling work stories and chatting about this and that. Sometimes I was drawn in with a question but nothing challenging, an invitation to offer an opinion or to provide some inconsequential information. Billie's mother said almost nothing but followed everything with a smile and a benign expression in her eyes, even when they fell on me. It was looking good, I thought, and tried to make eye contact with Billie but she only briefly acknowledged me.

I had expected smouldering accusing stares and acid questions about my parents, my work, my religion, but the nearest it came to that was when I looked at Billie's mother while Anand was talking and found her gazing at me with surmise. She caught my eye and smiled and then turned towards her son. In due course the cakes and tea came out and after a visit of two uneventful hours or so, we set off for Putney.

'I like your mum,' I said. 'She looks so elegant. I can see where you get your looks.'

Billie shook her head, worrying at something she was not ready to talk about yet. I guessed she was going over the visit in her own mind. When she was ready to speak about it she said the visit had gone surprisingly well but something in her tone made me think she was saying that to hold me off. The next day she called me from work to say that she was summoned home to Acton that evening.

'What's it about?' I asked. I didn't want to ask if it was about me, but of course it must be.

'I don't know,' said Billie. 'I'll probably be back late.'

But she did not come back at all and she did not call. I was full of apprehension, imagining the harsh realities Billie's face was being rubbed into, imagining the cruel lashes that were being laid across my back. We know nothing about his family. Certainly he is no high-flier – the Sports and Leisure Department of Lambeth Council, for God's sake. He will be a financial burden to you. You have a promising future at the bank. Look, they are already training you in investment and finance, why compromise that with dubious connections in your young life? A Muslim from Africa!

I rang Billie at work but she was unavailable. Later in the morning I had an email: *Sorry about last night. I'll see you later*, which rather than reassuring me only worried me more. Why wasn't she calling me? When I got back that evening Billie was already at home when usually she came in later. I embraced her but her body was limp in my arms and in her eyes I saw exhaustion and defeat.

'What happened?' I asked.

'I'm sorry. I'm really sorry,' she said.

I waited for a while before I asked again what had happened although I was beginning to think I knew.

'They were all there,' she said wearily. 'Suresh came over from Madrid to lay down the law. My mother called him after our visit. She only wanted to meet you to confirm that she had the details right. After that she rang Suresh and told him that I was living with a Muslim nigger from Africa and that he was to come over the next day and talk me out of it. He already knew from Anand. It was all planned. They used that word freely: a nigger is a nigger however nice he is. I had thought religion would be the issue ... I'm sorry. I have to leave you.'

'No. You can't do this.'

'You don't know ... my mother said she would kill herself if I did not.'

'She won't do that!'

'How can I be sure?' said Billie, tears running down her face. 'You don't know what she can be like, how obsessive she gets. When I said, no, don't talk like that, she said it would be an act of sacrifice, a sacred act to maintain the family's honour. I don't know if you can understand her idea of family honour.'

'No, she only said that about ... it's to get your brothers working on you,' I said.

Billie shook her head. 'I am not sure she won't do it if I disobey. When my mother is depressed she talks about suicide. I have heard her do that before. I have heard her say suicide looks you in the eye and draws you from birth and then lurks over you for all your life. She said that every moment I spend here with you is a torment to her, and if I don't leave at once she will kill herself.

How can I be sure she won't do it? I have agreed to return home tomorrow.'

I tried to talk with her but she said she had no choice and talking was not going to do any good. When we went to bed, she lay silently while I talked and pleaded, and then at some point she turned her back to me. I must have fallen asleep in the end because I was woken suddenly by the sound of the early-morning traffic past our street. Billie was sleeping on her back, her right arm flung over her head as usual. I washed and dressed in a hurry because I was late, trying to be quiet so as not to wake her, although I suspected she was only pretending to be asleep. She had said she would call in sick so she could do her packing. I went through the day with the conviction that she would not be there when I got back, but she was. She was waiting for me to come home.

'I was just waiting to say goodbye,' she said, speaking quietly, unsmiling, determined.

'There's no need to do things this way,' I said gently. 'Let's talk about what we can do. We can't just throw everything away like this.'

'I don't want to talk about this or anything else. I need to get away and think about everything that's happened. I think it's best to do this quickly. That's the only way I can do it,' she said. 'But it didn't seem right to go without saying goodbye. It was not your fault. Please don't say anything. I've called Anand, he'll be here soon.'

I nodded and sat in the room for a few moments, silent in the face of so much determination, then I went to the bedroom to change out of my work clothes. When Anand came, he smiled his greetings and picked up Billie's things but did not come back to say goodbye. A nigger is a nigger although not to his face. I exchanged the lightest of kisses with Billie before she left.

Out there in Acton the life she had chosen with me would have looked different from the way it felt to live it. It would have looked reckless, naïve, even treacherous. I guessed that in the brothers' telling I would have seemed like a vagabond, snuffling and sidling into their family warmth, somehow tricking her into irresponsibility. In the end she could not resist her brothers, and there must be something more about the mother that Billie had not told me in full. Her threat of suicide sounded to me like a petulant declaration intended to manipulate and control. I did not understand how suicide could be a sacred act and did not fully understand its enormity for a pious Hindu woman, not at the time. Billie did not explain these things to me before she left so I had to guess at them as best I could and find out more later.

Billie did not make any of it easy, and afterwards, once she had made her escape from me, she rejected all my attempts to reach her or be with her again. It must have been what she had agreed with her brothers and her mother. She blocked my number after my second call so I could not get through to her mobile. She did not reply to my emails and in the end must have blocked my address. I rang her work number and persisted through all attempts to deflect me until she came to the phone. She listened to my greetings in silence then said quietly, 'Don't call this number again. You're going to get me fired.' I felt rejected and misused by this severity and, after the work call, I did not try to get in touch with her again.

Kwa mpenzi Mama,

Salamu na baada ya salamu, I hope you and Munira are both well. In the quiet time I have to myself these days, I remembered that Munira is now seventeen. That was nearly the age I was when I left, and I cannot imagine what she looks like now. A young woman, of course, but it's been such a long time since I saw a picture of her. I should have asked you to send me a photograph of her every year so I could keep track of how she grew, but I did not do that. It did not even occur to my neglectful mind. There are times when I still feel myself to be the same age as when I left home, not in a thinking way but if I catch myself by surprise and imagine myself, then I see that seventeen-year-old youth who came here so long ago, or at least I feel him. I am still here after such a long time when I never thought to be here long when I first came. Everyone says that: I didn't think I would stay for so long.

I'm sorry to have been quiet for a while, but it's not because I don't think of you. You must not think that I neglect you because of lack of care. It just seems as if every day happens like this, coming and going with nothing to report at the end of it. But today I do have some news. I am going to buy a flat, the same one I live in in Putney. I wonder what you would think if you saw it. Maybe I should take some pictures and send them to you, with me sitting in my comfortable armchair reading Chekhov. You'll probably find it shut in and wasteful of space – with just me in it. I often think of the little house we lived in, and how intimate and close everything was and yet it was not stifling or oppressive. Here in this place I sometimes feel drained. The air is thick with dust and clogged with human breath and there are times I feel as if I am suffocating.

It is summer now but the weather has turned stormy and unsettled, heavy rain and hail and then brief sunshine. The language people speak on the news and in public has changed too since those killings in New York, and the talk is all about Muslim fanatics and terrorists. They speak a familiar language of freedom but plan to enforce it with violence. I guess that is familiar too. You would not recognise the way some of the bearded ones speak either, how it was all a plot by Kissinger and the Jews, who planted the bombs to make it seem that Muslims had done it so that America could take over the Muslim world and crush it. They are so full of rage and hatred and contemplate cruelties with such righteousness that it sounds nothing like those stories of our lives that we took in so avidly when we were young: the return to Medina, the Night Journey, the Dome of the Rock. I feel even more of a stranger here now. I hate it but still I stay. I feel like a traitor but I am not sure who it is that I am betraying.

Mama, some weeks ago I lost the woman I loved. I feel as if I have lost a life. I told her about you and Baba, and how things went wrong for us. She is the only person I have ever spoken to about you, and now I feel as if I have lost something of you so cheaply, given something away. Sometimes I feel unwell from loneliness. Sometimes I lose track of days, and on Wednesdays I think it is Thursday, although when I was younger, I always knew

Wednesdays by heart because they felt so bad, with so much of the week still to go.

I don't know what it is about buying the flat, but it makes me feel safe, as if I can't now just float away unheeded into a vast dark nowhere. I have borrowed to the limit to buy it but it will be a necessary pain, a penance for a whole year and more of wanting too much. My notebook is filling up with unsent letters to you. I will have to get another one soon.

7

MOTHER

The shock of Billie's going took a few days to reach every sinew in my body and by the end of that I was listless, weary, at times paralysed. I would not have believed it if it had not happened to me. I felt her rejection as a bodily nausea, a carnal sensation of revulsion and depletion. I had to force myself to do the simplest things, make the bed, have a shower, cook. Even when I cooked I often could not eat. I could not sleep for longer than two or three hours and then woke up in misery. I could not concentrate at work or on what I was reading. The silence of the flat was oppressive and there were too many objects around that reminded me of her. I thought of going home for a visit, to break the chain of events, to please my mother, to reassure myself. That would take my mind off her for sure but I did nothing about it. Weeks went by like that until I found ways to coerce myself out of that nerveless state. Buying the flat was one of those ways. The owner got in touch to say he wanted to sell and I agreed to buy and that occupied a large amount of head space and pushed thoughts of her away.

Taking long walks was another. I think that walk I did to stay out of the flat on the day of Billie's mother's visit started something. I enjoyed it so I began to take long walks through London on my own. Sometimes I set off in the morning and headed across the river, going west or east as I felt like, as far as Chiswick or Hackney. I stayed out all day, or until I needed to force myself to keep walking, then I caught the train or the bus and headed back to Putney. I always took a book with me and if I was in the mood and I found the right spot, I sat down to read. Sometimes I walked to Camberwell and strolled past the OAU house, or to Holland Park to see the house where I lived when I first came to England. In the spring, I sometimes came home from work and went out again to walk in the park or as far as Clapham Common, stopping at a café or a pub on the way.

One Friday I walked all night long, through Wandsworth, and Tooting Bec and Brixton and Denmark Hill and Lewisham as far as Greenwich. I passed clubbers and revellers and people like me walking through London streets in their sleep. Mostly I kept away from the major roads, and tried to find my way through the tangle of small streets, bearing left whenever I felt in doubt. I read how once Charles Dickens walked from Tavistock Square in central London to Gad's Hill Place, his house near Rochester, a seven-hour walk through the night, because he had had a row with his wife. I read about a group who re-enacted the journey of Chaucer's pilgrims from Southwark to Canterbury. I dreamt of taking that walk one day later in the summer when the sun had warmed up the ground a little more, carrying my pilgrim's flask to refresh myself on the way.

Dear Mama,

I am so glad you are pleased to hear about the flat but I should tell you that it is only a small one and it does not mean that I am now well off. In fact, the very opposite because I have to pay a lot of money back every month. It must be very frustrating to keep having these tests and not get any firm results. Maybe it does mean that there is nothing to worry about. Here the days (years) pass. I'm surprised how easily and swiftly they do. When I add them up I am astonished how long I've been here. I think you are right, it is time I came for a visit before you forget what I look like. I've made a plan to come after the New Year. I'm due some leave from work then and I'll take a month off and come and see the old homeland and my old Mama.

Thank you for Munira's photo. It was wonderful to speak to her and to you just recently. I enclose a photo of the flat.

Love,
Salim

*

The following New Year's Eve I went down to Folkestone in Kent to stay with a friend. I met her on a training course and things worked out, and after that she called me when she was coming to London and felt like meeting and a couple of times she stayed with me. Her name was Rhonda. I make the relationship sound casual but Rhonda was a troubled woman and I told myself this New Year's Eve would be the last time I met her.

The morning of New Year's Day was mild, with heavy clouds and a thin, almost invisible haze. The ashy light had an unexpected brightness at the back of it, like the silvering in a mirror, and it made me feel sad, as certain kinds of light do for inexplicable reasons. I was sitting on the back porch of Rhonda's ground-floor flat, overlooking the lawn that sloped towards the surgery next door. There was no fence or hedge to mark a boundary between the two because all the lawn belonged to the surgery. It was Saturday and quiet at this end of the town with its rows of gabled Victorian houses, some of them three storeys high and still occupied by single families. The streets were avenues of huge leafless trees, which I knew in the summer made the pavement as gloomy as a forest floor. From where I sat, I could see the surgery building and I wondered if the house Rhonda lived in would have been the doctor's house perhaps, and it and the surgery would have been one property.

Every so often I heard a car go past, a faint, wet whispering noise as if the road were some distance away when I knew it went past the front of the house. There were no other sounds even though it was New Year's Day and a Saturday. Rhonda was still in bed, wearing her eyeshades to indicate that she was not to be forced awake, and her daughter Susannah was sleeping over at a friend's house. A few days before this Saturday, Rhonda telephoned me in the early hours of the morning. I knew it was her because that was the kind of time she rang. The first time she did it, I thought it was a call from another place, and now every time she rang in the middle of the night I had to suppress a spasm of guilt that I did not call my mother more often.

By the time I was awake enough to reach for the phone, on that early morning some days before New Year's Eve, I knew it was Rhonda. I did not want to see her but I also did. I said hello and waited for the ritual gap that Rhonda liked to leave in our conversations, then after a few seconds she told me that she could not sleep. She hated it. Was I alone? Did she wake me up? I said yes and left it at that. After another moment, she said that she was going to be on her own on New Year's Eve as well and she knew she would not be able to bear that. She couldn't, not on New Year's Eve. Was I doing anything? Did I want to come and stay for a day or two? I left my own pause then, and in those silent seconds images of Rhonda rushed in on me: her eyes with their luminous grief, her warm nakedness beside me, her anguishes. There was something not quite right about her. Her jaw was slack, her eyes quite small, but she carried herself as if she was a beauty and her self-love made her provocative.

Her call came after weeks of silence. The last time we had been together had been an evening of bitter talk, and long before we stopped and decided to call it a night we had heaped scorn on each other and on whatever it was that brought us together. When she was in this bitter mood she spoke with incomprehensible assurance, in a language that made me think of abstraction in its ruined temple, of fantasy taking flight. I hesitated for a long moment, wondering if I should allow myself to be drawn into being with this woman who spoke as if words meant something different to her, as if she knew a language with an emphasis all her own. After a while, as the memory of her came surging back into my body, I said, yes, I would come. A moment later the phone went dead and she was gone.

That was how she did things, abrupt, unsettling, inviting outrage, all intended to demonstrate her wacky independence when to me she often seemed on the brink of sadness. Every time I left her, I thought that would be the last time. I smiled at the thought as I sat in the back porch on that mild Saturday morning, waiting for Rhonda to wake up. I smiled a little sad self-pitying smile because I was not sure which of the two of us was more in need.

*

My mother died on New Year's Eve. I did not find out for four days because I only returned from Folkestone on Monday afternoon. By then my mother had been buried for that number of days and the khitma prayers and readings had been said. There was nothing left to do but grieve. It was Uncle Amir who rang on Monday night to tell me.

'Salim, is that you? I have bad news,' he said. Then after a short pause he continued, 'Your mother has passed away.'

A wail ran unbidden through my body but no sound came out. When I said nothing he continued speaking, his voice solemn and deep.

'I called your number on Friday morning from Delhi in case you could get back in time for the funeral, or at least for the readings in the days that followed, but there was no answer. I even began to wonder if Munira had given me the right number or if you had moved and changed it. I myself was able to get an Oman Air flight that got me in by late afternoon and so I was able to be here in time for the funeral. I called you every day, two or three times, but there was no reply until today. I even asked someone at the embassy to check that you were still listed as living there.'

'I was at work on Friday,' I said. 'Then I went away for a few days. I'm sorry not to have been here to take your call.'

'We buried your mother on Friday afternoon,' Uncle Amir said, 'and we had a khitma for her that evening at Mskiti Mnara. We added your prayers to ours because we knew you would have wanted to do so if you could.'

'Thank you,' I said. 'It must've been very sudden.'

'Alhamdulillah, we prayed for God's mercy on her soul. Your sister Munira was with her until the last moment, and heard her say the shahadah just before her soul left her body. That was a great blessing. No one can die except by the will of God, and at the appointed time,' Uncle Amir said, reciting a line from the Koran. Then he told me who had washed the body, and who had led the prayers, and how grateful he was to them for their kindness in the absence of her brother and her son. I was surprised by Uncle Amir's distraught and pious language. I had not heard him speak like that before.

'It was a blood clot in the brain, an embolism,' Uncle Amir said. 'You knew she had high blood pressure, didn't you? And diabetes. You knew that, didn't you? But then perhaps you didn't. You never bothered to keep in touch. You hardly ever wrote to her and never thought to ring. How could you know? Well, never mind, nothing can be done about that now, but you could at least have left a number when you went away so we could do what we are obliged to do under such circumstances. Don't you have a cell phone? Everybody has a cell phone.'

I said all the abject words the moment required of me: my regret that I was not there to mourn her as a son should, the anxiety I had caused them all because I was not able to take the call. I had always made sure I had the air fare in my savings in case, but when the call came I was not there and I had not taken my phone with me when I went away. I was not so used to mobile phones then and I was not a regular user and sometimes forgot it or forgot to switch it on. Instead I had been with Rhonda and the thought of her and her relentless games filled me with disgust at my needs.

'Nothing can be done about all that now,' Uncle Amir said, his voice gravelly and flinty again. 'I assume you are well and that your life progresses in some fashion. Now that I have your number, maybe next time I come through London I'll give you a ring and we can meet for coffee or something. Perhaps you'd better give me your cell-phone number as well, in case you're not at home. There's no need for you to worry about the funeral expenses, by the way. Hakim and I took care of that. All right, your family here send their regards. Look after yourself and keep in touch.'

I had been waiting for this news, dreading and expecting it in low-key resignation. All those tests had filled me with worry and my mother must have lied to me when I asked because she always said they found nothing. She was fifty-three, no age to die in this place and in these days and times. But she did not live in this place, and her times had been fraught. I waited until Uncle Amir hung up before I put down the receiver. I was distraught to have missed the funeral, but I did not feel tragic about it. *There's no need for you to worry about the funeral expenses, by the way. Hakim and I took care of that.* It would have given them satisfaction to do what was necessary for her honour. In any case, it was not really her honour they were worried about so much as their own. Uncle Amir told me about the expenses in the way he did to remind me how derelict I had been in my obligations.

I took out the shoe-box in which I kept my mother's letters, and for the rest of that evening and night I read through every one of them. There were dozens. Uncle Amir was lying again. We must have written to each other more than I remembered. Habibi, that was how all her letters to me began. Beloved. Mamako, that was how they all ended. Your mother.

Habibi,

I am so grateful to receive your letter and to have your news. I am so pleased that you are enrolled in a college and that your studies will begin in earnest so soon. I know you will be brave and do all that is required to make this journey into a great success, and that you will work hard and return to live a good life here with us. I have never travelled anywhere, and it is not easy for me to imagine how you live there and what you see. You must tell me about those things so I can picture them. Can you understand the people when they speak to you? I have heard that no one speaks the way they do on the radio and TV, and that when you get there you can't make out what people say. The house is so still since you left us, although Munira does her best to make a racket. She misses you too.

Mamako

Habibi,

I have just read the letter you sent me at the beginning of the month. It was sitting in the post-box all these days and I did not know about it. It is such a long way to the Post Office and I can only go there every now and then. I am sorry to be so long replying. I loved the picture of you in the snow. It made me wish I could touch it, although of course I have seen pictures. Unlike you, I have not stood on ice! What an adventurer you are.

You must not complain about the angry crowds or about the noise. Nothing comes easy in life, only you must stay alert and do your best, and don't get into any trouble. All we hear about here is the drunkenness and violence of young people in Europe. Your uncle will be there to advise you whenever there is need, so don't do anything without asking him. Please give him and Auntie Asha my regards.

Mamako

Habibi,

There were two letters waiting for me today. If you go on like this you will make me greedy. I am so happy to hear that your results have been so excellent. I know you will succeed and make me feel very proud of you. Here the rains are over now and the weather is perfect. It's not too hot, everywhere is green, and the breeze is constant and mellow. You would have loved to be here.

Today we moved to our new flat. It is very comfortable and has all kinds of modern equipment in it, as well as a bathtub! There is a balcony at the back where I will grow plants in pots. I have always wanted to have plants in the house but we never had the room. It was sad to leave the old house, in some ways, but it was fortunate in others. What a relief to get away from that champion backbiter Bi Maryam!

You must send us a photograph. I want to see you in the big ugly coat you say they force you to wear. It's probably for your own good, you ungrateful wretch. Munira sends love, as I do too.

Mamako

There were several such letters during my first year, cheerful and encouraging, mildly hectoring. The tone changed in the ones that followed, when I was struggling with my studies and with Uncle Amir and Auntie Asha. I read through the later ones as well, after I left Holland Park, and felt her disappointment at my failures, and heard their forced encouraging tone. I must have written less frequently after that because most of the letters that followed began with her complaining about not having heard from me in a long time. Every now and then, a letter would begin with an apology for not having replied sooner, or with a cry of joy at a recent letter. I should have done better. When I finished reading my mother's letters, I read through my notebooks. There were three of them, filled with what started off as incomplete or abandoned letters, but the later entries read as if they were never intended to be sent. My mother was the absent reader, the unsent letters a conversation I was having with her in my mind. Two of the notebooks were full but there were still some blank pages in the third for me to compose another letter to my dead mother.

Dear Mama,

Salamu na baada ya salamu. It looks like snow is on the way. I know how much you like the weather reports. I haven't seen the forecast, but from the chill and the stillness I would guess snow is imminent.

Why did you not tell me about the diabetes and the blood pressure? Did you know about the risk of the blood clot? I have been waiting for you to go, I think. Not because I wanted you dead (do you mind my using that word about you?) but because I dreaded that I would never be able to say to you that this torment is over, that I have done well and found some good that I can tell you about. I would've come if you had told me. I haven't found anything much here to tell you about, little bits and pieces to string a life together, but it's not hopeless. It's just not anything to make much of.

Love,
Salim

*

Two days later – I needed that time to prepare myself – I rang my mother's number. I expected Hakim to answer, the man whom I now decided to call by name. I thought my mother would smile to see that my petulant resistance was over. She would think that my rejection of Hakim and his gifts was intended as a rebuke to her, but she would be wrong. I felt a mild repugnance as I rang the number. It was fear perhaps, an involuntary helplessness in the face of such violent appetites. But I wanted to speak to Munira, who had also lost her mother. I wanted to hear her voice, and to wish her well and to leave matters there. I wanted nothing from her and could give her nothing. That was what I thought. Munira answered the phone but I heard my mother's voice.

'Munira,' I said.

'Salim,' she said instantly. 'Salim, Salim! How nice to hear your voice, you sound just the same.'

'Munira,' I said.

'I recognised you. As soon as I heard that empty noise a long-distance call makes, I knew it was you.'

'I am sorry I did not hear in time,' I said. 'I would have come.'

'It happened so quickly,' Munira said. 'She was taking her medicine for the pressure as normal and looking after herself, but then that day she had a very bad headache. She had been having headaches for several days but she did not think it was anything serious. We did not know that it can be a symptom. That day she also started feeling dizzy and was numb in her right leg. They told us later that it was an embolism, a blood clot had moved from another part of her body and blocked an artery in her brain.'

'I am sorry,' I said.

'I know you would have come back if you could. It would have been wonderful to see you,' she said, 'even for such a sad event. We missed you so much. She spoke about you often, nearly every day, as if she had seen you earlier that morning. Do you know her word for you? She said you were loyal, ana amini, and that one day you'll come back. But this is how things have turned out and we can't do anything about that.'

I could not think of anything to say, speechless with guilt. I had waited too long and now it was too late. I listened as my sister told me about the funeral. 'Uncle Amir arrived just in time, from the airport straight to the funeral. Daddy arranged for an escort to pick him up at the airport. Auntie Asha and the other aunties from Daddy's family have been so good. One of Daddy's cousins has moved in to stay with me for a while. I haven't decided what to do yet. I can't stay in the flat on my own, and anyway I still have the final year of my degree to complete in Dar es Salaam. I'll decide after that. The flat is in Mama's name, it's her property, so now it belongs to the two of us. If ever you come back, even for a visit, you'll have your own place to stay.'

Munira spoke with what seemed to me surprising assurance, like someone who knew how to talk on the phone, someone with decisions to make. She had grown up among powerful people, which maybe explained why she was so confident. Or perhaps she had inherited an audacious gene from her daddy. At some point she must have become aware of my silence because she stopped and after a second said: 'Salim, are you still there?'

'Oh, yes,' I said, 'I was just listening to you.'

'I can be a chatterbox on the phone,' she said, laughing. 'This is a long-distance call, it must be costing you a fortune. I'll call you next time.'

'Never mind the cost,' I said. 'Let me give you my email address. We can't have a student making long-distance phone calls.'

It was in one of her emails that she told me Baba was back. She wrote: He returned three weeks after Mama's funeral. I don't know whether it is anything to do with her passing away or not. Daddy told me. He just said someone informed him that Salim's father was back. I don't know if he's here for good or only visiting. I am off to Dar in a couple of days to begin the second semester of my final year in the Business School. I'll keep you informed and you keep me informed.

The news of my father's return was quite unexpected. It had never occurred to me that he would do something like that. It made me smile, the thought that my old Baba had decided to

163

return. I was sure it must be because he had heard the news of Mama's passing away, and the sentimental in him forced him back. I decided that I would go back too, to catch up with the nervy old man after all these years. I replied to Munira immediately, to tell her about my decision and to ask her to find out if Baba was staying or visiting. Munira replied at once as well. We must both have been sitting at our computers: *Hurray. Yallah, it's about time. Will find out before I go to Dar.*

Dear Mama,

He's come back for you. I don't know why he would do that after such unhappiness. If I ask him, do you think he'll tell me? He was not much of a talker when I knew him. You saw to that.

PART THREE

8

RETURN

I arranged leave from work and booked a ticket way in advance. I would have to wait until June to get a month's leave but there was no hurry because I knew now that Baba had gone to live at the back of Khamis's shop, as he used to before. Munira had gone to the shop to ask after him and to take him my message. She would have been six years old when my father left for Kuala Lumpur but she would not have known him, or rather he would not have known her. He did not have very much to do with anybody at that time. She reported that she introduced herself as Salim's sister, and he said: Ah. That's all he said: Ah. He looked well enough, a little frail, and he smiled when she told him that I was coming back in a few months. Tell him I'll be here, inshaallah, he said.

I was not sure where I would stay. Should I stay in the flat Hakim had given my mother? I was sure I did not want to do that, just as I was sure that was what Munira wanted. *It was Mama's flat and now it's ours*, she had written in an email, *and where I have lived most of my life*. To me it meant something darker, and I did not want to own any part of it. First it was her father's property and now it was hers. I would have to find a way of making her understand that. I made an advance hotel booking on the internet, so there would be no argument when I got there.

I tried to imagine Baba, but I did not try too hard. It was difficult to dislodge the picture of him when I went to say goodbye to him that afternoon, looking weary and threadbare in his room at the back of Khamis's shop. I could not quite remember the incomprehensible advice he had given me then. Was it blessing was the beginning of love or the other way round? It didn't matter anyway, they were just words, and they were not really what made someone unhappy, not in the long run. Memories did that, those dark immovable moments that refused to fade. So in those weeks of waiting for my flight, my Baba remained that mumbling recluse I had seen every day of my youth. And he went back to that life! What faith he must have to do that! Ana amini. The old scholar must have passed away and then, when Mama died, Baba had come to be near where she was.

I had not travelled much since my first arrival in England. I had gone to Paris on the Eurostar twice with friends, and had taken the ferry to Boulogne for the day with Rhonda. I took a city break holiday to Amsterdam some years before with a woman friend, and visited various places in England at one time or another. The trip back home was my first long journey. My inexperience of travel added to my other anxieties about returning after such a long absence, but as the day approached, I felt much calmer about what was to come than I had expected. I told Munira about the hotel booking, just to get that out of the way, and she replied to say she would meet me at the airport.

The flight was exhilarating, and as the plane flew over Zanzibar in the dawn I searched the landscape for familiar signs in the brief moments before landing. I recognised the air with my first breath, even though it was not something I had thought about and would not have had the words to describe. I knew this smell, and would have known it if I had been shaken awake in the middle of the night and asked to name it. Someone behind me on the steps of the plane nudged into me. The flight was packed with British tourists. They must have been eager to get to their holiday pleasures while I wished to linger and relish my return.

I saw Munira across the barrier as I was going through Customs. She was standing on the pavement outside the Arrivals gate, her left hand on the metal railings that fenced off the passengers from the outside. I recognised her from the photograph she had attached in her last email, but I would have known her anyway. She looked so like Mama, but perhaps taller. I waved to her and she waved back, and even from that distance I saw that her smile was calm and patient, as if she was in no rush for what was to come, as if she was just meeting her brother who had been away for a few days, really just like Mama. We embraced and kissed, and then she stood back and examined me with a confident gaze. Still handsome, she said, and then led me to the car. She drove herself. It would have been unusual for a woman to drive in the time before I left, but I expected things like that to have changed. She talked as if she had known me all her life when in reality she was three years old the last time I saw her.

'By the way,' she said in between our excited exchanges and my distracted attempts to take in familiar sights and listen to her at the same time. I was familiar with *By the way*, spoken in a casual way like that. It was usually a preamble to something that was anything but casual, and I gave my sister my full attention.

'By the way,' she said, unable to suppress a smile, 'I've cancelled your hotel booking. You're staying with me.'

'But why did you do that? I've already paid,' I said.

'No, you haven't,' she said firmly. 'I checked with the hotel. There's no point protesting or being stubborn. I can't have my brother staying somewhere else when we have our own flat. What will everybody say? Can you imagine?'

I protested again but nothing I said disturbed her composed smile. 'See if you like the flat first,' she said. 'You can stay there as long as you like. I have to go back to Dar for four nights next week to take the last of my finals, but after that I'll be here and we can catch up with everything that's happened. You'll see, it will be better than shutting yourself up in a hotel.'

I wondered once again how she had got to be so brisk and confident. Mama had never been anything like that, or if she had it must have been before my time, so I guessed that it was a quality Munira inherited from her other parent. The flat was in Kiponda, and she parked her car in the yard in front of the Ismaili Jamatkhana. The huge main door looked new and Munira said it had recently been renovated. The Aga Khan Trust was spending a lot of money repairing old Ismaili buildings and re-laying the pavements all over the old town. You wait until you see Forodhani, she told me.

'It's not my car,' Munira explained, 'it's my sister's but I can borrow it whenever I want. She is away studying in Boston, so you just have to say if you want me to drive you anywhere. I'll be taking it back later in the afternoon and you can come and meet the rest of the family if you want. Daddy is in the Ministry of Defence now but he is nearly retired and only works part of the day. We could go and greet him when I return the car.'

I did not reply for a moment. 'I'll go and greet Baba this afternoon,' I said, regretting that I had not been able to stick to my plan to stay in the hotel. It was to avoid this tangle of obligations and courtesies that could not be refused without guilt that I had wanted to do so. I could not have my father finding out that the first person I went to visit on my return was not him but the destroyer of souls. 'Maybe later,' I said.

I did not go directly to Khamis's shop but took my time walking through the streets. I met people who recognised me and jumped to their feet to greet me. How could they still remember me after all these years? And how did they all manage to look the same when I felt so transformed? When I reached the shop, I saw Khamis sitting on a bench under an awning, older and heavier but still the same, while a young man was serving customers behind an aluminium-clad counter. Khamis knew me immediately and got to his feet, chuckling with pleasure and extending his hand. After our greetings he said, 'Go in there, he is sleeping probably. Give him a shout.'

Baba was not sleeping. He was sitting at the table reading, just as he used to several years ago, only now he was wearing glasses. He took the spectacles off and continued sitting for another minute or so after I appeared in the open doorway, contemplating me, and then he stood up and extended a hand to me. I ignored the hand and embraced him, and felt how slight and thin his body was. His hair was white and receding and cut very short. I gave him the bag of presents I had brought for him, a couple of shirts and books and confectionery, and Baba accepted the bag with gracious words and then put it aside without looking into it. After a few more minutes of greetings and questions he said, 'Let me get changed and then we can go for a walk.'

At first we did not speak as we walked. I saw that I was now taller than my father and I could not remember that being so obvious before I left. We walked slowly and I thought he faltered at times, as if he was struggling to keep his balance. I had felt his frailness when I embraced him and as we walked I could see it in his step and in his smile. He touched my arm now and then and said something affectionate or admiring ... how well you look ... with an openness so unlike the way he used to be. We stopped at a café and ordered tea. I could not relax because the café was noisy with shouted orders and raucous banter between the customers and the staff, and everything was greasy – the cups, the tables, the buns that came with our tea. It was not always grease that was visible to the eye, it was ingrained in the café's atmosphere and decor. I won't get used to this, I thought, but I did because it was Baba's favourite café. There were cleaner ones elsewhere, but this was where he came at least twice a day for a cup of tea and for his supper because he knew the owner from school days.

*

We spent several days in gentle nostalgic conversations and repeated visits to the café before we approached the hard questions. I went to him in the morning and we took a walk for him to do his chores, buy some fruit for his lunch, get new batteries for his radio, stop at the café for a bun and a cup of tea, and then we went back to his room and talked for a while until lunch-time when I went to be with Munira, who liked to have the mornings to herself for revision. Daddy's cousin, Bi Rahma, came in the morning to prepare lunch for us and clean the flat and bring greetings from the big house, which I had not yet visited but was due to do imminently.

Later in the afternoon I went to see my father again and we sat with Khamis for a while and then went for another walk to the sea-side or strolled the streets as people do at that time of day, exchanging greetings, catching up. When are you coming back to join your father? Did you bring your family with you? What do you mean, you're not married? This was how it was for the first few days, and conversations with both my father and Munira were mostly about me. What had it been like for me all these years? What was it like living in London? Where did I work? What did I do? Are the English as arrogant as they seem?

I gave an upbeat account of my life in England and to my surprise it lifted the burden of the years slightly. To my even greater surprise I found that I missed it. When I asked my father any questions he replied in his own way. He did not answer directly and I did not press, and hardly ever prompted him. I thought I was being careful not to panic him but Baba was talking with complete fluency and it seemed without reservation, and I began to feel that sooner or later he would tell me all there was to tell. I just had to let him do it his own way. I was surprised by his fluency, not only because he had been so silent before but because I could not remember him being so well informed.

At the beginning of the following week Munira went away to Dar es Salaam to take her final examinations in Business Studies and planned to be away for four days. On the first night she was away, Baba invited me to join him at the café for a supper of goat curry and parathas, with a side-dish of fried red mullet. The food was glittering with grease but Baba addressed himself to it without hesitation. He was enjoying himself, leaning forward to avoid dripping on his clothes. I ate with diligence because I did not want jokes about having become an Englishman. It was food I loved too, but I preferred it in the home-made style: a lot less oil and not quite so many bones and such cheap cuts of meat. Baba laughed when I told him that, heaving a little as he used to years ago. He said that he had developed a taste for café rubbish and had missed it when he was away in Kuala Lumpur. It made him nostalgic for his youth. I said I did not think it could be good for his health, all that grease, but he waved that away without replying.

172

Afterwards we went back to his room and he talked for so long that in the end I stretched out on the mat while he lay on his bed, talking through the night. At times he prevaricated in his way, approaching a crisis in the telling and then turning away from it. But as the night wore on, he grew confiding and intimate. He wanted, it seemed, to tell me everything. He could not tell the story directly, and sometimes broke off for lengthy periods when I thought he might have fallen asleep. He could not do the telling as if it was a testimony or a summary. He talked and then stopped, as if living again what he had described or checking it for accuracy, reluctant to revisit certain events at times and at others smiling and fluent, leaning up on one elbow to see how I had taken what he had said.

Some of it came from what my mother had told him because it concerned events he could not have been present at. Sometimes he remembered a detail that required him to rewind to a moment he had described earlier, and then to consider how that may have changed something else. Once I asked him a question because I had not understood a detail and that threw him for some moments, and he was silent as if recalled to his senses. Then he asked me if I really wanted to hear all this old stuff? Was I not tired? Did I not want to return to my mother's flat in Kiponda and get some sleep? I did not ask any more questions after that. I left my father to roam through his account as he chose.

In the morning I went back to the flat for some sleep and returned later in the afternoon to see Baba again. We took a walk around town while he pointed out places that he had talked about. Our old house and the warren of lanes nearby were still there, as were the blocks of flats on the main road, but there was garbage and litter in the lanes and the backs of the blocks of flats were filthy, with black iridescent pools and pieces of metal junk and abandoned furniture. There were so many people everywhere and so many more cars on the roads and so much more noise than I remembered. Then after our walk we went to the café for our greasy portion before returning to Baba's room for more of what he wanted to tell me. So then another night of talking and listening followed. At some point late on this second night when the streets were already dark and silent and in his telling he was approaching the time when love failed, when he lost my mother, Baba rose and switched the light off. It will be easier for me to say these things in the dark, he said. His voice in the darkness seemed very close to me. This is what he told me.

9

THE FIRST NIGHT

My father, Maalim Yahya, was a teacher, as you know. He taught religion in the same school you went to as a child, although by that time he was no longer here and you never met him. I should say he taught the religion of Islam not the idea or philosophy of religion. I don't know if religion was still taught like that when you were at school.

My father was a religious scholar. He had been a Koran school teacher for many years before he went to teach in the government school. He would have started teaching in Koran school when he was a boy himself, once his teachers discovered that he had an understanding of the word of God and the intelligence to learn it and instruct the little ones in its power. It was not difficult to recognise the ones who were gifted in this way, and for some of them, knowledge in the word of God was a blessed route for their scholarly talents. They became local legends and were celebrated by ironic and teasing tributes as they walked the streets. My father Maalim Yahya was a young person like that. People were teasing him about his learning when he was still a teenager, and in time he became a man of renown, and someone whom others always pushed forward to lead them in prayer. It was a tribute humble people without treasure or power bestowed on one of theirs. Lead us in prayer and we will honour you. When Maalim Yahya led prayers he recited the longest and most complicated suras without a hitch or a stutter and with perfect recall, as far as anyone could tell, and when invited to do so, he would explain chapter and verse of any theological issue a member of the congregation cared to put before him, and he would do so with unanswerable fluency. Such talent could only be a gift from God.

Not only was he a scholar, he was of the generation whose entire understanding of the world was informed by religion and its metaphors, which is not to say that he was an ignorant man with a medieval cast of mind although he did believe in the existence of evil as a force that preyed on human life, in the form of malevolent spirits who roamed the air and besieged the frail and the indecisive. He knew and cared nothing, or almost nothing, about Europe's learning and triumphs, nor was he interested in its history of frenzied wars and conflicting nationalities, and so he would not have known to turn to them for historical explanations of the world we lived in. He knew the results of Europe's violent will, as the whole world did. Nor did he pay much attention to the doings of other religions or peoples, which to him were distant crowds of strangers going about their incomprehensible business on the twilight edges of the world. Nothing that they did mattered to anyone but themselves. When an explanation was needed for a dilemma or an event, there was always an appropriate example to be found in the life of the Prophet or his companions or in the tales of the prophets who had preceded the Nabi, sala-lahu-wa'ale. In addition there was always wisdom and illumination in the reflections of the endless stream of scholars who followed from the days of the Prophet. As my father used to say: we thank God for His gracious mercy in making such guidance known to us.

Even stories Maalim Yahya told to us his children were always ornamented by reference to religious wisdom or were episodes from the life of the Prophet. He spoke about these matters without insistence, as if these were only innocent reflections circulating in his mind or something that had just occurred to him in the course of the conversation, not as if he was trying to force something down our throats, which he was. I was absorbed by his limitless knowledge, which was capable of addressing any issue I asked him about, and doing so in unhurried detail accompanied by several examples. Sometimes I hoarded a question for a day or two, until I found a moment when my father was in the right frame of mind to answer, not tired or preoccupied or suffering one of his monstrous headaches. For then I knew I would get one of his lush detailed answers rather than something curt.

Like what? Do you mean, what kind of question? Once I asked him what his name meant. I was going through an obsession with the meaning of names at the time. My father liked questions like that because of the way they could be opened out. He told me: Yahya is the name of the prophet that the nasrani call John, your mother's name Mahfudha means someone who is protected by God, your sister's name Sufia means someone with a clean heart, like a sufi. He told me that I was named after Abdalla ibn Masud, the shepherd boy who became the sixth convert to Islam. He told me how that untutored shepherd boy became the greatest scholar of the Koran and its most esteemed reciter and interpreter during the Prophet's lifetime. He told me about the time Abdalla ibn Masud spent in Kufa and about the other scholars he met there and their teachings and contributions to scholarship. That is what belief can do, he told me, it can confound and astound the ways of men, and raise the most humble to great and noble achievement. You are named after a great man, he told me.

It was strange that Maalim Yahya ended up teaching in a government boys' primary school because he did not go to that kind of school himself and had not studied in the Roman alphabet. It was at first a matter of fulfilling his obligations to the community, which required him to undertake this duty. He would otherwise have fed his family by teaching in the Koran school for all his days and lived the ascetic life of a religious teacher without complaint, accepting the tiny amounts of money parents paid for their children to be taught the words of God and the handouts and gifts when they came from wherever they came. That is how scholars lived. To Maalim Yahya, the life of a religious scholar could only be one of dedicated vocation, one of humility and respectable poverty. In time, my father came to be grateful for the government school-teacher salary, which he collected steadily every month and which enabled him to provide unexpected decencies for himself and for us. His real work was learning and transmitting the word of God and the knowledge of

177

His commands. It was work he was dedicated to and which gave him a sense of fulfilment. All the boys he taught in government school attended Koran school as well or had done so in the past, as we all had to. They already knew what the school syllabus required him to teach them, but he taught it to them anyway. What harm could it do? Everyone got very high marks in his class, otherwise what kind of Muslim boys were they?

You might wonder how my father ended up being a government school teacher. The colonial government had had to agree to the teaching of Islam as a way of reassuring parents that schools were not going to steal their children's minds and turn them into unbelievers. It was not easy to persuade the parents at first. Nobody wanted the government schools anyway. What was the use of them except to turn the minds of the children? There were well-known stories of the mellifluous boastings of the missionaries and their ruses, and no cunning could be put past the British when it came to getting their way. The parents stood firm, keeping their children away from government school until Islam was put on the curriculum. So Maalim Yahya, who himself had never been to such a school but could discourse on the hadith and its interpretation over centuries, and could recite chapters from the Koran and the funeral prayer without a text, was recruited to teach in one of the colonial government schools. Other scholars were recruited to fill similar posts in other schools, in order to allow colonial education to enter their children's lives. It is such an irony, isn't it, that it is religious scholars like my father who made colonial education possible.

When I was quite young I used to accompany the Maalim to the mosque and to other events where he led people in prayers and in the observance of the rites. Then I would carry his loose-leaf books for him or pass him his spectacles or his tasbih when it came time for him to tell the rosary, and carry messages back and forth as required. I knew that my father liked to have me beside him on these duties, and I won smiles and affectionate pats from many people, and I loved the feeling of belonging and being one of many. They called me the little saint and predicted that I would follow in my father's ways, laughing at my precocious piety but pleased with me too. I eased away as I grew into my teens, blaming schoolwork for my absence from my father's side. It must have been obvious to him and to everyone else that I was lying, that I was making my escape. I studied in the same school as my father taught, and he would have had a very good idea of what work was expected of me. He must have been deeply disappointed that my love of religion and its scholarship turned out to be so shallow.

Those were the years of independence and then the revolution, and so many things changed after that.

*

Baba paused in his recollections and looked away. I remembered Mama struggling with memories of those times, and when Baba's silence had lasted for several minutes I told him that, to bring him back from wherever he had gone. He looked up but continued to sit silently for a while longer. Then he took a sip of water and continued.

*

A year or two after the revolution my father lost the government school job, as did so many senior teachers and civil servants. He would have known it was coming. The government announced that it was to save money and to sweep away the privileged remnants of another era. That was how matters seemed to the new rulers and their fraternal socialist advisers from the German Democratic Republic and Czechoslovakia, who had allocated themselves the education portfolio in our affairs (while the Chinese took over the hospitals and the Soviets advised on security and the armed forces). The advisers probably used stronger words than sweep away the privileged remnants of another era. They probably used muscular and cruel words like purge the system and excise the rot, cut prune incinerate, just as the Soviets had done to them in their mania for slash and burn as a process of reform. The only reform possible for those you suspect is extermination or expulsion, cut prune incinerate. In short, most senior administrators and teachers tainted by any association with the previous era knew that sooner or later they were to be removed from their jobs. Some of them were people who had become used to a dignified and wealthy existence, and could not imagine themselves or theirs reduced to such an extent. The disregard and poverty they subsequently felt no doubt seemed harder for them by contrast with their old existence, although in reality it was just as hard for people like my father, whose life had always been close to the edges of decency: cramped spaces, humble food, and hardly anything left over when all was said and done.

There was no choice but to sit silently while history was narrated anew, no choice but to wait in a dumbly unenthusiastic silence for the mocking dismantling of our old stories, until later when we could whisperingly remind each other what the plunderers had tried to steal from us. As times became harder and the humiliations and dangers mounted, the search for work and a place of safety made many people remember that they were Arabs or Indians or Iranians, and they resuscitated connections they had allowed to wither. Some of these connections were works of the imagination or fantasies in the minds of people made desperate by need, but many were real if long-forgotten. That was how people lived, with relatives and acquaintances all along the shores of the ocean, obligations to whom they preferred to ignore most of the time but whose addresses they now anxiously searched for in old letters and scraps of paper. The government did not prohibit this frenzy. The politics of decolonisation could not tolerate these divided loyalties, and required commitment to nation and continent. With the revolution, that politics turned violent and punitive, and forced many people into flight because they feared for their lives and their futures. To the government, this search for connections across the ocean demonstrated the underlying foreignness of these people and it waited patiently for their departure, stripping them of whatever it could in the meantime.

In time, Maalim Yahya was offered a job in Dubai, and received a passport and permission to leave, which was not easily done at that time, not for any good reason but because nothing was easily done at that time. He had found a good job in Dubai where they sought and rewarded his kind of scholarship. He made his preparations as modestly as he could so as not to draw the attention of anyone in authority. He left on the ferry, carrying only a small suitcase as if he was going away for a few days. He bought his airline ticket to Dubai in Dar es Salaam, where no one knew who he was and no one would have any reason to wish to delay him. Maalim Yahya was not one of those ascetic religious scholars who worried that the wrist watch was a challenge to God's mastery of the day, and that flying in an aeroplane was a blasphemy because it mocked God's design (if God wanted us to fly He would have given us wings). But nor did he give a second thought to the ingenuity which provided the aeroplane which was waiting there to take him to Dubai. It could have been a donkey or a dhow, any means of travel that God provided. Allah Karim. For Maalim Yahya, the builders and operators of the aeroplane occupied far-away fringes of the everyday and did not live real lives. They were no concern of his. It was still possible at that time to live in a small place without television or the internet or email and to be cut off from the world and its hectic enterprises, and yet to live a life of vindicated self-assurance.

Several weeks later, safely in Dubai, my father sent word to us that he had found a house to rent and had arranged a loan in advance of his salary to bring his family to join him. He did not tell us about the difficulties he had had to face in finding somewhere to rent, how expensive it was and how humiliating the arrangements he had been forced to agree to for the loan. As husband and father it was his duty to put up with all that and no more needed to be said about it.

What humiliating arrangements? He told me about that later. He had to find six people to guarantee the loan. They had to be paid a fee and insisted on seeing his bank account. He had to pay a lump sum in goodwill and to commit himself to large monthly repayments, which he could only do by taking more loans. It was a nightmare but he did it all and did not tell us anything about it until later. So far as my mother was concerned, the money was now available for the family to join him.

When my mother Mahfudha told me of my father's instructions, I said that they should go without me. I refused to leave. I was seventeen then, living in the house where I grew up and where later you grew up, and I was in the final year of secondary school. In the recent past, I had had trouble with my father, he whom everyone respected for his learning and found deserving of God's blessing. I did not wish to quibble about my father's deserts but I found him demanding and unreasonable and increasingly bad-tempered at times, and felt that he expected me to be more enthusiastic in my obedience to God than I was or felt inclined to be. As I mentioned earlier, I grew less desperate for God's blessing in my teens. That was probably one of the reasons why he was bad-tempered with me, and because he had lost his government school job and was worrying about finding work in the Gulf.

I found it difficult to contain my impatience with these demands my father was making on me even when I rebuked myself for my petulance and lectured myself about my duty to obey. I knew that my slouching and shrugging and *I don't know* in answer to most questions made me seem childish but the knowledge did not make it any easier to bear my father's irritation and harassment of me. He chased me to go to prayers – I would be failing in my duty if I do not and God would punish me, he told me – and he corrected me for transgressions that sometimes came as news to me. I liked to stay in bed late when there was no school, as all young people do, but my father disapproved and shook me awake to get me up so I could do something useful.

'Do your schoolwork,' he would say.

'It's the holidays,' I would reply. 'I don't have any schoolwork.'

'Don't be cheeky with me, you little goat turd. You can prepare for next term. Or you can read the Koran with me, go to the market for your mother, or even just go for a walk and get some exercise. Don't just lie there like an old rag all day. Don't waste the life that God has given you.'

My father also disapproved of my love for the cinema. When I was younger I loved to go there. To Maalim Yahya it was corruption and venality, kufuru, an affront to morality and a complete waste of money. I agreed on the last point. After the revolution the government became stupid about censorship. It was the influence of the Soviets and the East Germans, I expect. We were ignorant cinema-goers who went to watch whatever the proprietors put on for us and these were mostly Hollywood and British films and Indian films, cowboys, spies, musicals, love stories, Tarzan. So many films were mutilated by the censor or were banned at the last minute and something else was shown instead, another film or an old newsreel or a cartoon, but I still liked to go.

Everyone knew who the censor was, and that he was a loud-mouthed, timid man who cut anything that he thought the powerful might dislike: no Sindbad or Aladdin or Ali Baba because film-makers who liked those stories could not imagine these people without a turban, which meant a suspicious nostalgia for the overthrown sultans, none of those silk robes and flowing beards and kissing of fingertips for the same reason, no spy thrillers because the Russians were always the villains and the Russians were now the government's friends, no empire adventures because the British were so sneeringly superior and always defeated their dark-skinned antagonists, and no undressed black people because that made them look like savages. Instead there was a steady supply of melodramatic Indian musicals in which the heroines exploded into energetic dances every few minutes, strident Chinese operas in which short thin young women with heavy make-up screeched for hours, and underdressed Italian versions of mythic Greek heroes, with ridiculous special effects. Not all the films were plain rubbish but many were, and many were incomprehensible or endless (the Russian ones), but I still liked to go. It was a waste of money but not a lot of money. I loved that darkened pit and its flashing lights, and how I could come out of one world and enter another, and then return to my own an hour or two later.

But it was not just the cinema my father disapproved of. He disliked my friends, or rather the people I moved around with as I made my escape, the noisy ones who laughed loudly and swaggered on the edges of discourtesy as they roamed the streets. Hooligans my father called them, which was not true. They were only playing at being hooligans, messing about, pretending to be bad. What my father really meant was they did not go to the mosque, which was true. Perhaps it was the inevitable bickering between father and son, and if I had been wiser I would have said to myself that one day we would have a laugh about this. But I was not wiser, I was going on seventeen and I lived in a place where fathers were used to having their way in this kind of exchange. I knew enough about my father to understand his detailed sense of the respect owed to him as a parent and as a man of virtue, and I knew that what he wished from me was complete submission. That was what I believed was happening between us, and maybe that was what always happened between fathers and sons.

I refused a confrontation, I could not even contemplate one. It would have been unthinkable disrespect for me to defy my father, but I found my own way of evading and escaping his demands. I hid from him, I lied to him, heading in the direction of the mosque and then slipping into a lane that took me towards the cinema or the café. I think he knew what I was doing but he did not try too hard to catch me out, and I in turn carried out my evasions with enough care to appear obedient and respectful to my father's wishes. So my disobedience when the summons came for the family to travel to the Gulf was unheard-of audacity. I flatly refused to leave. It would have been harder for me to do so to my father's face, but as he was not there, I could say to my mother that I was not going and nothing was going to make me change my mind. This was my country, I told her, and I was not going anywhere like a homeless vagrant, to beg for mercy from people whose language I did not even understand. What was out there that was so desirable I should give up everything I knew? I would stay here and wait for life to return. My mother and my sisters waited for me for a whole year while I finished school, hoping for me to come to my senses and to stop being so stubborn. They passed on stories of the good life in the Gulf that were current then: how respectful and pious people were, how easy it was to get a job, a house, a car, how brightly lit the hotels, how full the shops, how ingenious the gadgets, how good the schools, how generous the state. They believed these stories themselves,

184

and either through inexperience or desire did not suspect them for fantasies of migrant labourers. They passed them on to me, pressed them upon me, because they wanted me to change my mind and leave with them, but I would not, even though those were terrible and violent times. There was another reason I did not want to leave and that was your mother.

*

I could not restrain a smile when Baba said that. 'I've been waiting for her to come into the story,' I said.

He held his hand up palm outwards as if to restrain me. Be patient.

'She never talked about how it was with you two,' I said. 'She refused to tell me anything.'

He looked surprised and thought about that for a moment. 'I loved your mother,' he said. 'I loved her even before she became your mother. Does it embarrass you for me to talk like this?'

I shook my head and he smiled but I could see that his eyes watered with emotion. I waited for him to continue.

*

She was one of the reasons I did not want to leave although I did not say this to anyone, not even to your mother – that is to say, not at the time I was being summoned to Dubai. I would not have known how to say such a thing to her. The thought of saying anything to her, let alone something as provocative as that I loved her, terrified me and made me struggle for breath. I mean that exactly. I had this problem when I was younger, that if I panicked my tongue felt as if it had swelled and filled my mouth and I could only make drowning, gurgling noises. It had happened a few times with my father, sometimes with teachers, and once with a policeman who stopped me for riding a bicycle at night without a light, and I knew it would happen if I tried to speak to her.

And if I did manage to get those words out against the odds, I had a good idea of what she would do. Yes, I expected she would look pityingly at me and burst into uncontrollable laughter. I was pitiful and worthless, an ugly young man with a thick tongue, meagre schooling and no prospects, the very emblem of ineligibility. In addition I was too thin, my feet were large, my ankles were fat, and I was no good at anything in particular whereas she was a beauty. But I could not give up the possibility of winning her love, not give up just like that without trying. I mocked myself, abused my absurd fantasy, but I could not stop thinking about her and talking to her even when she was not there. It was not something I learnt, this way of being with her, it was not something I heard people talking about. Something of her slipped into my body and fitted there so snugly that I knew it would never leave or diminish.

I met her at a debate organised by the Youth League of the party ... Oh, you know about that! So she did tell you something ... As you well know, any association of the Youth League with lively juvenile fun, even of the unruly kind, would be mistaken. The Youth League liked to speak of itself as a cadre of radical political workers that had been transformed into a revolutionary vanguard ... that kind of Bolshevik double-speak. It was an organisation packed with hot-headed ideologues, not all of them youthful, who spoke a language of force and confrontation and blood-letting and cruelty. Their pronouncements and proclamations were intended to expose, accuse, implicate and call for the arrest of the enemies of the Party and the State, which were one and the same thing. Only one political party was permitted, a convenience many African states allowed themselves at the time so they could proceed about their affairs without any annoying questions or opposition from imperialist stooges, social malcontents and sexual perverts.

Several Redeemers and Their Excellencies the Guardians of the Nation had already made the intellectual case for one-party state rule, and only revilers of African civility still sought to argue that it was an authoritarian practice. Elections were regularly held, which the President and his government always won. Why shouldn't they? Who did they expect to win if not the President and his government? Some unemployed homosexual? A reformed housebreaker? The obstinacy of these opinionated disparagers stemmed from their failure to understand the complexity of African cultures: African citizens preferred the one-party state with a powerful virile leader mounted on it.

As one exalted His Excellency the President argued, the one-party state was an authentically African concept, a continuation of the traditional practice of rule by consensus – that is, since he was the President, everybody was bound to agree with him anyway, so what was the point of having another party? Another Excellency, who wrote poetry in his spare time from guiding the state, suggested that it was logical for all citizens to prefer a one-party state. Rather than introduce contention and fitna with an opposition outfit, a one-party state encouraged dialogue and bonding between the people, freeing the spirit for that uniquely African civility of communal unity and obedience that was the envy of the world. His Excellency the Poet was fond of obedience and thought it a virtue of great value.

For similar reasons, only one Youth League was permitted, and one of its most important recent initiatives was a schools debating competition to get more young people involved in party-sponsored activities, to give them a sense of national unity and responsibility and to stimulate their rhetorical and intellectual skills in the service of the people. My school and Saida's were paired in a debating contest, and the two of us were selected for our respective teams. As I told you, I was inclined to freeze when I became tense, which I did when I had to address several people at once, and my headmaster put me forward for the debating contest because he thought it would do me good, get me over the psychological barrier, unblock me. There's nothing wrong with you, he told me. It's all in the mind. I've heard you chattering away like a fisherman on hashish. The headmaster was known for his anarchic practical jokes, which he used in place of punishment. Not everybody found them funny but we preferred them to abuse and the cane and laughed along with them to keep the peace. So even as he encouraged me to defy my disability, he was already grinning at his own joke. I think he despised my quiet ways and wanted to see me hopping around a little more. And even if it doesn't work, the headmaster told me, and you stand there with your mouth shut as if you had swallowed a whole bun in one bite, the sight will cheer up the Youth Leaguers and you will have done good. Go on, off you go. Give them hell.

The debate was held in the Youth League offices, the rambling, three-storeyed building near the market we went past today that is now a collection of small shops and money lenders and stores. Before the revolution it was the headquarters of the other party, and in those days it was a buzzing, crowded building, covered with flags and banners, people coming and going or pausing outside to catch the latest gossip.

At the time of the debate, when it was the Youth League head-quarters, it was sparsely furnished and empty, a parody of its old self, almost derelict. It was part of the government's revenge against its defeated rivals, to turn some of their venerable sites into ruins. I had been in it a few times before to play games of coram with Yusuf, a school friend whose father was a big man in the government. He was a good friend and will appear again in what I have to tell you but I don't expect you knew him. Yusuf and I played in the games room on the ground floor, which also contained a table-tennis table and a broken-down fan on a stand. I had never been to any other room there or to any of the other floors. Later I found out that Saida was entering the building for the first time, and doing so nervously. The Youth League had a reputation for intolerance and enjoyed humiliating its victims. Its rages were at times random and unexpected. Worse than that, this was the party which had murdered her father and she usually kept her distance from all its activities. I think she expected to see smears of blood on the walls and the gloating faces of her father's killers whose names she knew.

The debate itself was entirely unmemorable: the venue was a room on the second floor and the only people there were the chair, the four organisers and the four debaters, two from the boys' school and two from the girls'. Most of what I remembered later concerned Saida. I had seen her in the streets a few times without knowing who she was, just a pretty girl in a cream-coloured mtandio veil, which was the fashion then. But sitting in that debating room with her I could see she was beautiful, and that was the moment for me. When it was my turn to make a contribution to the debate ... I was the second speaker and only had to talk for one minute ... I saw her waiting for me to speak with her head bent to one side like this, as if making fun of someone participating in an intellectual conversation. I felt slightly mocked but I knew it was meant as a joke so I tilted my head towards her, acknowledging her interest, waiting for my tongue to unglue itself from the roof of my mouth. To my relief, the words began to stumble out of my lips and continued to do so for the required length of time. I threw in an expansive gesture towards the audience of eight as I felt myself coasting along on the tide of drivel and added a small bow towards the chair as I came to a close. Saida liked that, I could see. Her eyes had a bright spark in them, amused by my airs, so I added an additional flourish with dead-pan passion, just to make her smile. That is how it started for us, those little gestures and smiles during that absurd debate. The organisers split the vote precisely between the two teams so no one won and no one lost, in the enviable spirit of communal unity. Afterwards we four debaters walked together for a while, laughing at the comedy we had participated in, before heading for our separate destinations, but by then I knew Saida's name.

I looked out for her after that, I thought about her every day, I became obsessed. When I saw her she was often with school friends, still in their uniforms, and sometimes as I cycled past she gave me a restrained little wave. The other girls saw and laughed. I did not know what to do, or even whether I should do anything or just wait to see what would happen next. I don't know what it is like for young people today but we were brought up thinking that to address a respectable young woman who was not a relative was to insult her. It was not something people spoke about, how to go about it. I had seen young men in the cinema meeting girls, smiling at them with teeth gleaming, riding in open-topped cars with them and even kissing them, but I had not seen anyone I knew doing that. I thought I would just wait and see what happened next. I came up with several schemes but I did not have the nerve to carry them out. They were all silly anyway.

In time I came to know that her grandmother made sesame bread for sale, and in desperation I thought I should go there and try to catch sight of Saida and perhaps speak with her, just like any other customer, but I could not make myself do it. It would be too obvious and perhaps she would not like it.

I was then nearly eighteen, in my last year at school, resisting my mother's pleas for me to leave and join my father in Dubai. I had my home, I did not want to wander the world like a beggar without a country. That was what I said to my mother again and again: I will stay here and wait for life to return. And in a way I knew to be absurd, I did not want to leave because of Saida. This was a secret I kept to myself and mocked myself for, but I could not deny its reality. It caused me pain to think of her. It caused me pain to think how she would mock me if she knew. It caused me to whisper to myself that I had fallen in love with her. Does that sound ridiculous to you, hearing your white-haired father saying something like that about your mother? I missed her every day but had to restrain myself from searching the streets for her, for fear of being discovered and made fun of for my childish love. So I learnt to make the ache I felt for her a part of my life, an obsession I could live with at a tolerable intensity. I did not know what else to do.

When I finished school, my mother Mahfudha's pleas for me to depart for Dubai became plaintive. She did not want to leave me behind. What would my father say – that she had abandoned their only son? And who would look after me if I fell ill? Who would cook for me? Had I thought of that? I would have to eat a filthy stew in a café every day and that was bound to make me sick in the end. She was right about the filthy stew in a café but she did not know that I would come to like it. Where would I turn to if I needed help? I would learn bad ways. Anything could happen to me in this dangerous world. What did I think I would find in this place? You can imagine the rest of it. I hated it when she spoke to me like that. Her voice changed pitch, her eyes looked pained and she made me feel selfish and cruel. When I tried to explain myself she raised her voice even louder, shaming me with her pleas and, in the end, her tears. Sometimes I thought she raised her voice on purpose, so that our neighbour Bi Maryam would hear her and add her voice to my mother's, so that the whole world would know that I refused to leave.

My sisters, both younger than me, also pleaded with me to go. They wanted their beloved brother to come with them, it would not be the same without me. They would lose me if I stayed behind. I listened to them and shed tears with them and felt chastened, but I refused to leave. I tried to explain but did not know how to make them understand that I did not want to lose my freedom to be where I belonged, where I knew how to live. I would not have known that that was what I was clinging to by staying, and so would not have known the words to use. And even if I had known the words, my tongue was too thick to shape them so they would come out right. I would not have been able to say that I did not want to live under my father's tyranny again, because my mother and my sisters would have found that hurtful. Nor could I say that I did not want to lose Saida before I had even spoken to her and discovered if she had any feelings for me.

When it was clear that I would not change my mind and agree to leave with them, my mother became angry with me and refused to speak directly to me for two days, and my sisters sulked and only spoke to me in wounded and sarcastic tones. But it could not last like that, and in the end we all became resigned to the way things had turned out and made peace with each other. I helped with their passports, queuing up day after day at the Immigration Office until I was granted an interview. The officer asked me questions addressed to my mother and sisters, and I answered for them as I was allowed to because I was a man. They were issued with temporary permits that would be valid for three months and could only be used to travel to Dubai and back. If they did not return while the permits were valid, they would not be able to travel at all and would have voluntarily forfeited their citizenship. I found it difficult to understand the point of this meanness, and it confirmed me even more in my decision to stay. I did not want to become a homeless wanderer in the world.

When the tickets came, my mother distributed what she could not take with her among her neighbours and acquaintances. The tickets were delivered by hand, passed from person to person from Dubai until they arrived at our house. Why? So that the authorities would not learn of our plans. There was so much vindictiveness in those days that you could just picture some official tearing those tickets up for no reason, or, if he had enough wit and know-how, selling them to someone else. My father also sent some money for me and that could only be sent by hand to trusted hand, otherwise it would never have arrived. My mother gave what was left of her dowry jewellery to me as a memento and for safe-keeping, four gold bracelets and a chain, because she was afraid the khabithi immigration officials would steal them from her when they searched her before boarding. It was illegal to take anything but the skin on your back and a few rags when travelling out of the country, just in case you were spiriting away the nation's wealth. You can imagine the immigration officers performed that part of their duties with great thoroughness. Then, on the scheduled day, we all took the taxi to the airport, and I stayed there and watched until the plane disappeared, knowing that my mother and sisters were not coming back, not ever, and thinking that perhaps I would never see them again.

*

In the silence around us I could hear the night settling down. It must have been around ten, and the distant traffic noises had ceased, and the café TVs and radios had been turned off and most people except the tourists would be on their way home. Baba was quiet with his own thoughts for a while and then he looked enquiringly at me.

'Is it getting late for you? Did you want to get back to the flat? We can continue tomorrow,' he said. 'The mosquitoes are bothering you, aren't they?'

'No, no, they're not,' I lied.

'I'll spray,' he said. 'Let's go out for a bit of air.'

He got up and closed the window, and told me to wait outside while he sprayed the room. Afterwards we went for a walk to let the poison work. The street lights were on and a handful of shops were still open, the ones that stocked meagre groceries for the poor, stale bread and tinned fish and condensed milk. We walked up one side of the road and down the other, stepping over rubbish and round the folded-up furniture of the street-sellers. Someone was lying curled up in a doorway, a shadowy lump covered with a mat, and as we walked past he said my father's name. He was the watchman for the line of shops and the trestles and derelict trolleys of the traders. It was a self-appointed task and in return he had somewhere to sleep and the shopkeepers gave him a few pennies for breakfast when they opened up. We leapt over a muddy culvert and crossed the empty road and were soon back in Baba's room. I sat on a mat on the floor, leaning against the wall, waiting for Baba to resume his tale.

*

It was just before my mother and sisters left that I went to work for the Water Authority, just a few months after I finished school. It was the era of national sacrifice. The United States and its friends had their Peace Corps and VSO and Dan Aid and other volunteer programmes, the Soviets and the Cubans had their Young Pioneers marching in uniform and preparing to serve the party and the nation, and many newly independent African states created national volunteer service schemes to promote an ethos of discipline and service. The volunteer aspect of the scheme that I and my generation experienced was a wordy metaphor, which lent dignity to the enterprise. It was compulsory volunteer national service and this was how it worked for us.

The government assigned all school-leavers a job for minimal pay, mostly as assistant teachers in country primary schools to fill the posts taken away from senior teachers like my father. Once the Ministry of Education had taken its quota, the rest of the school-leavers were distributed elsewhere, to government offices in town, or to the army if they were thought politically reliable and physically fit, or for further training if they were lucky and well connected. I got lucky because one of my friends, Yusuf, the one I sometimes played coram with in the Youth League games room, had a father who was powerful enough to have our names removed from the Ministry of Education list. It was a simple matter. Yusuf mentioned it to his father, who arranged things in one brief conversation on the phone. Yusuf went to the Ministry of Foreign Affairs, where his father worked and where he himself intended to make a career, and I was sent to the Water Authority, not so glamorous perhaps, but not very far from where we lived.

Nowhere was very far from anywhere in that town, at least not at that time before it sprawled into the countryside, yet after every two streets the area had a different name and insisted on using it. It was pointless pedantry, like poetry, a delight in complexity, a relish for detail, a stubborn refusal to forget what was known. The precise naming had no practical use since no one could get lost in that town, at least not the people who lived in it or not for long. Visitors would know only a few of the names, and most of the time would not know where they were in the perplexing maze of lanes, and anyway, most of the names did not appear on any street signs and no one ever used a map. It was only a small town, and if you did not know where you were, you just walked on until you did, or if you did not mind looking foolish, you asked.

Working in a government office meant that I wore a clean shirt every day and did not have to take it off because my work made me sweat bare-chested in the sun. I did not have to wait on the caprice of a contractor or put up with shouted commands while passers-by laughed at me. I did not have to wait patiently at the end of each day to be paid for my work and to learn if I would be required for the next. I sat at a desk not far from an open window letting in the breeze from the sea. When the tide was out in the heat of the day the air also brought in the odours of the filthy creek across the road from our office, and sometimes the smell of garbage from the landfill a little further up the road towards Saateni, and sometimes other, less identifiable smells, which made me think of wood-smoke and burnt hide. When the tide was in, the sun glittered on the water and illuminated the ceiling of our gloomy office with its rippling reflections, and a cool sea breeze blew in over the water.

The building was known to be the place where a famous Scottish traveller from a small town called Blantyre (population 9,000 in 1881) had lived for several months while he gathered himself for a journey to bara and the deep interior, where he hoped to find souls in need of succour as well as the source of an ancient river, the discovery of which would bring him everlasting fame. It was a conceit of the time that the existence of anything, a river, a lake, a mountain or a beast, could not be assured unless a European person had seen it and wherever possible named it. The river that the Scottish traveller was there in that house preparing to seek already had a name of great antiquity but did not have a source verified by a European. When the tide was in and the breeze blew over the glittering water, I imagined the Scottish traveller sitting by the window, glancing towards the small blue mosque across the road or looking over to where the creek opened out to sea, and dreaming of home and salvation. I could not imagine the traveller's thoughts when the stench overpowered the air but I suspected they would dwell on his unworthiness for the fate he had selected for himself. It was that kind of stench.

Our office was probably like many other government offices at that time, staffed by recent school-leavers without much knowledge and with not much to do, who were respectful and fearful of authority. Everyone was fearful of authority because in recent times we had seen how stern it could be, especially with those it suspected of being reluctant in their submission to it. Authority relished its fearsome reputation and thrived on it. It went about its ugly business as if no one could see what was happening, or remember who was doing it or why.

My team in the Water Authority office dealt with the supply to the town. We had less to do than our colleagues who dealt with the countryside, where the government was digging wells and laying pipes to villages and districts that had never had running water before. The countryside team was busy in its righteous task whereas a lot of the time there was no water supply to the town, either because the electricity was cut off and there was no power to work the pumps, or the pumps were broken and awaiting repair, or an unforeseen event other than these predictable mishaps had occurred. The pumps were often broken, sometimes for several days while a part was sent for from the mainland or from further afield. People learnt to cope: storing water, digging a well, doing without.

The water distribution system was old, most of it built by Sultan Barghash in the 1880s in the twilight days of Omani rule as the British were impatiently shuffling in the shadows of our small corner of the world, waiting to take charge. Before he became the sultan, Barghash had been exiled to Bombay by the British for attempting to displace his elder brother Majid, something the Omani princes felt compelled to do whenever opportunity presented itself. Their own father was reputed to have killed his cousin with his own hand, at the age of fifteen, to become the sultan: a sharpened jambiya in the chest during a royal banquet and then a chase through the countryside until the cousin dropped dead from his wounds, the accursed Wahhabi usurper.

The British had no business interfering in this internecine mayhem – they had not yet taken our little territory in hand for its own good – but they did so anyway because they wanted the world to run as they liked it, even if it was only a caprice on their part. Exile this one, replace that one, hang the malcontents, even bombard the whole town ... why not? It was necessary in order to establish who was superior and had the power, and who should do precisely what he was told. Historians can always be found later to offer weighty policy explanations that prompted one petty meddling or another, to describe avarice and destruction in reasonable words. Alexander the Macedonian wept when he thought there was no more world to conquer, but he did not know how much of it there really was and how much of it needed to be put right and with what sternness. He had no idea how many sweet morsels lay hidden behind mountains and beyond deserts and across oceans, let alone that there was a whole New World to plunder.

In Bombay Barghash had his eyes opened to many things, among them the luxury of running water. When his brother Majid conveniently died young, Barghash returned as sultan and, among other magnanimities conferred on his subjects and himself, he built palaces and gardens and hamams. He installed running water and flushing toilets in his little town when such luxuries were unheard of in most European cities, although they were probably available in San Francisco and St Louis and New York City because the Americans wanted the world to see how advanced they were. The Americans were contemplating the construction of the Panama Canal around then, with its artificial lake and its six huge locks to raise and lower ships from one ocean to another, so a flushing toilet system would have been child's play to them. But Sultan Barghash ruled over a few small islands, not a continent, and perhaps even to describe what he did as *ruled* was to flatter him, so providing running water for the town was an arduous enough undertaking for him. In any case, Sultan Barghash's magnanimity was exercised over a hundred years before, and this world had aged and changed since then and his small town had grown. Some of the underground concrete pipes in the old town were cracked, and there was constant seepage and unaccounted water loss, so that even when the pumps were working, it was difficult to maintain adequate pressure. There was no money for repairs, or what money there was was in demand elsewhere, and there were so many other matters gone wrong in our lives and in our minds that to dwell on them was to despair.

So like everyone else I did what could be done and ignored the rest of the wreckage if I could. Houses were falling down in the night in the Old Town, weary and uncared for and out of strength. Once the rendering was cracked, rainwater soaked into the mortar, and sooner or later, however thick the walls, the houses cracked – *datta* – and collapsed. What could anyone do about any of it? I owned a small share in a market stall where I sometimes found more profitable employment than my office work. I paid for it out of the money my father sent me from Dubai. Other people did that if they could, or found extra work to top up their meagre salary, or if they were lucky enough to be employed in certain government offices and had the knowledge and audacity, they squeezed what they could out of the needy. It was not only government clerks who did this either. Teachers did not always turn up at school because they had another job that paid them better, or that paid them something, and children sometimes had unsupervised periods that they spent joyfully shouting and bickering and tormenting each other as if all day was an extended recess. In better-organised schools, children filled in the empty periods by spending several hours a week cleaning their classrooms, or the school toilets, or even the street outside the school.

*

I lived on my own in the house where I was born and which I had shared with my parents and my sisters, and under whose roof I had spent every single night of my life until then. I had never slept in that house for even a single night on my own. I thought I would be unnerved by its emptiness and silence, and would not be able to resist the night-time fears we all know since childhood. At first I was stunned by the silence in the house, and by the way outside noises came to me so differently, muted and close, and at times sinister. The sound of someone walking in the lane and clearing his throat made me tense, and I waited to hear the slap of sandals receding before I could breathe out. But once I bolted the windows and doors, tucked in the mosquito net and covered myself with a sheet, I felt safe and released, secure from all danger.

The house was rented but since it was now illegal to be a landlord, the owner was too frightened to ask for rent. Officially the house belonged to the government, but with so many houses confiscated in this way, the government office that dealt with gazetted property – that was the coy phrase for the plunder – was still catching up with the administration and had not yet got round to billing sitting tenants. If the house had been a mansion by the sea it would have been a different story, and one of the swaggerers would have had it without delay, but since it was only a two-roomed hut down a dark lane, it had to wait its turn for official recognition. It was an arrangement that suited the government office well enough as it provided opportunities for earning a little more money by selling favours and expediting processes.

198

In the meantime, I decided to clean the house. I had never lifted a finger to clean anything while my mother and sisters were there, even though at times I had winced at the greasy walls and the mouldy bathroom and the smell of unclean bedding. Now that I lived in the house on my own, I found its filth unbearable. I stripped the beds in the big bedroom where my mother and my sisters used to sleep, washed the sheets and the mosquito nets and aired the mattresses. I washed a few items every day when I came home in the afternoon and hung them on the line in the backyard. They were usually dry by the time it got dark. I collected the books my father had left behind and whatever clothes my mother had not given away and all the little ornaments I did not like and packed everything in a trunk. I did not know what to do with that. Although I would have liked it to disappear without a fuss, I pushed it against the wall for the moment and threw a cloth over it. I folded all the clean sheets and bedding and put them away in the wardrobe. I knotted the jewellery my mother had given me for safe-keeping and hid it under the bedding. When I finished with the big bedroom I closed the door on it and started on the small room where I slept.

After that I cleaned everything in the large entrance hallway: the cupboard with the pots and pans, the braziers, the primus, the mat, and with some of the money my father had sent with the tickets, I paid a house-painter to whitewash the walls and ceiling. The whitewash only turned the walls grey, but I was sure there was a thinning of the smells of grease and sweat and condensed breath. When all this was done, I was ready to start my new life. The house was streamlined and sleek, free from clutter and a lot less grimy.

My neighbours Mahsen and Bi Maryam watched this frenzy with friendly amusement and mocking sarcasm but I took no notice. I loved the freedom of my solitariness. Sometimes the sound of cockerels crowing at dawn made me smile in my sleep, as if I had never heard cockerels at dawn before. Some evenings I went to the cinema, and despite the censors' watchfulness, found enough of the film there to make it worth the outing. I did not know living alone would be like that. I went out to be with friends when I felt like it, or now that I could, I stayed in and read.

It was difficult to find new books at the time but so many people who departed left theirs behind that second-hand book-shops were overflowing. I visited one run by a young Indian man in Mkunazini whose name was Jaffer. I had been in secondary school with Jaffer's younger brother some years before and had briefly been friends with him before he was sent off to a private school in Nairobi. His family were ambitious for him and relatives in Nairobi took him in to help him, and maybe the family were the kind who were always hedging their bets and sending one son here and one son there in case things went wrong in one place or the other. The family owned a clothes and sewing supplies business, a haberdashery, but its entire stock was looted during the revolution, and in the uncertainty and anxiety that followed, the remainder of Jaffer's family took flight for Nairobi after the son who had preceded them, leaving Jaffer behind to stand guard over the house and furniture until he could dispose of them.

In the meantime, he transformed the family haberdashery into a second-hand bookshop, and surrounded himself with piles of books that he arranged on the shelves where bolts of cloth used to lie and placed some of them spine-up on the old shop coun-ters. Jaffer suggested that if I would like to make up a boxful, he would let me have it at a discount. So the two of us walked up and down the counters, and even went into the back-store, while Jaffer, who loved his bookshop and had always wanted to have one, offered advice and opinions. He talked as if he had sampled much of his stock personally or perhaps he could not resist slipping into his trader patter and pretending that he had. I made up an arbitrary library of detective novels, a four-volume collection of Sir Walter Scott (because I had seen the film of *Ivanhoe*), Westerns, mysteries, an abridged *A Thousand and One Nights*, an old children's encyclopaedia (Jaffer threw that in as a gift) and a Collins edition of *The Complete Works of William Shakespeare*. The letters in the Shakespeare were tiny and the paper wafer-thin, but the book was still fat and heavy, at least two inches across the spine.

I had never read a Shakespeare play before, so when I got home I opened that tome with curiosity, fully expecting to be daunted. I tried the opening scenes of a few of the famous plays – *Julius Caesar* because we had read Mark Antony's speech in a class anthology, *Macbeth* because I had seen an illustrated comic edition and knew there were witches and ghosts in it, *The Merchant of Venice* because of the shocking idea of the pound of flesh – but I could not manage more than a few pages in each case. Then I started another one and was drawn effortlessly into the text. It was *The Two Gentlemen of Verona*, and I read the play late into the night. I did not try another for several months, resting on my laurels for the time being and consuming the mysteries and the Westerns, reading and re-reading the ones I liked. That was when I started buying those boxes of books from Jaffer whenever I could afford it. When I was not out in the evening, I ate a cold supper of potatoes and radishes and pickles and, if I had no chores to see to, read for hours on end. I found such unexpected contentment in this lonely and eventless existence.

*

The three months of their permits went by and my mother and sisters did not return. I had received one letter from my mother soon after their safe arrival, giving me their post-office box number. She told me that my sisters were now in school and were content, as she was, with their new house and neighbours. My father was well and sent his blessing, and asked that I should come and be with them as soon as I felt able to. There were so many people they knew there, you'd be surprised, so you would be among friends and in safety. The letter was written by my younger sister Halima (whose name meant calm and forbearing, my father had told me years ago) because my mother could not write. It ended with her sending her love and saying how much she missed me: *Your mother Mahfudha.* Below that was a *P.S.: So do we*, signed by Sufia and Halima. I put the letter away in the wardrobe with the jewellery. Once the three months were past, their travel permits lapsed and they were no longer citizens. A new tense calm descended on me. I was now really on my own.

As my days grew calm and my life slipped by quietly, Saida came back more into it and the thought of her began to make me anxious again. Now when I caught sight of her she seemed more stunning than ever, but I could not just keep looking longingly at her. I had to do something, I had to be bold. I had to take fate in hand and make it mine. Luck played its part. I saw her standing in a queue at the Post Office and joined it, and casually fell into conversation with her. That took some doing, the audacity of it. After that I stopped to talk with her whenever I saw her, unless she was in a crowd of school friends. She asked me about my sister Sufia, who had attended the same school, and I said that the only news was that they had arrived safely and were now settled. I asked Saida about school, and she told me about an incident people were talking about when a man went to the school to accuse one of the male teachers of cheating on his wife, who happened to be the other man's sister.

'Can you imagine how embarrassing it was? He came right into the classroom,' Saida said, her jaw dropping as she re-enacted her surprise. 'The teacher just stood there looking shocked while the poor man ranted about dishonour and shame, and made ugly threats. He made such a fool of himself.'

'Everyone knows that teacher has a reputation,' I said.

'Exactly, his sister should've known better,' Saida said and I nodded, although I imagined that such knowledge always came too late.

One afternoon I saw her walking on her own and I dismounted my bicycle and walked with her for ten minutes until she reached her destination where we stopped to talk and grin at each other, ignoring the knowing looks people gave us as they passed. She could not have failed to see my devotion to her, but I thought I had to wait until she gave me more encouragement, a definite sign. Other people knew about us now and passed word between us. A sister of a friend said something to someone else, who passed it on until it reached me: she thinks you're really nice, or vice versa that sort of thing. I still did not know if that was enough encouragement.

Saida was beautiful, she was famed for it. People pointed her out in the streets, and youths sometimes walked behind her, smirking their adoration. In those years, the rules of sexual decorum people had lived by for generations were set aside. The new owners of the government and its offices did so contemptuously, pursuing women they desired without fear of causing offence, or perhaps they did so with such indiscretion deliberately to cause offence, in the way that men look to humiliate their defeated rivals by treating their mothers and sisters and wives with disrespect. They boasted of their conquests and pillage among themselves, giving themselves farmyard names and guffawing at their outrageousness. For the women it was sometimes impossible to say no, because of the insistence of the men or because of the threat to their loved ones or the needs of the family, and because they understood their obligations. Some people thought it a curse when their daughters grew up prettier than expected. It was a time when a beautiful daughter was cause for anxiety. But not all the young women were coerced. For some of them, it was as if after turmoil and deprivation, they who had been under surveillance all their lives now relished this unanticipated liberty and participated in it without heed for what might lie ahead. Something went out of our lives in this abandon, some quality of reflection and tenderness and fellow feeling.

Saida would have been a target of predatory approaches both because of her beauty and her age. The approaches would have been gentle and indirect to begin with, and like most young women of her age she would have spurned them for the moment, would have refused the lift in a gleaming government car and ignored the invitation to have a coffee at a hotel. But she was now in the final year of school, preparing to graduate and to look for work or opportunities for further study, something that could be done more easily with the help of an influential father or lover. It was now that the approaches to young women like her became insistent, and cars parked outside at the end of school, waiting to pick up the lucky ones. By this time Saida was very aware of my admiration, and I guessed she preferred my lop-sided smile to anyone else's but she did not know exactly what to do about it either.

Her school friends decided to have a party to celebrate their graduation. They asked for permission to use the school hall, so that parents would know that it was likely to be supervised in some fashion. Their parents and guardians allowed them to proceed with their plans if brothers and sisters were also invited, and the party was held in the afternoon so that everything took place in broad daylight. All these measures were intended to diminish the possibility of shame and disaster. A record player would be acquired from somewhere and people would bring their own or their parents' records. They were also allowed to invite a few friends who were not members of the school – that is, boys. The next time she met me, Saida asked me to come as her guest.

'We'll just play some records and dance and have some snacks,' she said.

'I would love to come,' I said.

I had never danced in my life. What an idea! Who would I have danced with and what would Maalim Yahya have said? So I had to have a hurried tutorial from my friend Yusuf, who knew about such things and who taught me how to wriggle and wiggle to music played on the radio. Yusuf wept with laughter at my efforts, which made the exercise even less bearable. 'Never mind, just keep wriggling your body. That's all you need to do, it's not going to be the kind of party where you'll get to hold her in your arms,' he told me. 'It's just a children's picnic, really.'

When I got to the party I found it was packed with noisy young people of all ages, like the Idd fair, eating, shouting, pushing each other around, with the music scratching feebly in the background. What little room there was for dancing was occupied by a hand-ful of exhibitionists, who thronged the record player while Tom Jones belted out 'It's Not Unusual' and Ray Charles beseeched 'Unchain My Heart'. Saida and I found a wall to lean against, and somehow our hands touched. It was only furtive hand-holding but it was enough to make everything clear. She took off her wrist-chain and gave it to me as we parted: 'It's only tin, painted to look like gold,' she said. I solemnly accepted it as if it were made of precious metals.

When I saw her again, I secretly passed her a note in which I told her that her beauty outshone the moon and that she was the light of my life. I had read *Romeo and Juliet* by this time, which was where I got the line about her beauty outshining the moon. That she was the light of my life was my own line. She had one ready for me next time, in which she told me she loved my gentle voice and sometimes heard it in her sleep. Young love is such a beautiful thing. We saw each other almost every day, often only briefly, our encounters hard-won and sweeter for the contriving. Whenever we thought we were unobserved we held hands, and if the place was secluded enough, we kissed! Just a brief touching of parted lips and then fond smiles in retreat but it felt like sweet daring. I wrote her a note about her perfumed breath. I had a whole house to myself, but I dared not invite her to visit me there. I thought she would feel humiliated by my lack of respect and might misunderstand my motive. It never occurred to me that she would agree. At times I imagined that she was in the house with me and it thrilled me to go about my chores in the evening, pretending that she was in bed waiting for me.

One day I went to the house in Kikwajuni, as arranged, so that Bibi could have a look at me. Normally an aunt or someone like that would have dealt with this delicate business but I had no relatives to perform the task so I had to present myself for scrutiny. Bibi had a good look at me and chatted in her good-natured way, in the meanwhile slipping in several detailed questions about me and my family. She knew about my father, of course, the eminent Maalim Yahya, and my mother, but did not remember meeting either of my sisters or maybe she did when they were small. Has God blessed their move to the land of the Arabs? Inshaalah they will prosper and find a rich Arab to marry. Isn't that what all young women think about? Saida said No, vehemently, they think about getting on with their lives. Bibi chuckled mischievously, puckering her lined and wizened lips. If I was younger I'd be looking for a rich Arab husband myself, she said. After that Saida and I were more or less betrothed. I wrote to my parents requesting their blessing, and after two months received a letter and a sum of money, which had once again been passed from hand to hand. The letter contained my parents' blessing and an invitation for my wife and I to come and join the rest of the family in Dubai after the wedding. I put the letter with the other one from my mother, and used some of the money my father sent me to increase my share in the market stall.

*

Baba was lying back on the bed, smiling at the memory. I was smiling too as I pictured them at their happiness. He was content to stay there for a while and I was in no hurry. I knew now that Baba was reliving those times himself and that he would not hold back in describing them. I just had to let him do it his own way.

It was late by then and I realised that I would be staying until he was too tired to continue talking. His eyes were blazing with life, and I guessed that I was going to be there all night.

*

We were young when we married, like grown-up children really, but not unusually young by our ways. In those first few months we lived in a paradise of our own. Nobody bothered us. Bibi came round every few days to see us, and Bi Maryam made her presence felt in her interfering way. Saida was offered temporary work in the office of a Norwegian organisation that was studying our education system, God knows why. One of her former teachers was employed by the Norwegians and was hoping for a scholarship to Norway, and it was she who got Saida the job. So although money was short we were comfortable compared to many people. Amir also came round a lot. He was living with Bibi but I knew from Saida that he found that difficult and wanted to come and live with us, though Saida persuaded him that Bibi needed him with her.

You never knew Bibi. She was an angel, everyone said that. She was getting old then and struggling. Saida said she had been struggling for years, groaning with pain in the night and taking minutes to get up from all fours in the morning. They had partitioned a corner of the room for Amir and shared the rest of it between them, Saida on the rope-bed and Bibi on the floor. They had got rid of the bedbugs by putting the bed out in the backyard every day until the sun burnt them off, and they replaced the coir mattress with a kapok one. Every morning Saida was awakened by Bibi's groans as she struggled to rise. She refused Saida's help in getting up, saying it was God's will that her body should be so stiff and feeble, and she waved away all talk of seeing a doctor. It's only a little stiffness, she said, it will soon wear off. When Saida left to come and live with me, she felt like a deserter, an ungrateful wretch, but Bibi would not hear of any delays. I want to see my grandchild, she said, I've got my handsome young man here to look after me.

That was Amir. Bibi did not know how difficult he found it living alone with her. He complained to Saida about how she groaned and snored and had no control of her body. As she grew weaker she cried so much and he did not know what to do to make her stop. She forgot things, including the location of the toilet, and sometimes made a mess of herself.

He told Saida it would be a mercy for her to go. Hush, she told him, it sounds bad to talk like that. But Bibi lingered on: waiting for you, that was what she said. We tried our best and after a year and some earlier mishaps, Saida fell pregnant. Bibi lingered on until you were born and a few days afterwards she died. She waited until you arrived before slipping silently away some hours before dawn. God took her away suddenly and swiftly. May He have mercy on her soul, people said, but they did not know the many months of feebleness she had to endure first. Dying is such a degrading business.

That was when Amir moved in with us. He was almost seventeen years old, handsome and friendly and full of joy. When he smiled everyone smiled back, and he smiled a lot. Saida told me that he had the same elegant looks as their father and the same fair complexion, although he was taller and leaner and laughed more loudly. Whatever he wore hung well on him. It had taken a while after the death of his parents for him to acquire the poise he now had, Saida told me, to grow from the edgy and frightened boy he had been to this friendly and confident youth, although you could see that promise in him even as a tense little boy. He liked to do things, he had energy and a determination that even the tears could not obscure. He also had Saida. The tragedy of their lives brought them closer in an urgent way, made her obsessively protective of him, and made his demands on her absolute and undeniable. He did not hesitate to ask and she did not hesitate to give, and because he was so tender and in need of her, she loved him more for it and tried not to deny him any request. They both understood that their bond of grief and love would be everlasting. Saida used to say that she would do anything for her brother.

He had also had Bibi, whose regular reminders to both Saida and Amir had been that they should mourn and love their parents forever, but that they should also learn to live their own lives with virtue and eagerness. This is the burden we all have to bear, to live a useful life, she said.

It all took time, but Amir probably learnt Bibi's lesson more completely than Saida, who was sometimes helplessly overcome with the memory of her grief, even in later years. When Amir came home after a troubling encounter at school or at play, his sister and Bibi listened and soothed and condemned the source of his misery. Amir thrived and grew strong on this love and in time he grew into the open and self-possessed youth who came to live with us. He had a way of behaving with anyone, people of his own age or older, that flattered and pleased them. He was quick to laugh at people's pleasantries and jokes. He listened with humble attention to what was being said to him by his teachers, at least before their faces. He was quick to offer assistance, and had a graceful agility that was like a kind of glamour. He was a good athlete, sang well, and was somehow able to express strong opinions without antagonising his friends. To all appearances, he was a handsome and becoming youth.

To me he was like a beloved younger brother. When he was talking I listened to him with a smile on my face. His smile was at times too wide, trying too hard to please, but I took that for naivety on his part and I smiled back anyway. In time he would learn that he did not have to try so hard. When Amir lamented the lack of music in the house, I bought him a second-hand radio-cassette player. I would have bought him a new one, if one had been available at a reasonable price. Amir searched the wavebands into the early hours and recorded the music he liked, which was mostly British and American pop, and played it again and again in his room, sometimes for hours on end. If the mood was right in the house, he performed the songs for us and taught us to sing along, writing out the words for us and conducting us like a band-leader. He began learning to play the guitar at school, in informal classes organised by one of the teachers, Maalim Ahmed, who otherwise taught them biology. How good it would be if he had his own guitar to practise with at home, but that was beyond our resources. I could spare a small allowance for Amir, though, who saved the money to buy clothes. Music and clothes were his greatest pleasures.

He did not have the same enthusiasm for his schoolwork, although he always did well in examinations and reminded us of that when we tried to persuade him to complete his homework or revise for tests. It will be all right, he said, I know this stuff. At times, Saida completed his work for him because she could not bear the wrangling and the nagging. He could not wait for his time at school to be over and told that to everyone who cared to listen. The teacher who organised the guitar classes asked him one day if he would like to come along to the rehearsals of the band he played with. They did not really need another guitar player but were desperate for a singer. Did Amir want to come along and try? In the meantime, he could improve on his guitar by learning from the others. By the way, the teacher's band name was Eddie, not Maalim Ahmed, but Amir's name was good, it sounded showbiz. When he reported this conversation to his sister and me, he put much emphasis on the anticipated improvement. He was not going to be just hanging about but improving on the guitar. He could not help grinning when he told us about his fine showbiz name. The band played at a dance club on weekends, and after the rehearsal Amir was invited to join them for their next show at the club.

'But you're still at school,' I told him. 'Shouldn't you wait until you finish your examinations?'

He made a face and turned towards his sister, who made a face with him and then they exchanged smiles. It was their way of telling me that I was being bossy, laying down the law when it was not called for. I remembered how my father used to be with his rules and prohibitions and I said no more. They did that sometimes, looked at each other and turned against me. I could not resist the feeling that Saida had rejected me at such moments, but I tried not to be hurt and reminded myself that I was a newcomer in her affections. In any case, Amir was nearly eighteen years old by then, quite old enough to go and sing with a band on a Saturday night if that was his choice, and he would be singing in the same band as his teacher, Maalim Ahmed Eddie. When he came home in the early hours, he knocked on our bedroom window and I unbolted the door for him. It had gone really well, he told me every time.

In the months that followed, Amir became a regular singer with the band, rehearsing several evenings a week and sometimes doing two or three sessions over the weekend, playing those British and American songs that he loved so much. He still came home in the early hours and knocked on our bedroom window for me to let him in while Saida pretended to be asleep, not wanting to know how late it was, not wanting to hear in case I complained. Apart from the lateness of the hour, which was worrying because it was irregular and somehow unsettling, there was nothing to complain about, I persuaded myself. Amir's attendance at school for those last few months was normal, and he made enough effort to hold his own and complete his examinations. He did not pretend any enthusiasm for the schoolwork but he did what was necessary. After the examinations he was finished with school, he said with a swagger. He was now a singer with a band. It was not, in any case, that he was spurning any brilliant academic opportunities.

The regulation assigning all school-leavers government employment for minimal pay was no longer in operation. There were no government jobs left. Amir was earning a little from his share of the band's fees so he had money coming in. I offered him some work at the market stall but he said no, he needed the time for rehearsals regardless of the meagre return from the band. Some nights now he did not sleep at home, and some mornings he did not bother to wake up until it was time for lunch, yawning and laughing at himself for sleeping so late. His clothes smelt of smoke and alcohol, although I could not smell alcohol on his breath. I talked to Saida about him and only succeeded in annoying her.

'He is wasting his life,' I said. 'He was such a nice boy. Something will go wrong.'

'What do you mean, wasting?' she said, although she knew what I meant. 'There is nothing for him to do otherwise, except sell okra in the market for you. Let him play in the band, what harm can it do?'

'He could turn out to be a musical genius but I hope not of the lawless short-lived kind,' I said, making peace, knowing how protective she was of Amir. 'And here I am, trying to interfere with his growth. But I don't like this business of him not coming home some nights. I worry about him and I cannot make myself not care.'

Saida nodded silently and we left it there for a while. In the end I said something to Amir, and when I did so he too nodded silently at first and then he said that he understood why I would worry about him but there was really no need. He only stayed overnight when they were playing at a wedding or an event like that which was far to get back from, especially when there was nothing to rush back for, was there? He would try to warn me beforehand if he could but it was that kind of business. It often ran late. 'Don't worry, I won't bring shame to your house,' he said, smiling, and I thought he was mocking me.

For a while after that conversation, Amir stayed away on Saturday nights but came home the other nights of the week. Saida and I tried to restore our previous ease together, asking about the band's fortunes, flattering Amir's singing, but the joyfulness was diminished. We were all more watchful now about what could not be said. I started to feel a mild sense of foreboding.

Perhaps I was just worrying about money, I told myself. The Housing Department had returned the house we lived in to its owner, who was now talking about the accumulated unpaid rent of years. Several other previous owners of houses had appealed successfully to get their properties back, after offering money as goodwill and doing a bit of grovelling. When the landlord spoke to me about the rent, I told him to be reasonable. Where did he expect me to get that kind of money? It was his right to ask for the back rent and mine to delay and negotiate but it was a worry. I had many reservations about the landlord, who was a Hadhrami rumoured to have acquired several of his properties by lending money to the owners and then demanding the house when they failed to meet the repayments. He had now moved his main business to Dar es Salaam, where he had invested in a drinks manufacturing factory and was apparently making a fortune. He left one of his sons behind to run the dry-goods shop in Darajani, which had always been the visible face of his many commercial interests. The landlord preferred that we should leave, in which case he would forgive part of what he was owed and then put the house out for rent at current prices.

These worries about the rent caused me real disquiet. Saida's Norwegian job was over and I did not earn enough as a clerk in the Water Authority to feed all of us, let alone have anything over for the back rent, and I was not sure if I had enough of the law on my side without having to pay for it. I also knew that the landlord had the money to arrange for our removal if he really wanted to. I told Saida we should sell the jewellery my mother had left in my safe-keeping. She had given it to me as a way of insuring me in case of need. Saida said no, we would get a pittance for the gold bracelets. We should just hang on and manage. Until life returns, I said, and she smiled because that was what I always said when things looked bleak.

Perhaps it was this feeling of crisis looming that was giving me a sense of foreboding, something worse than the usual disquiet with the general shortage of everything we lived with all the time. My whole life from childhood had been hand to mouth like that. My father had never earnt enough for us to be comfortable while he lived here, although if reports of fabulous salaries in Dubai were true, that would no longer be the case. What I earnt myself was barely enough when the scarcity of essentials made life so expensive. Amir kept whatever he earnt. I would not have accepted anything from him anyway, but I would have liked to have been able to say so. It would have made the burden of it a little easier to bear. But I really feared that something would befall Amir that would cause Saida pain. She took too much responsibility for him, and saw her obligation to care for him as unconditional and undiminishing. I did not say this to her, nor did I say anything to Amir about finding regular work. His singing with the band had made a name for him and given him a thrill, and perhaps it might lead to something. The band had already featured on a live radio programme. But I feared and dared not say that Amir now lived by rules very different from ours, and that I thought I would find repellent. I felt I could smell that life on him, see it in the hardened look in his eyes and the scornful glances that sometimes betrayed his feelings. When I spoke about my worries to Saida she defended him angrily, and I hated the venom of these exchanges so much that I hardly dared to mention his name to her again. Amir must have sensed this atmosphere in the house, and guessed that it was to do with him, but it just became another thing we did not speak about.

It was around that time that we had a conversation about television. Despite food shortages, crumbling houses and the lack of every conceivable luxury from toilet soap to chilli pepper, the government decided it was time there was a television service in the country. Not only would there be a television service, but it would be the first colour broadcasting anywhere in Africa south of the Sahara. It was, no doubt, the President's whim to grant his subjects this luxury while denying them others, and also to have a laugh at all those other big mouths north and south of us who did not yet have colour television. It seemed to many people a frivolity in those hard times. Amir, however, began to agitate for us to get a set.

'We don't have the money for that,' Saida said. 'They bring us televisions when there is no rice or onions or flour, when sugar has become like gold dust, and we'll soon be eating grass and weeds like goats.'

'You can ask your father to send you one from Dubai,' Amir said to me, ignoring Saida. 'I hear they are really cheap there, and top-quality Japanese models as well. Why didn't you go with your family when they moved there? I hear everyone is living a life of luxury in the Emirates.'

I could tell that Amir was teasing me, provoking me, yet it was not a question he had asked me before, not straight out like that: why didn't you go with your family when they moved there? Because I did not want to live like a stranger, like a vagrant in someone else's country. I did not want to live among people whose language I did not speak and whose wealth would allow them to despise and patronise me. I wanted to stay here where I knew who I was and knew what was required of me.

Now Saida too repeated Amir's question. 'Why didn't you go with your family when they moved there?' she asked, glancing at her brother and smiling with him.

Because of you. I had already told her that. The words would not come, though. I sat frozen in front of them, my tongue the size of a fist while they exchanged glances again and laughed. After a moment they moved on, assuming perhaps that I did not wish to reply, and my terror slowly subsided. I felt foolish and rejected and did not know how to explain my ineptitude. I thought I had seen a glimpse of Amir's dislike in those exchanged smiles. I thought I had seen a glimpse of his contempt.

In the mid-1970s many things began to change. The President was assassinated in the early years of the decade and never got to watch the colour television service he had ordered for his subjects. The appointment of a new President did not at first diminish the arbitrary violence of the state, which had the assassins to deal with now, many of them former allies, in addition to the other enemies it had been busy persecuting for a while. There were show trials to be held, expulsions to be ordered and vengeful exiles and reluctant clemencies to be decreed. The new President, though, was a milder man, a former school teacher, a Master Boy Scout, and was reputed to be pious.

His government began to make gradual changes whose small humanity would sound paltry to those accustomed to living in more fortunate places. People were allowed to travel, to send and receive money (although mostly it was to receive) and those who had been expelled earlier were allowed to return. The government's autocratic grip was loosened slightly by allowing citizens participation in local affairs. Elections were announced, campaign rallies were allowed, vociferous speeches and denunciations were made, although in the end the results of the ballot were not allowed to disrupt the proper order of things. New businesses opened, small in scale and sometimes cautious revivals of former enterprises, but more often they were the investments of those who had been plundering the state over the last few years: boutiques, coffee bars, travel agencies, hotels to cater for the tourist overflow from mainland package holidays.

In the atmosphere of change the new President brought about, Amir too found work with a travel agency, which added to the considerable glamour his singing career had already brought him. The job only paid a small salary and Saida said it would be mean to ask him to contribute to the household expenses. To keep the peace, I agreed. I could see, though, that the job was doing Amir good. He wore a short-sleeved white shirt and black tie to work, together with a silver tie-pin showing an aeroplane ascending, and he took calls from the head office in Nairobi and sent cables to Addis Ababa and Hong Kong. People courted him to secure their travel arrangements, which so often seemed mysteriously vulnerable to the caprices of agents and officials. He came home with stories of the cock-up in Kigali that meant a twenty-four-hour delay for passengers en route to Brussels, or the flight to Cairo that only had seven passengers on board. I could see just how much pleasure it gave Amir to be able to say the names of the places people were travelling to, how the association with those places allowed him to patronise us with his sophistication.

The year you started government school Saida talked about looking for work too, because perhaps after two miscarriages it seemed a second child was not destined to come. You were at government school in the morning and Koran school in the afternoon, and only at home to have lunch and change out of one uniform into another. I went to the market for her and did all her errands. I have nothing more to do but cook and clean and sleep all day, she said. A friend had told her about a clerical post in the Ministry of Constitutional Affairs, and she decided to go and enquire.

In that year when you started government school, and where you turned out to be a gifted pupil from the first day, one of Amir's new acquaintances in the world of travel opened a hotel for tourists in Shangani. It was called the Coral Reef Inn, and was funded by big international money, which people said was money laundering of gangster loot: drug money, kickbacks, prostitution, slave labour. Perhaps it was the same crowd of financiers who were turning so many places in Kenya into package-holiday ghettos for tourists from Europe. None of us knew the details of such arrangements. Someone upstairs took his commission and no nuisance questions were asked. The whole world was run like that, not just our little puddle of it.

Amir was appointed assistant manager in charge of social activities: arranging music and bands, hosting events, supervising the pool staff, organising spice tours to the countryside. It was a job made for him, he said when he told us about it, someone with personality and style. He was then twenty-five years old, a handsome and charming worldly young man, inclined to think of himself in glowing terms. This was just the beginning, he said, and filled the house with words and laughter. It seemed to me that he had been living off us for years, wearing down my affection with his conceited chatter. I wished the talk was more about finding a place of his own to rent, but I dare not say that, especially to Saida, who would glower at me and accuse me of meanness.

*

Baba was lying down on the bed towards the end of his account, and after a moment he turned away to face the wall. I heard the bitterness and weariness in his voice, and before long I guessed from his breathing that he had dozed off. I too was weary and

216

stiff from sitting on the floor although I would have stayed there for as long as Baba wanted to talk. I switched off the light and stepped out of his room. Ali, the young man who served in the shop, slept in an alcove by the front door, and he let me out and locked up after me. I walked the silent streets back to Kiponda, keeping to the main roads and avoiding the gloomy shrouded alleyways.

10

THE SECOND NIGHT

I tried to sleep late into the morning but I was no longer used to long hours in bed. Sometimes I lay for hours waiting for the light so that I could get up. Even though I had been up so late the previous night, I heard the muadhin calling for the dawn prayers at four and was only able to doze intermittently after that, running images of the events Baba had told me about through my mind. Then quickly the noises in the tiny square in front of the house made any idea of sleep impossible. Three lanes opened into the square so it was a crossroads of a kind: the grocery shop opposite was open for business, the machines in the tailor's shop downstairs were whirring, pedestrians sauntered by amidst shouted conversation and cyclists rang their bells and called out greetings as they wheeled past. It was not unpleasant and I could imagine how Mama would have loved it here, living in the midst of things.

When the water came on I switched on the pump to fill up the tank, then showered and washed some clothes. I went for a walk down to the sea and spent the rest of the morning reading. I was giving Baba time to himself. I didn't know if he needed that time but I had sensed his bitterness as he fell silent in the early hours and I knew there were difficult things still to be said. Late in the afternoon I went round to the shop and found him sitting outside with Khamis, already dressed for an afternoon stroll. We walked through hectic streets at first until the crowds thinned towards the old prison and barracks.

'I kept you up late last night,' he said.

'You fell asleep,' I said, laughing at him.

'No,' he said. 'I was tired of talking.'

We stopped at a café in Mkunazini for a cup of tea and listened in to the usual mad tales of the conspiracies and intrigues that seethed in the world and then headed off for a meal of Baba's favourite café rubbish nearer his home. I knew that he would not resume talking until we were back in his room and I think there was a kind of preciousness in his self-discipline. He wanted the ceremony of it and he did not want me to be distracted, and after a while I got over my impatience and was content to wait. When we were back in his room, he continued talking into the second night.

*

Late one afternoon, there was a knock on the door. I was just recently home from work, had showered and was lying on the bed while Saida was ironing and telling me about her interview for a position at the Ministry of Constitutional Affairs. You were not yet home from Koran school, which you were still attending in the afternoons. The young man who knocked on the door held on to his bicycle with one hand while we shook hands. His eyes were bright with the news he had come to deliver to us.

'I work at the Coral Reef,' he said to me, which was the hotel where Amir worked at that time. The young man was thin and nervous, perhaps unwell. 'Amir has been taken away,' he said. 'I saw it. A white Datsun with government plates. They came this afternoon.'

'Taken away where?' I asked him although I understood what he said. My pretence of not understanding was a way of putting off knowing, but also of wanting more details. 'Wait,' I said, reaching out to delay him as he made to mount his bicycle and leave. 'What's the hurry?' I said. 'Wait, don't go yet. Who took him where?'

The young man hesitated and then shrugged, not believing that I did not understand what he had said. He glanced over my shoulder and then his eyes slid away. I guessed that Saida must have appeared behind me. Perhaps she had heard him say Amir's name.

'He says Amir has been taken away,' I said, turning to see her standing behind me and still adjusting her kanga, lowering my voice as if conveying delicate information. 'But he won't say who has taken him. A white Datsun with government plates.'

The young man nodded, satisfied now that his message had been delivered. We all knew that a white Datsun with government plates meant the security service so why ask who had taken him? I was being ridiculous because of my anxiety, or in case there was a kinder explanation.

'Is that all you can tell us?' Saida asked. 'Where did it happen? Can you tell us any more?' The young man shook his head at so many pointless questions and mounted his bicycle. 'Are you a friend of Amir?' Saida asked him.

The young man said: 'I work outside, in the garden. Two men came and spoke to him, and then they took him to the car. I think one of them was armed. He had his hand in his pocket, like this,' he said, demonstrating the bulge in his pocket, his eyes bright again as he gave the details.

'We thank you for coming to tell us,' Saida said because she could see the young man was poised to cycle away. 'Could you also tell us your name?'

'Bakari,' the young man said reluctantly.

After Bakari rode away, disappearing round the bend of the lane in an instant, Saida sat at the table in silence for a few moments and I sat opposite her, waiting. I was stunned by the news and confused about what to say or do. People were detained and released, or sometimes not, regularly over the years, but no one close to me had been taken before. Despite everything that had happened, no one had stood in front of me and threatened me with arrest. We had learnt to gratify the powerful with timorous obedience. Why arrest Amir? It is strange how you can deliberate even in times of danger, because I found myself putting this new event into everything I knew about him and trying to guess what he could have done to offend, as if there was time for careful calculation.

'I was thinking about when they came for my father,' Saida said in the end. 'We knew they were arresting everyone who was important in the other party. It was the revolution. What could Amir have done to annoy these people?'

I shook my head to say I had no idea. 'I thought there was something,' I said in the end. 'Some excitement was happening to him. Then I thought maybe it was the new hotel job, that he was excited about that. But I suppose he could be involved in something we don't know about.'

'What something?' Saida said wearily. She did not like to hear one wrong word said about Amir. 'You are always ready to believe the worst of him,' she said.

I shook my head again because that was not true. 'Don't say that,' I said. 'I don't know anything about these things. He could have got involved in politics. We don't really know who his friends are or anything like that any more. Or he could have offended someone, they are very touchy, some of these powerful people.'

We talked for a while about what to do and decided that I would go to the hotel to see if I could find out any more. Usually I never went to places like that, hotels and bars and clubs. They were places for foreigners and those who wanted to be like them. At least it was like that then. Now there are so many places like that for the tourists and everybody goes everywhere. So when I said I would go and find out, I really had no idea how I would do that because those tourist hotels were unknown places to me. Bakari said he worked in the gardens, which meant he was a gardener or a labourer who cleaned up the grounds, someone who would be powerless and afraid of being found out as the bearer of such news. From the look of him, he probably needed the job too much to tell us more than he had already done. It was surprising enough that he *had* come to tell us. Perhaps Amir had done him a kindness and this was Bakari's way of doing one himself.

Anyway, I set off for the hotel to see if I could find out anything more from someone else. I had seen in films – I used to go to films a lot when I was younger, I told you – how unhappy guests always asked to see the manager, so perhaps I would have to do that if all else failed. I asked the man at the reception desk if he knew anything about what had happened to my brother Amir, and the man said he had no idea that anything had happened to him. I knew him by sight, this man. He had droopy eyes that made him conspicuous but I did not know his name. I told him we had received word that Amir was taken away by two men in a white Datsun. The man asked me who had told us that and I said it was something a neighbour said he had heard, a rumour. The neighbour came to ask if there was any more news, that was the first we heard of it. I did not mention Bakari's name. The receptionist with droopy eyes said if that was so, then it was all news to him. He was not there when it happened and had nothing to add. It was then that I asked to see the manager and Droopy Eyes looked at me with interest, assessing if I perhaps knew someone important. He went into an office behind the reception counter and after a short delay I was shown into the manager's office.

The manager was a stony-faced man in his thirties, a stranger from somewhere, with a trimmed moustache and a chin that came to a sharp point. He was one of those creamy-faced men who smell of perfume but whose eyes are like daggers and whose build and bearing betray them as thugs. He had the hardened stillness of a man capable of doing dirty work. He looked at me from under lowered eyebrows and shook hands while still seated. Then he pointed me to a chair. I understood from all this that I was to be intimidated by this trusty flunkey of corrupt money. Because even someone like me could tell that this unpleasant-looking man was not the one who cooked the books and signed the cheques. The manager said he knew nothing further about the incident except that two men in a government car took Amir away. They could have been friends of his who had come to pick him up for a picnic for all anyone knew. The manager was not there when it happened. He would wait for clarification from the authorities. In the meantime, he sincerely hoped that everything would be resolved happily. He was concerned for his employee, of course, but he was also anxious that the matter should have no detrimental effect on the business. If there was anything further he could do to help ... After that, he stood up, shook hands with me, and showed me out of the office. From the reception area, which was now empty – Droopy Eyes had gone – I could see a section of the swimming pool and some European children splashing noisily in it, having fun in the sun. I don't know why exactly, but even now after all this time that image revolts me.

On my way home I passed people I knew, and some of them had already heard. News of such events travelled quickly, then the rumours and the explanations began, and then slowly, after some days, information emerged from witnesses about the where-abouts of the poor man who had been arrested, and maybe even why. Sometimes it was only the rumours and the wild theories that accompanied them that people remembered. I disentangled myself from the curious questioning as politely as I could, after all I really knew nothing, but I was grateful that Amir's arrest was so widely known. It was safer that way.

Saida was distraught when she heard there was no news. 'You found out nothing,' she said, making me feel useless and cowardly. She must have seen that her words hurt me because she reached out to touch my hand and called me *habibi*. 'We don't know who took him, or why, or where to,' she said. 'It's unbearable, we can't sit and do nothing. Isn't there someone we know?'

That's how it was, you see. Whenever some hardship came, people asked if there was anyone to go to, someone who would help them. That's how it still is. I said that I would go and see if Yusuf would agree to help us find out something. You remem-ber him? We were at school together and were very good friends when we were younger. As I cycled towards Yusuf's father's house, I debated if I should ring first. There was a shop on the way where I could stop and do that. Yusuf's father was now a powerful man in the government, Deputy Minister of Foreign Affairs. Yusuf himself was also a junior official in the ministry. I would see him sometimes, driving by in his gleaming red Honda with his sunglasses on. It made me smile to see him drive by like someone on TV. He always gave me a wave if he caught sight of me, which made me think some of the old feeling between us was still there. When we ran into each other in town we still had time for greetings and conversation. The last time we met I had teased him about his diplomatic career and Yusuf said he was expecting a posting to Washington soon. He was playing up his position as a way of making a joke, of being sarcastic about his own importance, but that did not mean he was not important. All the children of the powerful were being groomed to be powerful too. That is what families do, if for no other reason than to ensure the security of their plunder. That's how things are.

Yusuf lived in a wing of his father's house, with his wife and child. Imagine how big that house would have to be to accommodate a grandee and his consort, and have wings large enough for his children and their families, and perhaps outhouses for their servants and their guard dogs, and garages for their cars. If I rang beforehand, it would perhaps turn out that the telephones were bugged, not to spy on the deputy minister but to protect him and his family from nuisance and insult, so that any such callers could be traced and punished for their discourtesy. And if they were bugged, Yusuf would have to be cautious and perhaps would try to get rid of me quickly if it turned out that I was asking indiscreet questions. Perhaps he would try to get rid of me anyway if I spoke to him on the phone, even if it were not bugged. Promise to help then do nothing. It would be easier to do that on the phone than to my face.

On the other hand, if I just turned up outside the deputy minister's mansion, which I knew had walls topped with barbed wire as well as an armed guard in a kennel beside the gate, I was not likely to be allowed to reach Yusuf. I might even be arrested for something: disturbing the peace, suspicious behaviour, audacity. It was still late afternoon and I thought that might help, as if I might be there on pre-arranged business rather than disturbing the family while they were relaxing. I thought I would rely on the old-fashioned politeness usually extended to a caller. And if that failed, then I would ring and arrange to see Yusuf at his office the next day. That was what went rather anxiously through my mind as I cycled to ask for his help.

The deputy minister's house was set back some fifty metres from the main road. The ground either side of the drive was cultivated, with hibiscus and bougainvillaea and oleander and cannas and other plants and bushes I did not recognise. This spectacle was protected from the attentions of adventurous children and wandering goats by a chicken-wire fence on the verge. The house was on the edge of town, and some people brought goats there to graze. I am talking about twenty-five years ago. Now that area is built up, although the houses you see there are still mansions with large gardens.

When I turned into the drive of the deputy minister's house I saw there were two soldiers at the tall green gate. One of them was armed and the other was without his beret, as if he was off-duty and standing there informally, rubbing his head in an absent-minded way. I dismounted some metres from the gate and wheeled my bicycle towards them, to give them plenty of time to observe my approach. I had never in my life touched a gun or even the sleeve of a man in uniform, though both were ubiquitous in our lives. I hoped there would not be a tremor in my voice when I spoke. Both guards saw me, and the one who was armed adjusted his beret carefully as I approached, as if he needed to look his best as he fired his gun at me. While I was still a couple of metres away, the one without a cap said, Simama hapo hapo, bwana. Stop right there, mister.

'Salam alaikum,' I said, and was relieved to receive unhesitating replies from both soldiers. It is always so reassuring to hear a prompt reply, because hesitation means the person you have greeted does not like you and is only replying because God commanded that a Muslim must reciprocate that call of blessing when another Muslim makes it (and must not when it is uttered by an unbeliever). 'I've come to speak to Bwana Yusuf,' I said.

The soldier without the cap, whom I could now see was the senior of the two, did not look impressed.

'What about?' he asked.

I dropped my eyes deferentially to suggest that, with all due respect, I could not discuss the matter with him. These powerful people are always doing something they shouldn't and I thought if I made it seem that I was doing some dirty work for the deputy minister's son, then the soldier would not ask too many questions. When I looked up I saw the bare-headed soldier reach into the guard post to retrieve his beret. He fanned himself with it a couple of times before putting it on. He glanced at his watch and gave me a long scrutiny before reaching into the guard post again to retrieve a heavy-looking black phone. He held it in his hand for a few moments, his head cocked to one side, and then reluctantly seemed to reach a decision. He was not happy with what he had to do. He asked for my name and retreated out of earshot before making his call.

To my complete surprise, Yusuf was at the gate within minutes. I had expected to wait or perhaps be given an appointment, but he was there, calling me inside as if he did not want us to be seen from the road. He stopped right there in the yard, with the gate ajar, in sight of the guards. He must have guessed that some trouble had brought me to the house, which I had not been to before and would not have dared to visit in other circumstances. As we shook hands he gave me a reassuring pat on the shoulder, like a teacher confronted by a nervous student.

'You are welcome. How can I help?' Yusuf said.

'My brother Amir was taken away by two men in a white Datsun with government plates,' I said, speaking in a whisper although there was no one nearby to overhear. I raised my voice and spoke properly. 'We think he has been arrested. We don't know why, or where he has been taken, and we don't know who to ask. I have come to ask for your help.'

We had known each other since primary school where we used to compete and to share books, and of course play coram together in later years. At one time we had looked a little alike, and people had taken us for relatives with the same large eyes and lop-sided smiles, the same dark complexion, but then I put on a spurt of growth while Yusuf remained short and plump and our similarity disappeared. After I finished speaking, Yusuf nodded and said: 'Amir, your wife's brother.'

'My wife's brother is my brother,' I said.

'What has he done?' Yusuf asked.

'I don't know. I have no idea.'

We looked at each other in a long moment of silence, two young men who had known each other all our lives and still felt a residue of the friendly affection we had shared as children. Well, I did anyway, and I think Yusuf did too, because he nodded and said, 'I'll try to find out. I don't know if I will be able to but I'll try. I'll have to speak to Baba. Come to the office tomorrow and check with me. It will be easier to speak there.'

'What time?' I asked, using the same business-like tone as Yusuf.

'Make it afternoon. It will give me more time,' he said.

As we stood in the yard just inside the gate of Yusuf's father's mansion, I saw the extent of the façade of the house, with its windows and balconies and hanging baskets, and how the drive continued down the left-hand side of it, perhaps towards the garages and the pool and the gardens. I did not know how far back the grounds went, and how many wings and outhouses they accommodated. It was a different world from the paltry one I knew, with its cramped rooms and exhausted furniture and ineradicable smells.

On the way home with my news, I went over the encounter with Yusuf. Was he a little unfriendly? Cold? He could have just told me that he couldn't help, and he did not do that. Was there a tone of distaste in his voice when he said Amir's name? And what was the meaning of that correction, saying Amir was my wife's brother and not mine? Was it a way of saying that because you are a friend, your brother would have had a claim on me but your wife's brother does not? Yusuf could not know that Saida was everything to me, and could not know how much what mattered to her, mattered to me. Perhaps Yusuf was one of those people Amir had offended in some way.

The next day, I went to the Ministry of Foreign Affairs and waited in the reception area as I was instructed. The receptionist sat at a large desk with a telephone and a few scraps of paper in front of her. On the wall behind her was an airways wildlife calendar and above that a row of photographs showing the President in the middle and a host of dignitaries either side of him. The large barred window beside her was open, letting in light and a hot breeze from the road. If I made the slightest move she looked up from her desk to see what I was doing. She had no reason to be watchful, her glances were intended to intimidate. I tried to sit quite still. After what seemed a long wait, perhaps because I had to sit so still, Yusuf came out, dressed in a white shirt and no jacket, shaking hands and smiling, looking every inch a young diplomat. When he shut the door to his office, the smile faded and his face turned stern; maybe he even looked displeased. He did not sit down and did not invite me to sit either. This was going to be brief. We were in a small airy upstairs room with a view of the sea, and through the open window I could hear the sound of traffic below. I thought it would be a nice office to work in. I watched as Yusuf went to stand by the window.

He said: 'Your brother has been arrested for raping an under-age schoolgirl.' He waited for me to speak, his face wearing a sneer of distaste. When I did not say anything, because I was shocked speechless by this announcement, he continued, 'Not just any under-age schoolgirl either, but the youngest daughter of the Vice-President. That is how her family will tell the story because they are so angry. They will say that he raped her, although possibly there was no coercion, maybe they both knew what they were doing. That's all I've been able to find out. It was difficult enough. I can't help you more than that. I don't know any more and I don't want to have anything to do with this matter.'

All I could say was: 'Amir?'

'Yes Amir,' Yusuf said.

He moved away from the window and stood beside his desk, hands on his hips, angry that he was in any way a part of this. I took in the information. Rape the Vice-President's daughter? But it was unreal, unfounded, a mad accusation, like something imagined or fantastic. At the same time I felt the impact of Yusuf's words somewhere in the cavity of my body, a churn of terror for what was now going to happen to Amir. I wondered at Yusuf's anger, perhaps he had had to humiliate himself to discover the information. Then he shook his head and turned towards the door. 'It has been a horribly busy and messy day,' he said. 'I must get back to work now.'

I understood this to mean that the interview was over, that there was nothing more to talk about, that there were powerful people concerned, and it was now time for me to go. 'Thank you for what you have done,' I said to him, reaching out to shake his hand in gratitude. 'We did not know ...'

'You keep saying that,' Yusuf interrupted, holding my hand for just a second longer than necessary. 'Your brother has a reputation,' he said, and I could not miss the sneer on his face again as he said *your brother*.

'I had no idea,' I said.

'Well, my old friend, you are the only one in this town who doesn't,' he said. 'You must excuse me now, I should return to these papers.'

'Where is he held? What can we do?' I asked.

Yusuf shrugged and looked helpless, then he opened the office door, ushering me out. On my way out of the building, the receptionist who had been keeping an eye on me said, Give my regards to Saida, and I said I will, but I forgot to ask for her name.

After I got home and reported my conversation with Yusuf, Saida too was speechless with shock for a moment, and then she said: 'I had no idea.'

'Yusuf said we are the only two people in town who don't,' I said.

But Saida meant something else. She said: 'I mean, I had no idea he mixed with such powerful people. The Vice-President's daughter. Where could he meet with such people? At the hotel perhaps. They must go there to relax. It can't be true about him forcing her,' Saida said, evading the word. 'And anyway, being a schoolgirl does not mean she is a child.'

'Yusuf's words were that she is an under-age schoolgirl,' I said. 'I don't know what the legal age to be under is, perhaps sixteen. People used to marry off their daughters at fourteen and no questions asked, and the husband could be anything from fifteen to fifty. I did not even know there was an under-age law now. Perhaps there always was and no one took any notice.'

'Yes yes yes,' Saida said impatiently, not interested in my ramblings. 'We must find out where he is,' she said, 'so we can hear what really happened. I am sure it did not happen like that. Rape? Amir! I don't believe he could have done something like that. He is the only brother I have, we must do whatever we can to get him out. Whatever happens afterwards.'

I asked: 'What does that mean, whatever happens afterwards?'

'I mean whatever kind of person he really is or becomes,' she said. 'We did not do anything when they took my father, and then just watched while my mother died so wretchedly. Now we must do what we can, whatever we can, to get Amir out before he comes to harm.'

'That was a different time,' I said. 'What can we do anyway?' Perhaps I was speaking out of fear. We had become cowed by our rulers' willingness to be stern with us.

She said: 'We can go and plead with the girl's father.'

We sat quietly for a while contemplating this bold suggestion, then I said, 'That may make the father even more angry. Perhaps we should wait for a while, see what further news comes out. Maybe tempers will cool.'

But Saida shook her head and said, 'I'm not waiting. Tomorrow morning I am going to the Vice-President's office to try and find out what happened to Amir. You can come if you want or you can wait until tempers have cooled.'

Throughout the day, neighbours and friends came to the house to find out if there was any news, and we said no. All we knew was that Amir had been taken away. We were not yet ready to reveal our shame.

The next day Saida and I went to the Vice-President's office together, although I was very nervous about what I expected would be a humiliating encounter. I did not even think we would be allowed to see the great man, but would be shouted at and chased away by his guards and minders. The armed guard at the door looked as contemptuous as I had imagined and refused us entry into the building. What was it about anyway? he asked. Saida said it was a confidential family matter of great importance and we needed to make an appointment to see the Mheshimiwa. The guard was adamant: this was a place of state business, not of family troubles. I wondered if he expected to be paid something or if that would make matters worse. I did not know how to do such things, but I wondered if the guard expected it, and if he did, how it was to be done.

'Well,' Saida said to the guard in the end, 'you had better be sure you know what is state business and what is family business. Because if anything terrible happens as a result of our failure to see His Excellency, the responsibility will be yours, and then you'll come to know without any doubt whose business it is.'

The guard looked displeased and I thought he would shout at Saida for threatening him in that way, but perhaps he too was afraid in a different way. After considering for a moment or two, he told us to go and speak to the receptionist. The guard glanced inside and saw someone passing by and called out. It was the appointments secretary, just the man who would be able to tell us if the Mheshimiwa would have time for us, the guard explained, conciliatory now that he had decided to be helpful, demonstrating to us the joyful caprice of power. The appointments secretary waited for us to approach and then signalled for us to follow him to a desk in the reception area. He was dressed in a short-sleeved white shirt and khaki trousers, the humble costume of a lowly clerk or a teacher, unexpected in the office of such a high grandee. He looked at us coolly, watching us with a sinister stillness that was surprising in someone of such modest and benign appearance, and then he enquired the nature of our business. For some reason, I guessed that he already knew who we were and why we were there.

'It's a private family matter,' Saida said.

The secretary shook his head, so she said it concerned her brother Amir Ahmed. The secretary pondered this for a moment. Amir Ahmed Musa? he asked, and Saida nodded. The secretary reached forward and put his hand on the telephone without picking it up. I thought I had seen a slight leap in his eyes when Saida said Amir's name. He picked up the receiver and dialled a number. Then he said into it, The sister of Amir Ahmed Musa is here, asking for an appointment to see His Excellency. After listening briefly, he rose to his feet and called out to someone in the office behind him. We are going upstairs, he said, and asked Saida and me to follow him. We went up two flights of stairs and stopped outside an office with a sign that read *Chief Protocol Officer*. The appointments clerk knocked on the door and waited for a few seconds before opening it. He held the door open and then followed Saida and me inside, shutting the door behind him.

The office was large and air-conditioned, and at the far end of it was a desk behind which stood a commanding-looking man with a shaven head. Nearer the door, chairs and sofas were arranged in an oblong. It was the office of a senior official used to receiving powerful visitors. The man was dressed in light green trousers and the wide-lapelled shirt so beloved by our dignitaries at that time. Now they all wear suits and ties because they want to look like statesmen, but then everyone wanted to look like a guerrilla.

He came out from behind the desk and walked slowly towards us. He pointed to the sofas and chairs as he approached, but then he stopped and glanced back towards his desk. The secretary nodded to Saida and me and pointed us towards the sofas and chairs, then he stepped to one side as if he was taking himself out of the picture. In the meantime, the Chief Protocol Officer turned and walked towards us again. All this walking about was intended to demonstrate that he had complete mastery of the situation, that we were powerless before him. It was something we understood anyway. We were sitting on a small sofa side-by-side and he stopped a few feet away from us. The sofa was low, which forced our knees to rise, and made me feel as if I was cringing. The Chief Protocol Officer stood in front of us without saying a word for what seemed a long time. I thought I felt something in the air, a kind of tremor or disturbance, a chill, but then I realised it was a shiver of fear running through my body. When I glanced towards the appointments secretary I saw that his eyes were shining with laughter or mockery or relish.

We had both immediately recognised the Chief Protocol Officer, if that was what he really did in this office. I gave you that description so that you would have an idea what it felt like to be there and to be confronted in this way, but really we knew who he was as soon as we walked into the room. He was the son of the Vice-President, and we would have seen his image on television news bulletins several times, usually scowling over the shoulder of his father or sitting in the second row on a podium at functions and events. We knew all those people, their glamorous excellencies and their wives, whose images and names appeared to us several times a week in replays of old concerts and old speeches and in commemorations of old sorrows. Here was the brother of the abused sister, in person. He was known as a man of strength and discipline, a ferocious man whose preferred sphere was the army, with its brawn and guns and shouted commands. His name was Hakim, which I expect you know means the one who is wise and learned.

'Sasa,' he said. *Now what*. He said it like a question, inviting us to talk, to state our business. His eyes were fixed on Saida as he spoke, and even when *I* explained that we had come to request an interview with His Excellency the Vice-President, his gaze did not move from her. Eventually he glanced at me briefly before immediately turning back to Saida. 'What do you want to see His Excellency about?' he asked her.

I started to explain about the news we had received, but the Chief Protocol Officer hissed suddenly, a startlingly violent sound in that air-conditioned office, a hiss of reprimand and warning and exasperation. 'We have come to ask for information about the whereabouts of our brother Amir,' I persisted, refusing to be intimidated although I thought I heard a little quiver in my voice as I spoke.

'*Her* brother,' the Chief Protocol Officer said with exaggerated gentleness, glancing again at me, as if speaking to a fool who did not understand how close he was to danger. The hard look in his eyes was a warning to me not to try his patience. Then, turning back to Saida, he said, 'You have come to plead for your brother, have you? Do you know why he has been arrested? You don't, do you? He has been arrested because he raped a girl of fifteen. She is a girl of good family, still at school, and beloved by all her brothers and relatives. Your brother's behaviour is outrageous and despicable and unforgivable. That's the kind of thing people like him have been doing to us for decades, degrading our sisters with impunity. But the time is different now, and he will have to pay for what he has done. He will receive a punishment appropriate to the outrage he has committed.'

I released a sudden unintentional snort of disbelief at this bombast. What people like him are you talking about? What kind of people are *you*? And what kind of cruelties have *you* been committing that are different from the ones people like Amir are supposed to have done? That was what I would have said. That is what I almost said. The thought was complete in my mind but I don't know how much of it I spoke. I had never been close enough to powerful people to understand their methods or how their minds worked, and I did not know if it was best to grovel or to stand firm. Saida put her hand firmly on my knee before I could get going and I don't know if I managed anything more than something blundering and incoherent, some expulsion of noise. I am not a brave or even a reckless man. Whatever I said came out before I could think to be afraid, although our world then was full of fear. Hakim glanced my way, as if waiting for me to continue, but I heeded the warning in those stony eyes.

'May we know where he is, so we can hear his story from him?' Saida asked. 'So we can see how we may help him?'

'No you may not,' Hakim the Chief Protocol Officer said.

'It cannot be right that you will not allow us to see him and offer him what assistance we can for his defence,' Saida said. 'May we at least see him and see that he is well and hear what he has to say for himself?'

'No you may not,' Hakim the Chief Protocol Officer repeated, and I thought I heard the appointments secretary chuckle softly to himself. 'When or if it is considered advisable that you should see your brother,' Hakim continued, 'proper authorities will inform you.'

'May we see the Mheshimiwa to ask him this favour personally?' Saida asked again. 'I cannot believe the accusation you have made against my brother. It cannot be as you describe.'

'No, you may not, and it is as I describe,' Hakim said. 'It is not I who has made the accusation but the girl herself. But above all you cannot see His Excellency because he is out of the country on a tour of Asia for the next four weeks.' With that the Protocol Officer turned back towards his desk and said over his shoulder, 'You may go now.'

'What will happen to him? Doesn't there have to be a trial?' Saida asked, speaking stridently for the first time, desperately. 'You can't brush us away like this as if we are just curious bystanders.

He's my brother. Go to your heart and ask there how it feels for a sister to worry for the safety of her brother.'

The Chief Protocol Officer sat down at his desk without replying, and the secretary opened the door and held out his arm for us to leave. He did this with his head cocked solicitously to one side, as if he meant us to go for our own good, but the gesture was accompanied by a sneering flourish he did not try to disguise. When we were back in reception, he took down our names and address and told us he would be in touch if we were required or if there was any information to give us. He told us that his name was Abdalla Haji. I saw that there was still a small light of excitement in his eyes and I could not be sure exactly why. Was it pleasure at the bureaucratic power available to him? Was it the pleasure of seeing the Protocol Officer flex his muscles? Or just the excitement of participating in cruelty?

We walked in silence all the way home, and when we got there we went over everything again. What will they do to him? What is the punishment for what they say he has done? I said I did not know. It must have been Hakim who ordered his arrest, an angry brother affronted by the dishonour to his family. Did you hear that *people like him* stuff? Perhaps his anger will diminish with time, I said, although to me he seemed a man capable of any cruelty. Maybe his father will be capable of more mercy when he returns from his tour.

No, I don't think it's hopeless, Saida said. Maybe he's just trying to frighten us. That secretary will send us news of Amir's whereabouts, or why did he bother to take our address? He'll send us word in a day or two, and then we can go and see him and take some food and fresh clothes.

Yes, I said, and my scepticism must have come through in my voice because Saida looked wounded but did not reply for a moment. Then she proceeded to make a list of the things Amir would need in prison until something was resolved. I listened to her and wondered if I should get a piece of paper and write them down. It seemed a long list. Perhaps Saida was beginning to resign herself to a lengthy wait. I still thought that the best we could do was to wait and hope that tempers would cool, and perhaps pray that the Vice-President, when he returned from his tour of Asia, would show Amir clemency. He was said to be a thoughtful and considerate man whose gifts were wasted on the work he had to do. He had trained as a veterinary officer and worked for the agricultural research unit before politics claimed him and rewarded him with high office. Perhaps we would just have to pray that what was said of him would turn out to be true, and that he would prove to be a man capable of compassion. I did not think Chief Protocol Officer Hakim was likely to prove capable of that. But suppose it really was true that Amir had raped the girl, then kindness was most likely out of the question. I did not say this to Saida, because she seemed to have cheered herself up with the long list of items Amir would need, and I did not want to depress her again. But no, I did not think Chief Protocol Officer Hakim was intending to show clemency, and maybe from where he stood, there was no reason to consider doing so.

'What will they do to him?' Saida asked again after a long silence. I did not think there would be a trial for a while, if at all. Ours was not a government that bothered much with trials. I thought Amir would stay in jail or wherever he was held until Hakim had glutted his sense of injury and outrage at the degradation visited on his family. Nor did I think the Vice-President would overrule his son if his anger proved as implacable as I imagined it to be. But perhaps Yusuf was right, and there was no coercion. What exactly did Yusuf mean when he had said with such distaste that Amir had a reputation? A reputation for what exactly? For seducing vulnerable girls? For having reckless affairs with inappropriate women? For avarice? Yusuf had also said that he thought perhaps Amir and the Vice-President's daughter knew what they were doing, and I hoped that was so, that they were just young lovers doing what young lovers do. And the girl, whose name I did not know then, was lying low for the time being until her brother's rage had cooled, and would seek to extricate her lover when her father returned. That was the best we could hope for, it seemed to me, although I did not think it would save Amir from bruises and humiliations in the meantime.

Baba's eyes were glowing. The tempo of his speech had slowed and his tone was harder, with a hint of reproach. I sensed that we were getting closer to the moment of pain. He reached for the large thermos of coffee that he had asked Ali to prepare for us, anticipating another long night, and poured us both a small cup.

'I was at work the next day when the following events happened,' he said. 'So what I will tell you now I know because of what Saida told me later. I don't know if she told me everything, and it has been such a long time and I have thought about these matters for so long that I may have forgotten something important. It will not be easy to talk about. This is what she told me happened while I was at my desk at the Water Authority that day.'

*

At mid-morning a message was delivered to our house from Abdalla Haji, the appointments secretary at the office of the Vice-President. The man who delivered it stood at the door and said: 'You are called. There is news. I've parked the car round the corner and will wait for you there.'

'I'm coming,' Saida said without a second thought. 'I'll come right away.'

She changed out of her household rags and hurried out. The car was parked under a tree and there were already a handful of people watching nearby, curious to see who it had come for. The words *The Office of the Vice-President* and the national seal were painted across the side of the car. She wished then that she had refused the lift and walked to the office so as not to draw so much attention. The messenger dropped her outside the door of the office as if she were a dignitary, and as she walked past the armed guard, the same one who had refused her entry the day before, stiffened slightly in a kind of salute. The secretary saw her from his open office door as soon as she entered the reception area, and rose from his desk with a smile. After a word of greeting, he indicated that she should follow him and started off upstairs. He knocked on the Chief Protocol Officer's door, opened it after a short pause, and stood aside to let Saida pass. Then he closed the door without following her in. Hakim came walking slowly towards her and she sensed that the intensity of the previous day's rage had diminished, although his expression was still taut. He indicated that she should take a seat and came to sit opposite her.

'Sasa,' he said again as he had done the first time, but now without venom. He was dressed more casually today, in a long white shirt made of thinly ribbed material that was almost transparent.

'I am told you have news,' she said.

He stared at her for a moment and then shook his head. 'I still find it hard to believe that this could have happened, that your brother would dare to act in such a savage and insulting manner. He has done wrong. You will admit that?'

'If what you say proves to be true,' she said stubbornly.

He smiled, toying with her. 'Do you mean I could be lying? But if it is true, will you then admit that he has done wrong and no longer seek to defend him?' Saida said later that it was at this point, when he smiled at her in that way, that she began to be afraid.

'Will you then stop defending him?' he asked again, and waited until she made a gesture of compliance, a small ambiguous nod that might have meant something like: If you insist, but I'll wait to see where this is going.

'Will you then accept the punishment the authorities decide fits his ugly deeds?' asked Hakim, still smiling, insisting on her compliance, but now the veins in his temples seemed to pulse with anger as he spoke, or if not from anger then from some other strong emotion. He leant forward a little and she saw the hardness of his neck and the depth of his chest through the thin, baggy shirt he was wearing. 'The authorities in this case is me,' he said, 'and in my hands he will suffer for what he has done and he will deserve it. Or that is what I thought yesterday, before you came to see me. But now that I have seen you, I am no longer sure if there isn't a way of saving your brother after all. Do you understand what I'm saying?'

Saida thought she understood perfectly what he was saying, and she sat in front of that powerful-looking man, disbelieving what she knew he was about to say.

'Only you can save him,' said Hakim. 'You are a very beautiful woman. When you came in the door a moment ago, I felt my blood rushing to my chest with eagerness. I have not felt like that for a woman before, never in my life. I mean for you to be clear what I am saying, plainly understand that I want you. I want to remove that mtandio veil and undress you and take full command of your body. I want you to yield your body to me. I want to take charge of it and do with it as I wish. I thirst with desire for you. I will not harm you or cause you pain, do you understand? I want to make love to you, not just once, but to my satisfaction. That is how much I want you. In return, I will release your brother.'

He made no effort to touch her. His face was dead-pan and unsmiling now, and after he had said what he said, he leant slowly back in the chair and calmly waited for her to speak.

She said: 'You humiliate me. I am a married woman and a mother. I love my husband above any other person in this world, and I will not bring shame to his home and my son's home.'

Hakim leant forward again, smiling now with a kind of teasing pleasure. 'I thought you would be a virtuous woman, and your words do you credit. I do not mean to harm you or humiliate you. I desire you but I do not wish to belittle you. I want you to yield your body to me, that is all. If you wish to redeem your brother, you have no choice but to do as I ask. Your father was shot as a traitor some years ago, and suspicion already hangs over your brother, in addition to his abuse of a minor. You must understand that nothing else can save him but what I ask for. No one will interfere in this matter, not even the Vice-President, because they will see that it is my right as a brother to have the last word on it. I will give you a few hours to think about this, and I will arrange for you to see your brother after our conversation here, so that you may see he is well and his skin is undamaged ... yet. Then I will want your answer before the end of tomorrow. And as for shame, I will do everything to arrange matters discreetly, so that you and your home will suffer as little embarrassment

240

as possible. I want you to understand, I do not wish to harm or humiliate you.'

Hakim said the last words with that same lingering smile then he rose to his feet and went to his desk. A few moments later Abdalla Haji appeared at the door, and after listening to Hakim's softly spoken instructions, he escorted Saida downstairs. He too was smiling, and Saida guessed that he had known all along what news the Chief Protocol Officer intended to give her. As she waited for the car which Abdalla Haji had summoned to take her to the prison, she saw from the clock in reception that it was not yet eleven o'clock, so she had only been in the Chief Protocol Officer's office for ten minutes, yet it felt like hours. A short while later she was back in the car and on her way to see Amir. The driver parked in front of the main gate of the prison and knocked on the wooden door. After a brief exchange with the armed guard who appeared at the small inset panel, Saida was allowed inside on her own. Another guard escorted her through a large dark hallway, which was cool and surprisingly tranquil, like the entrance hall of an old mansion. It was not what she had expected. She was directed to a small room containing a medical trolley and a small desk and chair. It smelt strangely. She guessed this would be the examination room when the medical officer visited and she thought the smell was the odour of anguish. So far she had seen no sign of the yard or the cells, or heard the groans of the prisoners or the angry shouts of the guards that her imagination had prepared her for. She expected to be searched, but the guard who accompanied her merely pointed to the chair and told her to wait there, then he locked the door on her.

When he came, Amir looked dishevelled, as if he had only just woken up, hair uncombed, shirt creased, eyes swollen, but otherwise he looked unharmed. His skin was unbroken, as Hakim had said. The guard pulled the door to without closing it and waited outside. Saida embraced her brother and asked him her anxious questions to which he replied reluctantly, aggrieved and petulant. She thought how like her father he looked, and how unlike him he really was, how reckless and demanding, how sullen. They sat in silence for a moment while she considered how to proceed.

'What happened? Tell me what happened?' she asked.

'What are they saying happened?' he asked.

She tried to gauge his tone of voice: suspicious, cautious, assessing how much to tell her. She had imagined her brother terrified and confused by his arrest, but he seemed alert in that familiar way of his, unravelling a small idea of his own, plotting.

'I would have liked to hear from you first,' she said. 'Nobody is saying much, not even that you've been arrested. Only that you were picked up from the Coral Reef. We had to ask around ... What happened?'

She saw the same calculating look on his face, assessing what she had said, deciding how much to tell. 'Nobody has told me why I've been arrested,' he said. 'Two men came to the hotel and told me to get in the car. One of them had a gun,' he said, his voice rising to an exaggerated pitch, but she heard its faked intensity as he played for time behind the appearance of drama. 'They brought me here and put me in an isolation cell. I've been in here for the last two days and nights. It's hell, the heat and the mosquitoes ... using a bucket. Can you imagine that? The smell ... I don't even know what I've done or what they are planning to do to me. Nobody will say anything to me, not even you. Who did you ask? What did you find out?'

'We were told you raped an under-age schoolgirl,' Saida said briefly. After a second's silence, Amir snorted derisively, disbelievingly. Saida continued: 'The Vice-President's youngest daughter.'

'I did not ... do such a thing,' Amir said, dropping his voice to a whisper. 'Who said that?'

'Her brother Hakim,' she said.

'He came to see you?' asked Amir, still whispering, his voice incredulous.

'We went to try and see the girl's father, to plead for you, but he is out of the country,' she said. 'How do you know these people?'

'Not so loud,' Amir said, nodding towards the partly open door. 'What did he say?'

242

'He plans to punish you,' she said. 'He is the one who ordered your arrest, and he is very angry with you. That was why I wanted to hear your side of this, to see if they had any kind of case.'

Amir shook his head. 'Of course I did not rape Asha,' he said. 'I didn't know anything about her age. I've met her a few times, and we became friendly. She came to a party at the hotel,' Amir said and then paused to consider his words. 'I did not force her. She came back to the hotel three times after that, looking for me. She wanted me to be her boyfriend.'

Saida nodded. 'Her brother says you raped her and she is under-age. Apparently that is what Asha reported to him. Two crimes. Against her and against his family.'

'No,' Amir said softly, and ran his hand wearily across his face. 'How can you believe such a thing? Of course I did not rape her. She came back to the hotel three times … it was her idea. She wanted me to show her a suite. It was her idea. How can you say such a thing?' Then after a moment he asked: 'What will happen now? How did you get permission to see me?'

'Hakim arranged it,' Saida said. 'He wanted me to see that you are unharmed … yet. Do you know him? Is he another of your new friends?'

Amir nodded. 'I know him a little. He is a hard man. He likes to be like that. Is there anything we can do? Did he say anything else?'

Saida nodded back. 'He told me it is all up to him what punishment is decreed for you. He has made me a humiliating offer. If I yield to him, he will release you. Do you understand? If I sleep with him until he has had his fill, he will let you go free.'

'Oh my God, what a swine,' said Amir. He was silent for a long while after that, thinking over what she had said. Then he asked, as she knew he would: 'Will you do it?'

'Oh, Amir, you have a heart of stone,' she said.

'They will hurt me here,' he said, pleading. 'They may keep me here for decades … or worse … even kill me. You don't know how hard that man is. How can it be wrong to save a brother's life? However *he* thinks of it, you can say that you are doing a noble and courageous thing, saving your brother's life.'

'And Masud? How will I explain this to him?' she asked.

'He doesn't have to know,' Amir said, smiling triumphantly now, thinking she was going to agree. 'No one needs to know. People do these things all the time.'

*

I did not know about this when I came home, and not for some while afterwards. That evening, while Saida was still debating with herself what to do and how much to tell me, I asked her about the car that had come for her. Our neighbour Bi Maryam had told me that a government car came and took her somewhere. Was there any news of Handsome Boy? That was Bi Maryam's name for Amir. Saida started to tell me about the events of the day, and once she began, she told me everything, blow by blow, back and forth, until I felt nauseated, until I felt as if I had been there.

I said to her, 'Don't do it. You mustn't do it.' I pleaded with her half the night. I gripped her wrists and gently shook her, I wept, but the more I said, the more clearly she saw that none of it was worth sacrificing her brother's life. 'His life is not at risk,' I said. 'If what he says is true, the girl will get him out. That beast will keep Amir in jail for a few days or even months, but then the girl will plead with the father and get him out. Do not make our lives into nightmare and dishonour for nothing. His life is not at risk.'

But she could not persuade herself, and could only see that she had lost her father and her mother, and was now about to lose her brother when all that was required of her was to submit to a man. 'You must help me, Masud,' she said to me. 'You must stay by me. You must not abandon me. You must not allow me to lose heart. I will not be able to do this without you. He will want to see me a few times and then it will be over. No one will ever know.'

'No,' I said, 'it won't be over. That man has told you he wants you to yield to him until he is satisfied. It will not be a few times and then it's over. It will never be over until he has exhausted and humiliated you.'

But all my pleadings failed. One afternoon, a few days later, a car with private number plates parked under the tree and Saida

244

got into it as arranged. When she came home that evening, you and I were sitting at the table drinking ginger tea with buns from the café. Saida went through to the bathroom to wash and change. Neither she nor I spoke about where she had been that afternoon. We did not speak about anything for days, just what was necessary. At the end of the week Amir was released from jail and came home, smiling and animated, as if he had taken part in a witty prank. On another afternoon, the following week, Saida left the house to go to Hakim as arranged. She had asked him not to send the car as he had the week before, and she walked to where she had to go.

While she was gone, I retrieved the jewellery my mother had given to me for safe-keeping, and the letter she'd sent to me when she arrived in Dubai, and my father's letter when I married Saida. I put them and a few clothes in a bag and left. I cycled aimlessly for an hour or so, not sure if I really wanted to go, not really ready to lose her and my whole life, and then I headed slowly back to the house. When Saida went to Hakim for the third time, I knew I could not bear to live there any more, could not bear Saida and her brother, who in my shamed heart I imagined was chuckling and sniggering about me and my stupidity and my cowardice and my shame. I did not know what to do. I never knew what to do at any important moment in my life. I was always inept. I did not know how to speak to Saida about what she was doing. I was overwhelmed by what she was doing. I did not know why she was doing it any more.

*

Baba was weeping, his gaunt body heaving as he tried to control himself. I rose and switched off the light, and sat down at the table close to his bed. After a short while there was silence, and then he said, 'I'm sorry. It gets harder to control the tears with age.'

'Do you want me to put the light back on?' I asked.

'No,' he said. 'Leave it like this.'

*

While Saida was away for the fourth afternoon later that same week, I collected the few belongings I chose to take and, without waiting for her to return, I cycled to this place. I knew Khamis would let me stay. My father had helped him when he was in trouble with the authorities and I knew he would help me. They gave me this room where we are now. I did not think I would stay for so long but could not face recriminations and explanations. Amir came to the Water Authority office the next morning to find me and tell me Saida wanted me to go home. I could not raise my eyes to look at him and went on reading through the notes on my desk, or pretending to. I heard Amir sigh briefly and then leave. Later that afternoon, Saida herself came to the office, so close to our home, and asked me to come back. I walked outside with her because I was afraid I would break down in front of everyone.

'I cannot bear to return,' I told her. 'I cannot bear to see what you are doing.' She asked me where I was sleeping and I told her where I rented a room. The shopkeeper and his wife lived in another room at the back and there was a shared yard and wash-room. It was enough.

'Come back home,' Saida said.

I shook my head because I could not speak. She had taken everything away, there was nothing there for me.

The following day, when I returned to my room after work, Khamis told me that someone had brought something for me. It was a dish of cassava and a piece of fried fish. I ate the food for supper and left the cleaned dishes in the shop before I went to work. When I returned from work, I found that Saida had taken the empty dishes away and left some rice and spinach for me. She brought me something every day after that and left it in the shop, and later you did. Sometimes, when I was in, Khamis called me out to accept the basket myself, and I went out and accepted the food with words of gratitude. Whenever I saw her, I struggled to prevent myself from breaking down with grief. I should have fought for her, but I did not have the strength to overcome those two shameless men who had taken over her life. I was not sure if she even wanted me to try. In a silent place in my mind, I knew that she had already given me up, and that the food she brought me every day was atonement for what she could not help but do.

I could not speak for days after I left her. As the weeks and months passed I felt a deep self-hatred that I could not voice. I deserved contempt and disdain for my cowardice and self-pity and spinelessness. But even as I hated and despised this person just as everyone else did, I learnt to live with him, and I closed the door on the world with him. I thought that way I would learn to make peace with failure, learn to live with it honourably. I did not know how to think of myself differently, how not to take myself so seriously, how not to take the world so seriously. I was tortured by vivid images of their embraces, and night after night I murdered him. I was a dog, I felt like a dog. I did not think there was anything I could do about all of this. You ask why did I not speak. If I spoke I could only condemn myself for my puniness and cowardice. My life was empty, without pleasure or purpose. I could not bear that Saida had abandoned me in such a way. Nothing seemed worth the trouble after losing her. I lost my way, that was how I was. I was ashamed of what had been forced on us and that we could not prevent it, that I could not prevent it. I had no strength left for anything, and if it had not been for Khamis and his late wife, I would not at first have been able to manage the merest minimum of care necessary for self-respect. I don't know why they bothered to help, but they did. Their debt of gratitude to my father had been more than repaid but their care for me was without end.

As for Amir, everything blossomed for him after that. You know that better than I do, how the favours came his way and how he knew to make the most of his luck. Then he took you away to London and I thought I would never see you again. As for Saida, it turned out that Hakim could not satisfy himself of her for a long time. What he had intended as her humiliation turned into a passion he did not wish to give up. I suppose he had fallen in love with her, and for all I know, she learnt to return

247

some of the love he felt for her because she did not leave him even after her brother was safe, and then they had the daughter. People can get used to many things. Then when I was in Kuala Lumpur she wrote to me to say she had applied for a divorce so she could re-marry. She did not need to. I had deserted her. She wrote as a gesture of kindness, I suppose. I don't know how she found out where to write. Kuala Lumpur was a convalescence for me but I have never been able to love again because shame emptied my body and left me without vitality. At a certain age, you don't understand how long life is. You think it's all over for you, but it's not, not for a long time. You just don't understand how little strength the body needs to keep on living, how it goes on doing so despite you.

I've been waiting to tell you this for many years, even though for a long time it was for the wrong reasons. I wanted you to know who was to blame but you were too young and I did not have the strength. In the end I thought maybe you had chosen your side. Now I just want you to know since you want to know. It was my father who taught me to speak in this way. I did not understand him, not until he came and took me with him to Kuala Lumpur. Some of us like to think we were once better people than we have become but I was wrong about him. He prayed for me and I was not grateful at first but then I began to see a man who never gave up trying, a man of faith, and I had misunderstood that for many years, because I thought he was a man of narrow ideas.

In Kuala Lumpur he worked as a scholar in an Islamic college, teaching and explaining the writings he had been studying all his life. But then in his own time, and with his own money, he started an orphanage school, where children could receive a free elementary education. School still was not cheap in Kuala Lumpur even where it was free. Parents had to pay for tests, for books, for writing paper, for uniforms. My father's school gave these orphan children a start. He did this in addition to his duties as an imam. Other volunteers taught in the school, members of the congregation and some of his students, and I taught there too, to help at first and then to liberate myself from the paralysing misery that had taken over my life. I never became a scholar and I did not share his piety but I did what I could to please him when for so long I had desired nothing but to thwart him. I was grateful that he had come and fished me out of that sadness. Away from the disappointment and shame I felt here, I began to feel a return of my strength. I had become accustomed to the feeling that there was no relief or absolution for what had befallen me and what I had done, but there I felt the beginning of something else.

What I understood in Kuala Lumpur was that my father had faith not only in religion but in people. I had lost that faith and seeing how he lived his life made me recognise it again and think of it as a possibility. He died some years ago, Maalim Yahya, and he was mourned by hundreds of people among whom he had been a stranger until a decade or two before. Hundreds and hundreds of people in Kuala Lumpur walked in his funeral procession. He left enough money for his wife to live on comfortably, and his daughters had both found homes and families in Kuala Lumpur. Then I heard from my sister that Saida had died, may God have mercy on her soul, and I knew that I was no longer of any use there. I thought I would come back and finish my days here. Let me tell you what it was like in Kuala Lumpur. It is a surprisingly hospitable city.

11

Our Doubts are Traitors

Baba asked me if I was tempted to stay.

I hesitated for a moment and then changed the subject. I told him about the friends I made when I first went to London, Reshat and Mahmood. 'Reshat could make a filthy joke out of almost anything,' I told him, 'especially if it had noble words associated with it. Those big words like justice or the future or responsibility brought out the worst in him. You'd hate to share a parent with him or take him on a journey with you or do something with him where you needed to trust him, but for a couple of hours a day he was entertaining. Mahmood was quite different, always smiling, a gentle, kind friend. There were others I did not know well, from everywhere, India, the West Indies, Malaysia, Iran.'

'I never thought of it like that,' Baba said. 'I imagined you surrounded by angry English men and superior madams.'

'That as well, but not all the time,' I said. 'It's not as simple as the lies they told us about themselves or the lies we chose to believe. Anyway, it's not all angry English men and superior madams, there are hungry ones and foolish ones and righteous ones too.'

'Yes, I know,' Baba said, smiling at my vehemence.

'The whole world ends up in London somehow,' I said. 'The British never left anyone in peace and squeezed everything good out of everybody and took it home, and now a bedraggled lot of niggers and turks have come to share in it.'

'Tell me about Mahmood, your gentle smiling friend,' he said.

'When I first met Mahmood ... we used to call him Mood ... I did not know that there were Muslims in Sierra Leone. I didn't at first believe him when he told me that three-quarters of the people there were Muslim. I had always thought that Sierra Leone was a country invented by the British to send liberated African slaves to, a missionary reservation peopled by devout Christians. I must have read that somewhere or heard it in a history class, and must have imagined that the land was emptied for their arrival. The only book I had read about Sierra Leone at that time was something by Graham Greene, and I did not remember any mention of Muslims in it apart from the corrupt Syrians whom all the English characters spoke about sneeringly. That was how people like you and I came to know of so much of the world, reading about it from people who despised us. Reshat said that Cyprus too was three-quarters Muslim only the Greeks and the British falsified the population figures, but he was lying. Reshat was always over the top like that, and even if you caught him out, he just laughed as if all along he had meant to make an outrageous joke.'

I told my father about Mr Mgeni and the OAU house. 'That's where I lived for a while,' I said. 'We called it that because everyone who lived in it was an African. Mr Mgeni lived next door. He came from Malindi ... no, not our Malindi, the Kenya Malindi ... but he was a mswahili, one of us. There were Peter and Mannie, and Basil and Sophie later in Brighton, but I've lost touch with all of them.'

'So you are not tempted to stay,' Baba said.

I said I was but I was also tempted to go. When I was a child, I sometimes heard dogs barking and howling in the late hours of the night. In my childhood terror I thought it was the howling of wicked souls calling others like them to a sinful gathering – they filled us with such stuff when we were children – and that if I did not stop my ears and cover my head, I would be compelled to go and join them. I felt something like that now although not quite so literally. If I stayed it would be to stop my ears and cover my head so that I should not be compelled to join the other scavengers living off the rich people's garbage. To stay would be restful, in a place of content despite its deprivations, somewhere I could walk familiar streets and meet people I had known forever and breathe the air that was like old love.

'But I lost my freedom to chance,' I said, 'or at least to chance ordered by events put in train by others, which I could not change or influence. My freedom is of no importance to anyone else and from a way of looking at it, it's of no importance at all. But it leaves me torn about what to do, whether to stay or to go back to a life I find debilitating and which I fear will shrivel me up as it did Mr Mgeni. I feel I need to go back to that incomplete life I live there until it yields something to me, or not. I have not done anything in all these years, or nothing much. I don't know what I was waiting for. When I heard the news of Mama's passing away and that you were back, it made me want to come back too. I came to hear from you what Mama would never have been able to tell me. Once you left us, I don't suppose she had any choice but to see through what she had brought about, to wear that garment as if it was one she had chosen for herself. I did not think it was something she would ever be able to speak about.'

Baba shook his head. 'Don't think ill of her,' he said. 'It was the way she thought of Amir. She took too much responsibility.'

'I don't think ill of her, and I don't think it was because she took too much responsibility for Uncle Amir. She just did not know what to do. They overwhelmed her in their separate ways,' I said, and then said nothing more for a long time because I could see Baba was perturbed by what I had said or by the way I had said it. Then he sighed and looked up and nodded, inviting me to continue. 'She knew what Uncle Amir was really like. You spoke of how shame emptied your life. Uncle Amir had no time for shame. It would have seemed like self-pity and selfishness to him, a weakness. He would have turned what sought to shame him into an insult, and blustered and hit out at it, as a man should. So when the moment came he pressed her to sacrifice what was required for his well-being, and she did because she did not know what else to do.'

'Maybe we are saying something similar,' Baba said after a little thought. 'So you will be going back to London.'

I nodded. He waited patiently for me to speak then he said, 'What are you smiling about?'

'Did she always like plums? I remember she loved them,' I said. 'Sometimes she brought a bag home and we sat there and ate every single one until they were finished.'

'Yes, she always loved plums but they were not easy to get here,' Baba said. 'We had to wait until they were in season on the mainland.'

'They don't taste the same in England somehow,' I said. 'Do you still have that *Collected Shakespeare* you used to have many years ago?'

'Yes, Khamis kept everything,' my father said, smiling at the thought of his friend. 'He said he kept all the books because he was sure I would come back, so he must have known something I didn't. I remember the first play I was able to read was *Two Gentlemen of Verona*.'

I asked: 'Did you ever read *Measure for Measure*?'

My father shook his head. 'I don't think so. I might've tried. Most of the plays were too difficult for me. I could not get past the zounds and exeunts and harks and rummage in yonder prologue, and usually found myself nodding off after two or three pages.'

I said, 'When I first read the play I heard an echo which made me sad. Isabella made me think of Mama because I always guessed that there was some force behind what she did though I did not know about Uncle Amir. I was just not convinced about the perfidious brother who tried to persuade his sister to submit to Lord Angelo whose heart was sick with a bullying lust. What brother would do a thing like that?'

'Tell me about the play,' Baba said.

This is what I told him. The Duke of Vienna, wishing to test his deputy Lord Angelo, arranges to go on a long journey and leaves him in charge of the city. Lord Angelo has a reputation for high-mindedness and virtue, which the Duke must have had some doubts about, because in reality he does not leave the city but disguises himself and hides in a monastery. Lord Angelo is zealous in his righteousness, and thinks the Duke has been too lenient in his application of the law, turning a blind eye to all kinds of improprieties. One of the first things Lord Angelo does, when he thinks himself free to operate without hindrance, is to order the arrest of Claudio, who has been living in sin with his betrothed, Juliet, who is now pregnant. He orders the execution of the young man for the crime of fornication, a penalty the law allows. Execution, you might think, how barbaric! But that is all that Viennese law allows him to do when he might have wanted to do more, disembowel and castrate him for a start. Also, he only arrests Claudio and condemns him to death when he might have done the same for Juliet as well, pregnant or not. In some parts of the Muslim world where they prize purity and obedience, they know how to deal with fornicators, who are almost always women. They dig a hole in the ground, put the woman in it up to the neck, fill up the hole leaving the head exposed, and then stone the fornicator to death. All Lord Angelo does is to arrest the man and order his execution, and he leaves the woman to the nuns. Yet even that sanction, which the law allows, the Duke, with his tolerant ways, has permitted to lapse.

As he is escorted to jail, Claudio meets an acquaintance, Lucio, a frequenter of brothels, a maker of mischief, and a loud-mouthed chatterbox full of tedious jokes. Claudio explains to Lucio about this arrest and asks him to let his sister Isabella know, so that she may appeal to Lord Angelo for clemency. Isabella is about to take her vows as a nun but when she receives this news she agrees to do as Claudio asks, go to Lord Angelo and plead for her brother's life. She knows, like everyone else, that to get the smallest thing you desire, unless you are born to it, you have to plead and beg. She is admitted to Lord Angelo, who tells her that Claudio is to be executed first thing the next day: no talk of mercy, no use wheedling me, it is the law, no hanging around.

Isabella addresses Lord Angelo with spirit, pleading and courteous at first, and then when she realises that he is a hard, self-righteous man, she accuses him of unnecessary harshness and cruelty. She does enough, she thinks, to be allowed to come back the next day to hear Lord Angelo's answer to her pleas. So, at least she has delayed the execution and has given herself some hope of saving her brother. What she doesn't know is that Lord Angelo has been struck by her beauty and, perversely, by her virtue, and now desires her to submit sexually to him. When she returns the next day he tells her so in unmistakable terms: *Plainly conceive I love you*. If she wants Claudio to live, she must yield to him. Isabella, the novice nun, is appalled at this cruel seduction and expects Claudio to be as well, but when she tells her brother he tries to persuade her to agree to Lord Angelo's demands. *Death is a fearful thing. What sin you do to save a brother's life becomes a virtue*. Now the Duke gets involved. He has had his answer about Lord Angelo's suitability to rule, the dirty hypocrite, but he needs to catch him in the act of misrule. By a series of stratagems the Duke foils Lord Angelo, saves Isabella's honour and himself proposes marriage to her. It is a play, after all.

I said: 'There was no Duke to put things right for this Isabella, no one to restrain the man of appetite who, once he had her in his grip, never let her slip away. Nor was there any role for you in the play, Baba, because Shakespeare had already reserved the heroine for the Duke.'

'I will not bother to read it then if there is no part for me.'

'Sometimes I wonder if things were meant to happen as they did,' I said, 'or if there was a mistake, a mess-up along the way.'

*

Munira returned from her examinations in a cheerful mood. They had gone well. She rang her daddy with her news and told him that we were coming round to see him later that afternoon. I knew that I would not be able to avoid meeting him in the end. I told myself that I was doing it for Munira. My reluctance to greet her daddy made her unhappy, as if there was some wrong that still stood between us when I had declared to her there wasn't. I knew from Baba that my mother asked for a divorce soon after I left for London because she wished to re-marry. She must have waited until I was out of the way so as not to upset me or to have to put up with my petulance, and then she did not tell me. So, in short, Hakim was her proper husband and he had lived with her in some fashion and had been there to bury her with respect in the end while I was in Folkestone, fucking and bickering with Rhonda.

I went with Munira to the grand house where Hakim lived with his first family. I heard dogs barking as we turned into the drive, and a lean uniformed man appeared from the garden side of the house. He smiled when he saw Munira and she waved at him. A Land Cruiser was parked in the drive and two other cars were in the garages to the left. I wondered how such wealth could be maintained without guards or locked gates and where even the dogs were kennelled out of sight. They relied on fear, I guessed, which terror had made into the citizen's normal conduct. Who would dream of risking capture and its aftermath by attempting to steal from such ferocious owners?

Munira walked round the side of the house to the garden door, looking over her shoulder and smiling, tugging me along. I knew from her that both Hakim's other daughters were away studying, one in Boston and the other in Utrecht on generous scholarships awarded by those countries. The son was around, and I met him when we were strolling in town one afternoon: the same age as Munira, handshakes and smiles, hurrying on after his own affairs. Munira entered without knocking, as if she was entering her own home. I was introduced to an aunt or cousin whom we found in the kitchen, and guessed she was another Bi Rahma, the household skivvy, a poor relation who had found a niche with the family. She told us Mama was resting but Bamkubwa was inside. Munira was already walking past by then, calling out Daddy, kicking off her sandals as she stepped through glass doors and down some steps into the sitting room.

I had only seen Hakim on television before and had only ever heard him speak on the telephone. He was in his mid-sixties, I guessed, his eyes shadowed by loosening bags of skin and his thick neck starting to sag and wrinkle. He swivelled his recliner towards us as we entered, and rose to his feet. To me it seemed that he did so without effort, a large powerful man despite his age. He was watching a recording of the European Champions League final on mute and he switched the set off as he rose. He smiled at Munira and opened his arms as if he would embrace her but the gesture was rhetorical because seconds later he held out his hand for her to kiss. As she bent forward to kiss his hand, he brought his other hand over and rested it on her shoulder. I thought I saw her stiffen slightly, like a reflex at an unexpected touch. Perhaps he did not normally touch her in that way. She stepped aside and turned towards me, her face all smiles.

Hakim looked at me for a long moment, his face composed and unsmiling. He then held out his hand and I stepped forward and took it. During the brief contact, I felt a hand that was thick with meat but was unexpectedly smooth, made that way I imagined by expensive soaps and creams. Hakim gestured towards a chair and sat down in his own huge lounger. Munira was talking, filling in the space with her words as we settled in our chairs.

'Salim, at last,' Hakim said gently, smiling. 'Your mother would have laughed to see this moment.'

Lord Angelo, I thought. He would have looked even more intimidating twenty years before. *Plainly conceive I love you.* Redeem thy brother by yielding up your body to me, you bitch. I did not speak, and the space between the three of us was filled by Munira and Hakim, as they discussed her plans for the future. Should she go to Columbia to do an MBA or should she go to Berkeley to do Economics? She wished she could go to Italy but it would take years for her to learn the language. Italian men were so handsome, she said. But honestly, she wasn't sure. She thought she preferred the United States, although if she came to London – glancing at me – she could stay with me. Hakim snorted at this and said I was staying on here, wasn't I? I was not going anywhere now that I was back. He glanced towards me to see if I would speak. When I did not, he continued: There'll be something here for you if you decide to stay. I can guarantee that.

At some point during the visit, I said how much I regretted that I could not get back in time for the funeral, and I was grateful to him and to Uncle Amir for their generosity on that and other occasions. It was as much my duty as it was yours, he said. When it was time for me to go, Hakim shook my hand again and said,

I meant that, if you decide to stay. I nodded with what I hoped seemed like gratitude, but what I thought was, If I come back, it won't be to become a beast in one of your pens.

*

'Aren't you going to stay?' Munira said as my month was drawing to an end and I talked to her about calling at the travel agent's office to confirm my flight. 'Stay for another month, think it over, don't leave yet.'

'I'll think it over when I get back there,' I said.

'What's the big attraction? Is there someone you are returning for?' she asked.

'No,' I said, 'nothing like that. Just a lot of bits and pieces to sort out, bits of life.'

'All right, go away and think about it and then come back,' she said. 'I know you've got a good job in London but as Daddy told you, there's work for you here if you want it.'

*

My father asked me the same question. 'What's the big attraction back there? Is there someone you love? Is there someone waiting for you to return?'

I smiled despite myself at the faces my father pulled from the embarrassment he felt as he asked the question. We were not used to having conversations like that, and had only just recently got used to having conversations at all. I loved that way of putting it: someone waiting for you to return, just you. I wiped the smile off my face and said: 'No, there is no one waiting for me. You mean a woman, don't you? I loved a woman some time ago. Her name was Billie, but I lost her. Her family discouraged her. Or maybe she did not love me enough in return.'

'You'll love again,' Baba said.

'You didn't,' I said.

My father said, 'You can't live alone.'

'You did,' I said.

259

'I didn't. I lived with the misery of love gone wrong, and I almost lost my life,' he said. 'Until that old man came back and took me away. Maybe sometimes you have to be forced to do things that are good for you, or force yourself.'

I shook my head. 'It isn't like that,' I said. 'I told you before. I want to see what will come out of what has befallen me. I have been corrupted by possibilities. Remind me again of those words you told me when I left last time, something about blessing and love.'

'I can't remember exactly any more. My father used to say those words at one time. Something like: the recollection of blessings is the beginning of love,' Baba said. 'He meant the love of God, not the profane thing we are talking about. Maybe it still works for mere sinful mortals as well.'

*

I was on edge, tense on the journey back to London. I had learnt to pay attention to such feelings, as if something was putting me on the alert.

Baba died minutes after I boarded the flight to Addis Ababa. I had a six-hour stopover in Addis Ababa airport but then the flight was cancelled and I spent a miserable twenty-six hours there before they found a seat for me. I boarded the overnight flight to London and arrived in Putney a day later than I should have done. I received Munira's call later that morning to say my Baba died on the afternoon I left and was buried the next day. The reading for him was held during the night I was stranded in Addis Ababa. It was a stroke. He said he was tired and went to lie down. When Khamis's young man Ali took him a coffee in the afternoon to wake him up, he was gone.

'You would not have been able to get back in time, even if you had not been stranded,' Munira said. 'Your Baba had some money put aside, and his old friend Khamis looked after everything. They were like brothers, those two.'

I thought of how my father used to be many years ago and how at times I suspected that those silences were reserved only